beat

vi keeland

Beat

ISBN 9781682304273

Edited by: Caitlin Alexander

Cover model: Nicolas Simoes

Cover designer: Sommer Stein, Perfect Pear Creative

Photographer: Brice Hardelin Photography

Print layout by Deena Rae Schoenfeldt, eBookBuilders

dedication

For my very first crush, who also happens to be my husband.

contents

chapter one

Lucky

"**W**anna fuck?"

Lovely approach. "Does that line ever actually work for you?"

The tactless drunk at least has the decency to look a little embarrassed. "Not really."

"Perhaps you should try opening with a compliment instead. We like that much better. Go ahead, give it another try."

"All right." He gulps back the rest of what will now be the last vodka tonic he's served tonight and slurs, "You got a nice rack."

I shake my head and move to the next table. So much for trying to help the clueless ass. After taking drink refill orders from a half dozen tables, I pause, my attention drifting to the small stage. A gyrating woman is pouring her heart out, butchering "Hey Jude." The sound is akin to nails scraping down a blackboard.

Don't get me wrong, I love the Beatles. Obviously. But this poor song is way too long. It needs to be retired permanently from the karaoke catalog. The drunkards in the front row sway their arms back and forth in the air—joining in on the off-key, off-pitch, off-beat marathon sing-along. Somehow, tonight it still makes me smile. I walk to the bar singing along quietly to myself, "Na na na nananana, nananana, hey Jude."

"We're getting drunk as soon as this place empties out tonight," Avery yells over the deafening crescendo of the chorus. Suddenly, the singer on stage goes for the last na na na nananana and her voice breaks into a horrific earsplitting screech.

"I may not be able to wait that long." I tip my chin in the general direction of the small stage at the other end of the bar and shake my head.

"She's not that bad actually."

I make a face that conveys what I don't say out loud, and Avery rolls her eyes as she finishes making my drink order.

"You know, you could always show her how it's done."

I load my tray with the four drinks she's made and stick my middle finger up at my best friend before heading back to the table of four middle-aged women searching for liquid courage.

Stopping at the wall lined with framed photos, I straighten a crooked picture of my dad and Bruce Springsteen with their arms slung over each other's shoulders. They're both sweaty messes from an impromptu hour-long jam session. It was taken at the bar's one-year anniversary party. Seeing Dad's smile brings out mine. I close my eyes briefly. *Step two, Dad. I'm making progress.*

"You ladies going to get up there and sing tonight?" I ask, trying to be friendly as I hand off three mojitos and a tequila sunrise. It's the third tequila sunrise for the redhead with the thick bun wrapped at the nape of her neck. She's already feeling no pain.

"I would love to," slurs the redhead, "but I need to have a few more drinks before I'll have the nerve."

I nod, never one to push people past their limit. Redhead's wearing a cream silk button-down blouse—buttons fastened all the way to the top—with a navy pencil skirt and matching blazer, a string of pearls completing her conservative ensemble. The outfit pairs perfectly with the demure bun. But as I start to walk away, something under the table catches my eye—and it's not her impeccably crossed ankles. It's the shoes. They *definitely* don't go with the rest of the package. Five-inch

Mary Jane stilettos, the red soles a dead giveaway that there is more to the woman than meets the eye.

Spending six nights a week for the last seven years here at Lucky's has taught me a lot about people. I can usually spot a closet Beyoncé wanna-be a mile away. I smirk to myself, picturing Redhead standing in front of her bedroom mirror—letting her hair down and singing into her hairbrush wearing nothing but those nine-hundred-dollar Louboutins.

The crowd has doubled in the last half hour. It's Saturday night and the late movie across the street just let out. I jump behind the bar to help Avery for a little while and tell the DJ to throw on some house music so he can pitch in waiting tables until things slow down. Twenty minutes later, I notice the drink order Avery is making.

"Those for the same group that ordered them a little while ago?" She's finishing off mixing another round of mojitos, and the colors settling in the tall tequila sunrise glass are already at full peak.

"I think so. Redhead with a bun?"

"Yep. That's her. I got twenty she's our flasher." Flasher is a term we use for the patron who takes us by surprise. Without fail, there's one every weekend. They come in looking conservative, wearing their sleek taupe Burberry raincoats cinched tightly at the waist. But a few drinks and a microphone later, they're up on stage whipping open their coats, flashing us their flesh as they grind their hips like a pro stripper. "Bet she's covering a red G-string under that knee-length skirt too."

"Her? Are you joking? She's wearing fucking pearls."

I arch an eyebrow. "Is that a yes?"

Avery reaches into her pocket and digs out a twenty. She shoves it into an empty glass and sets it on a shelf holding liquor bottles behind her. "Put your money up and cover the bar. I need to get a close look at Pearls and make a stop at the bathroom."

"You know, I'm still your boss for another...." I look at my watch. Nearly eleven o'clock. "Five hours."

"I've known you since middle school. Who are you kidding? You'll still be the boss even after I own half the place." She kisses me on the cheek as she rushes by.

Ten minutes later I'm still alone behind the bar and Avery is nowhere to be found. I'm sure she's in the back alley smoking, even though she swears every day that she's quit. I check the IDs of three very young-looking pretty girls—they're over twenty-one, but barely. I can't miss their conversation.

"Seriously, he has to be gay."

"Why, because he hasn't noticed you yet?"

"No, because he's too perfect to be straight."

"Could we buy someone a drink?" one of the young blondes asks me.

"Of course. What do you want me to send over?"

They giggle for a few minutes, then decide on a Screaming Orgasm for their intended target. I mix the vodka, Bailey's and Kahlua and pour it over a tumbler of ice.

"Okay. Who's the lucky recipient?"

All three of them point to the other end of the bar and say in unison, "Him."

Lord. *That* is one beautiful man.

The three blondes were clearly not the only ones to notice. The brunette next to him with her full boobage on display is giving him her rapt attention when I walk over. Yet I feel his eyes on *me* as I walk down the long bar. I'm used to being hit on. Men seem to find an attractive woman whose sole purpose is to deliver them alcohol an alluring combination. They tend to become even bolder after tossing back a few drinks.

Halfway down the bar, I stop to refill a beer for a patron. I don't need to look up as I pour to know Beautiful Man is still watching me. The hair on the back of my neck is all the confirmation I need. He never takes his gaze off me, even when I turn, catch his eyes, and silently call him on his staring.

"I'm here to deliver you a Screaming Orgasm." Damn, he's even hotter up close. Sandy-brown, shoulder-length hair tousled just the right amount to make him look like he's just gotten laid. Long, lean torso, tattoos on his forearms peeking out from his long-sleeve fitted shirt. Nice. Then he smiles. Dimples. Yep. He *definitely* just got laid.

"Thank you. But I have a ladies-first policy." He winks.

I stare at him for a moment, then drop my eyes down to the drink, leading him to follow.

"Oh. You meant the drink." He smirks—it's sexy as hell, and he knows it.

I roll my eyes, but there's a reluctant smile hidden just beneath the surface. "It's from the three barely legal ladies down at the end." I nod in their direction and all three smile broadly and wave.

"Well, that's disappointing."

I arch an eyebrow. *"Those* three women buying you a drink with a name that tells you what their plans are for you later is a disappointment?"

"I thought *you* were buying me the drink."

Cheesy, I know, but there's a flutter in my stomach nonetheless. "Sorry. But you get the Doublemint triplets as a consolation prize." I shrug, trying to come off nonchalant, and turn to walk away. This close to him, the guy is making me fidget. It's a big bar, but the way he looks at me makes me feel like we're in a confined space.

"Wait," he calls after me, and I turn back. "What's your name?"

I smile and point at the sign over the bar. *Lucky's.*

The bar is hectic, but it doesn't stop me from keeping tabs on him. He nodded and held up his glass in thanks to the three women, but never walked down to meet them. Eventually, the trio of buxom blondes made their way to his end of the bar. They did their best at keeping his attention. He smiled politely, but it was clear he wasn't interested. Which seriously shocked me, because I would have bet the bar that he could have taken all three of them home.

"Hey, Lucky," Beautiful Man calls from the end of the bar when I finish waiting tables.

"Another Screaming Orgasm?"

"If you're talking alcohol, I'll pass and take a beer instead."

I grab a pint glass and pour a tall Guinness without asking what kind of beer he wants. I slide it toward him on the smooth waxed bar and ask, with an impish grin, "What if I wasn't talking about the alcohol?"

"We would already be out the door, sweetheart." Another wink, only this time he adds a crooked smile to the dimples on his ridiculously sexy face. There's a boyish quality to his smile, but a quick glance at the rest of him finds nothing but solid man. He sips his beer. "Guinness. My favorite. Nice choice."

Avery saddles up to the bar, a few spots over from Beautiful Man, and tosses her round serving tray in my direction. "Pearls wants another drink. Looks like your twenty is coming home with me, because I'm pretty sure she's going to pass out from the next one, not get up on stage."

I look over at the redhead with the tight bun. She's shimmying out of her navy blazer. Not only does she have incredible shoes, but with her blazer unbuttoned, her tiny waist and sinewy curves are on display—she's got a great body hidden under her suit and pearls. I'd guess there's a red lace demi-cup bra to match the G-string.

"You see that redhead over there?" I ask Beautiful Man.

"The one with her hair up?"

"That's the one. I have twenty that says she gets up to sing and turns into a siren on stage before the night is out."

Beautiful Man arches his eyebrows. "Doesn't look like the type to me."

"Don't listen to her." Avery dismisses me with her hand. "She also thinks she's wearing a red G-string under there."

"I'd like to hear this one."

"You can tell a lot about a person by what they wear. A woman who spends on shoes but dresses conservatively likes nice things, even if no one is seeing them. Strip a woman down to her underwear, you'll learn a lot about her." I shrug. "I've been here practically every day for seven years. I'm good at picking the closet rockstars."

He sips his beer and studies the redhead. "You ever get up there?" he asks me, only I don't have the chance to answer before Avery chimes in.

"She could be up on a real stage if she wanted to. But she's got arachnophobia."

Beautiful Man looks to me with a furrowed brow. "Fear of spiders?"

"Ignore her." I roll my eyes at Avery and make her drink order. "Tell Pearls this one is on the house." It's almost all orange juice. I started cutting back the alcohol in her drinks two rounds ago. Wouldn't want Pearls to fall over before her debut performance here at Lucky's.

It's nearly two in the morning when the DJ announces last call for karaoke sign-ups. The crowd at the bar has thinned out, but the tables are still keeping Avery busy. It's do-or-die time for the nervous hopefuls who came in with plans to get up on stage. Half usually make it, the other half stumble out inebriated from excess liquid courage.

Beautiful Man has spent hours fending off women, many drunk, gorgeous and easy. With an inexplicable gravitational pull, my eyes seem to track his whereabouts at all times. It's impossible to disregard his presence. I'm surprised to find him at the sign-up desk chatting with the DJ after his second trip to the bathroom.

"You came in to sing tonight?" I ask, refilling his beer when he returns to the seat he's spent all night at. "Wouldn't have taken you for the kind who needs alcohol to boost your confidence to get up there."

He sips his beer. "What would you take me as?"

I squint, pretending to assess him, and lean on the bar. He looks amused. "I would have said a player, but I've watched you fend off easy pickin's all night, so now I'm not really sure what to make of you actually." I shrug. "Are you here to sing?"

"Wasn't planning on it. Was supposed to meet someone here, but he called a few hours ago and said he got stuck and couldn't make it. Didn't even know it was a karaoke bar until I walked in."

"Interesting. But your friend canceled hours ago, yet you're still here. So you're on the prowl after all? You know, I don't think you're very good at it. You're supposed to show interest in the ones you want to take home at the end of the night."

Beautiful Man smiles; he's completely irresistible. "I have been."

I chuckle and shake my head before walking away to close out a patron's tab. Beautiful Man doesn't waste any time when I return to his end of the bar. "So...can I buy you a drink?"

I take an exaggerated look around. "Don't think that's necessary. I own a bar."

He isn't even slightly deterred. "Dinner then?"

I look at my watch. "It's two a.m."

"Breakfast?"

"I need to sleep before I eat breakfast."

"No problem. I'll cook for you when we wake up?"

I chuckle and shake my head, turning to stock the rest of the shelf with wine glasses. "Thank you for the generous offer. But I have to decline."

"You have got to be fucking kidding me!" Avery's outburst saves me from having to explain, although Beautiful Man's stare doesn't waver. He eyes me over the brim as he drinks from his tall pint glass. The sight of his Adam's apple working as he swallows does all kinds of things to my insides. And some things to parts of my outsides too.

"What's the matter?" I'm thankful for the distraction.

"Pearls. Look." Avery nods in the direction of the redhead, who is talking to the DJ. I gloat a smile as I watch her hand reach up to her tight bun and slip some hidden pins from the knot. Her hair cascades midway down her back.

"Told ya," I crow victoriously.

Pearls turns out to be even better than I could have imagined. Apparently, her hair wasn't the only thing the alcohol helped loosen. By the time she gets on the stage, her unbuttoned shirt reveals a healthy amount of cleavage and her skirt is hiked above her knees so she can move. And can the woman move. The slow rock of her hips as she sings the old Faith Hill song "Breathe" turns the temperature in the bar up at least ten degrees. Pearls can sing too. Not just carry a tune…really sing. A breathy, sultry, perfectly-in-key flowing melody that, with a little training, could sound great on an album. My attention is riveted on the woman as the closed flower who came in begins to blossom, right before our eyes. More than the song she sings, the sight itself is beautiful to watch.

I envy her. I'd give anything to get up there again. But, for me, it's going to take more than a little liquid courage. Years of therapy produced little results, and for a long time I learned to accept who I was. Although, every once in a while, my soul overpowers my logical brain and yearns for salvation. Which leads me to make illogical decisions. Like tomorrow, for example.

For some reason, I keep away from Beautiful Man after that. There's plenty to do as closing time draws near, so it isn't difficult. I make Avery switch with me, taking a second turn behind the bar, so I can work the floor instead. She probably thinks I'm trying to give her a break on my last night; the floor is never easy around closing time. Too many drunks, and cutting them off almost always results in boisterous rants.

As he does every night at the same time, the DJ comes over the loudspeaker to announce last call for drinks at the bar, but then he adds, "Tonight Lucky's is excited to have a celebrity in the house. For those of you not yet familiar with Flynn Beckham, you will be soon. Rumor has it he'll be joining a big sold-out tour. Let's give it up for a rocker who's going to show us his softer side tonight up on our stage."

The whole place erupts in applause, except me. I'm rooted in place watching Beautiful Man stride to the stage. He takes the microphone from the stand and scans the room with an easy smile. Eyes falling on me, his voice rasps over the speakers, the words sliding over me. "This isn't usually my style. But it's almost closing time, so I thought maybe I could help inspire those of you who are hoping to get lucky tonight. Like me." He winks at me and nods to the DJ to start the song. I recognize the song in the first four notes. It's one of my all-time favorites. A true classic, although people my age usually don't appreciate the gritty, heartfelt sound of Rod Stewart anymore. The music of "Tonight's the Night" plays quietly in the background until Beautiful Man's sinful voice joins in.

I was glued to the stage watching Pearls belt out her song, but for a totally different reason than I am now. His voice is seduction in the form of sound, and it flows from him with the ease of a pro. The entire bar sways back and forth. Every woman moves closer to the stage. Even Pearls.

For a long moment I watch the way his foot taps in perfect time to the beat. A man with good rhythm has always been my weakness. *Musicians* have always been my kryptonite. Then my eyes slowly travel up, taking in the parts of the man I'd only glimpsed from the other side of the bar. Jeans hang low on his narrow hips, a simple dark thermal hugs his broad shoulders. Ink peeks out from the pushed-up sleeves on both forearms. When my eyes finally reach his face, I find he's been watching me watch him. He arches an eyebrow and sings the next verse into my eyes.

You'd be a fool to stop this tide

Spread your wings, and let me come inside

I blink myself out of my daze. Flynn Beckham has a way of gliding his eyes over every woman in the room, yet making you feel like you're the only one he's actually looking at. As though he just found *the one* in a crowd of women, and not just the one he's going to take home tonight...*the one* he's been looking for since the first day he got on stage.

"Jesus. He sings another song and I'm straddling the speaker," Avery says, leaning her forearms on the bar. "Bet I can orgasm just from the vibration of his voice between my legs." She's speaking to me, yet she never tears her eyes away from Beautiful Man. Together we gaze at the stage with the adulation of teenyboppers watching Justin Bieber. "That man wants you. Pretty sure you wouldn't have to straddle the speaker. He'd bury his head and sing right into your vajayjay if you wanted. I totally vote you upgrade in the rockstar boyfriend category. Where is Sleazy Ryder tonight anyway?"

My best friend doesn't care for my boyfriend. Dylan Ryder is the lead singer of Easy Ryder, but she has a dozen alternative names for him and his band. "He got stuck in Philadelphia...missed his connection back. Called to say he wouldn't make it here tonight."

"That's too bad." She smiles slyly. "One man's loss is another man's luck."

"It's 'One man's loss is another man's gain.'"

"That too."

chapter

two

Flynn

The sun blares in through the small gap of the drawn curtains and lands directly on my face. I shield my eyes and try to fall back asleep, until I feel tiny hands trace the ink on my forearm. When her little finger follows the path of ink up to my shoulder, I surprise Laney by grabbing her and lifting her over my head. She squeals at the initial shock, but it quickly turns to a giggle. The sound warms me, even though my head is already beginning to throb.

"Uncle Sinn, you scared me!"

I growl, in my best monster voice, "Well, you shouldn't wake a sleeping lion."

"You're not a lion, Uncle Sinn. Lions are scary!"

"And you don't think I'm scary?" I lower my four-year-old niece from above my head and bring her forehead to my lips for a kiss.

"You can't be scary, you have funny pictures all over your arms and back." From the mouths of babes. Tell that to a tatted-up biker dude.

"Will you seep in my room with me tonight?"

"Maybe. If Mom says it's okay."

"Will you sing me that song when we go to bed again?"

"Sure." I don't have to ask which song. She made me sing it four hundred times the last time I visited.

"How come only one tattoo is colored, Uncle Sinn?" She pokes the red tattoo on my forearm—it's the only ink that isn't black or a shade of grey.

I jump up from the bed unexpectedly with her in my arms. She squeals again. "You're chock-full of questions this morning, aren't you?"

She nods fast, bursting with excitement, as if shooting off an arsenal of questions early in the morning was a good thing.

"Come on, let's go find your mother." I lift her over my head and onto my shoulders. Her tiny hands wrap around my chin.

"You're up early." My sister, Becca, is at the kitchen table. I walk to the coffee pot and pour before greeting her. Laney hasn't said a word; she's waiting for me to play the "where's Laney?" game.

"I thought I heard Laney. Have you seen her?" I pivot left, then right, scanning the room.

My sister's eyes rise to the passenger on my shoulders and she smiles. I picture Laney's crooked-toothed smile gleaming back at her from above my head. "Nope. Haven't seen her. Maybe she's hiding under the bed."

"That's too bad. I was going to take her out for waffles and ice cream for breakfast. With whipped cream. Lots of whipped cream." I grin, knowing my niece's weakness.

"Uncle Sinn! I'm right here!" Laney screeches and tugs my chin up to look at her.

"Oh. There you are."

My sister chuckles at the routine. "You know, I'm tempted to tell the speech therapist not to work on her Fs…because her name for you is just too perfect."

I heave Laney from my shoulders and steady her on her feet. "Why don't you go get ready for breakfast?"

"I wanna wear my *Frozen* pajamas to breakfast!" She jumps up and down.

I say okay, just as my sister tells her no. I love my sister dearly, but we've always been opposites.

"She can't go to breakfast in her pajamas," Becca scolds.

I shrug. "Why not? She's four, not forty."

"Because people don't go out in their pajamas."

"*Your* people don't go out in their pajamas. *Mine* are perfectly fine with it."

"*Your* people are nuts."

"My people are fun."

"Because they wear pajamas to breakfast?"

"No. Because they don't care about what other people think of them wearing pajamas to breakfast. Lighten up, Bec. You sound like Mom."

Her eyes widen to saucers. She huffs, but I already know she's gonna cave. "Fine. You can wear your *Frozen* pajamas. But no slippers. Put on shoes and socks."

"So how long are you in town for?"

"If everything goes as planned, seven weeks. Then I'm on the road for six months."

"Six months? That's a really long time, Flynn. Is the whole thing by bus?"

"Most of it. But Easy Ryder has some dates in Europe. I'm not sure if we're playing those or the current opening act, Resin, is. That's one of the things my agent is still working out before we finalize the deal to join the tour." The original Wylde Ryde tour was supposed to last six months. But the band's sales have dipped a bit, so they added almost six more months to try to regain momentum before the release of their next album. And the current opening act couldn't join the extended dates.

"Agent." She smiles. "Listen to you, big shot. You're not going to get too famous for us, are you?"

"Never. I'll always come back for my girl." I lean over in my seat and kiss Laney on her very full cheek. She has a dollop of whipped cream on her nose and ice cream dripping down her chin. But she's smiling from ear to ear. I'm guessing my sister's idea of a fun breakfast is adding a banana to whole grain oatmeal.

The attentive waitress swings by our table again. "Can I get you anything else?" Her smile is directed at me. I'm not full of myself—well, maybe I am a bit—but I can tell she's interested in something more than breakfast. She's cute, although a little on the young side.

"We're good. But thanks," Becca responds just as I open my mouth to speak. I know my sister—her over-the-top smile oozes a bit too much sweetness to be real. She barely waits until the waitress is out of earshot. "Jesus, Flynn. Is *that* the norm for you these days? That waitress was practically drooling."

"Can't blame her. I *am* one of America's most eligible bachelors, you know." I sigh loudly, clasp my hands behind my head, and tip my chair back.

Six months ago I was on a reality TV program, where I was the bachelor. I fell hard for Kate, one of the contestants, but my feelings weren't returned. Last I spoke to her, she had just found out she was having a baby girl with her new husband, Cooper.

A few weeks after the show ended, a magazine came out with their annual list of America's most eligible bachelors, and my name was somehow on it. I thought it was pretty comical that anyone would describe me as an eligible bachelor, seeing as I was unemployed at the time. But that doesn't stop me from gloating about it to my sister and my buddies.

My sister rolls her eyes. "You were an honorable mention on the last page of the article. The writer probably just felt bad for you because you did that stupid show and didn't get the girl in the end."

"You just can't see the hotness of your own brother," I tease. "Laney, who is the handsomest man in the world?"

She immediately points to me, her sticky lips smiling brightly, barely containing her mouth full of food.

"See."

"Is that what you do, you shovel their mouths full of sweets to get them to fall in love with you?"

I arch an eyebrow.

"Gross, Flynn. Just gross."

The lead singer of Easy Ryder is a bit of a douche. He made me wait at a bar for hours the other night before canceling, then today he's more than an hour late. I get it, shit happens. But walk in the room and at least pretend you give a crap by expressing an insincere apology. Instead, the minute he sits down at the conference table with me, Nolan and nine suits from Pulse Records, Dylan Ryder starts bitching.

"I asked for Throat Coat tea. That's not what this is," Dylan berates the assistant who just delivered his drink without ever looking up at her.

"It is Throat Coat tea, I made it myself," she says in a timid voice.

"Then your water tastes like shit. Use Voss."

"I don't think we have Voss."

"Well, then go to a store," he barks and lifts the cup over his head for her to take it away.

The assistant's face flushes. "Okay."

"So." He turns his attention to me and dives right in. "I wanna be clear about one thing before we bring your band on board."

"All right."

"This is *my* show. The name on the tour is Easy Ryder, not Flynn fucking Beckham or In Like Flynn, or whatever it is you call yourselves. I like your sound or you wouldn't be here. But my tour is *my* tour. We aren't coheadlining, you aren't playing encores and cutting into my show, and you certainly aren't selling your crap in *my* arenas." He stops and glares at me. "You good with that?"

Total douchebag. "Got it."

"I'm gonna hold you to it. Pussy is going to love your pretty face. Will make you feel like you're more important than you are. Don't let it go to your head."

Like you? "No problem."

Again, he glares at me. My short, stoic answers leave him questioning if I'm mocking him or responding with the respect a petty soldier shows a commanding officer. Eventually, he nods and turns to his manager. "Sign 'em. You leave in less than two months."

And just like that, In Like Flynn is going on tour.

chapter three

Lucky

My father swears I was tapping a rhythmic beat in my mother's belly before I even took my first breath. Honestly, I can't imagine doing anything else with my life. It's always revolved around music. My father was a drummer in two different bands for more than twenty years. My mother—well, singing is still her first love. *Music*. It's in the blood that pumps through my veins, keeps me alive as much as my own heartbeat.

Not being able to get up on stage and do what I love is a curse, but in a weird way, it was also a blessing for a time. Staying behind the scenes has taught me so much about music. There's certainly something to be said about the old truism *Those who can, do. Those who can't, teach.*

"Thank you, Lucky. I swear, I've learned more in the last week than I have in the last five years."

"You're sweet, Chelsea. But you're the one doing all the work. I'm only here to guide you to be the best you can."

"Same days next week?" she asks.

"I look forward to it. Try to rest your voice over the weekend. You worked hard this week."

I pack up after my last session of the day and look around at the sound studio. When Dylan first mentioned his record label was looking for a full-time voice coach, I was leery for so many reasons. Since going back to school and getting my degree, I'd trained only a select few people on a very part-time basis. Lucky's was my home, my comfort zone, but I hated the damn place almost as much as I loved it. Not to mention that the thought of having to demonstrate vocal techniques for more than one or two people was enough to make my palms break out into a sweat. Yet I knew it was time for a change. I'd been standing in place long enough—so I took the job. *Step three, Dad. You see that? I'm making progress.* If the first week has been any indication of things to come, I'm going to be very happy here.

With my last coaching of the week done, where else would I go to celebrate, but Lucky's?

The bar is crowded, even for a Friday night. It feels odd to stand on the patron side of the bar when I walk in.

Avery spots me immediately. "Hey, stranger! What the heck are you doing on that side of the bar? Come help me out. I'm drowning back here."

I smile. Oddly, I'm glad she needs me. I throw on an apron and start taking orders and mixing drinks. Avery and I catch up as we work.

"What happened to the new girl you hired?"

"Fired."

"What? Already?"

"Her customer service skills were a little too friendly."

"She was giving away too many buybacks?"

"Caught her giving a blow job in the bathroom while she was supposed to be waiting tables."

"Maybe he ordered a Screaming Orgasm." I grin, remembering Beautiful Man.

Together we clear the bar orders in less than half an hour, and I tell her about my first week at Pulse Records.

"That reminds me," she says. "The hot guy who was lusting after you last week came back in."

"He did?" My interest perks up. I've found my thoughts wandering to Flynn on more than one occasion. There was just something about him, aside from the obvious—that he was ridiculously good-looking.

"Yep. Twice."

"Did he come in to sing?"

Avery shakes her head and smiles. "Came in looking for you."

"What did you tell him?"

"Told him the first time that you weren't here. The second time, I told him to try back tonight. That maybe you would stop in."

My eyes bulge. "What? Why did you do that? You know I'm meeting Dylan here."

"So?" She shrugs. "You didn't do anything wrong. Might do Sleazy Ryder some good to see other men interested in you."

"You just like to screw with him."

"That's just a bonus."

"Be nice." I slide two wine glasses out of the rack above my head. "Or I'll tell Dylan that you had his poster on your bedroom wall when we were teens, too."

Avery stops. "You wouldn't dare."

"Oh I would. I might even embellish the truth a little and tell him you still have a big ole crush on him. You're really just jealous *I* was the one working the second time he visited Lucky's a year ago. And that's why you give him an attitude."

My best friend flips me the bird with a smile and returns to the business of waiting on customers.

Easy Ryder is on a short tour break. They've been on the road for four months already, and still have almost eight more months ahead of them now that they've extended their tour. Dating a rockstar is counted in dog years—Dylan and I have been together for nearly a year, but that only equates to a few months in the real world.

Word spread quickly that Dylan and his entourage were at Lucky's tonight. Avery had to lock the door fifteen minutes after their arrival, and now the line waiting to get in extends around the corner.

"You've been behind the bar all night," Dylan says. "Come sit with me."

"I can't. Look at this place." I take a quick glimpse around. The last hour that I've been pouring drinks hasn't made a dent in the three rows of people waiting to be served.

"You don't work here anymore."

"No. But Avery does. What am I supposed to do, let her drown? Plus, I'm still half owner."

Dylan sips his beer. "She should have hired someone."

"She did. It didn't work out."

"Excuse me. Mr. Ryder?" We're interrupted by yet another duo of girls saddling up to Dylan. Both blond, both wearing bustiers, with skintight jeans and leather boots reaching to the knee. "Can we take your picture?"

Dylan looks to me and then to the two girls.

"Can I see some ID, ladies?" I lean closer to the bar and extend my hand palm up.

"We showed it at the door."

Jase is working the door tonight. His idea of proper identification when a young, hot girl wants inside is to measure their bra cup size. Anything better than a C is automatically of age. My eyes drop to their well-endowed chests. "Still going to need to see ID to stay inside."

The eye contact between the two girls as they stall, fishing for their fake IDs, confirms my suspicion. Definitely underage. I'd guess nineteen at best. Hesitantly, they pass me their licenses. The picture on one resembles the first girl, but her age is certainly not thirty-two. The second girl doesn't come close to being the woman in the picture I'm looking at.

"Sorry, ladies. You're going to need to leave."

The two girls pout but are smart enough not to argue. They're lucky I'm even offering the licenses back to them. With a scowl at me, they snatch the IDs from my hand and return their attention to Dylan. "Can we *please*"—they coo in unison—"take a quick picture before we go?"

Dylan looks to me and I lift my hand as if to say, *by all means*. The two snuggle against him and extend their arms for a barrage of pictures—all three smiling.

I tend to a few customers, then walk around the bar to greet Dylan properly for the first time.

He curls his arms around my waist and pulls me close to him, rubbing his nose to mine. "I like you jealous."

"I wasn't jealous." *Maybe just a little.*

"Mmm mmm." He kisses me. "I missed you."

"I missed you too." I rest my head to his shoulder and sag into him as he wraps his arms around my waist and pulls me close. I didn't realize how much I've missed his touch—until I feel it again.

"I thought now that you had a normal job I would have more nights with you to myself. Why don't we get out of here?" His hand slips into the back of my jeans.

"I can't. Avery needs me."

"I need you." His lips brush against my neck. "Need to be inside you."

I groan. "That will give me incentive to work faster."

Dylan shifts me so our bodies are lined up and draws me even closer. "Feel what you do to me?" Evidence of his arousal digs into my stomach. "The longer you keep us here, the more difficult it will be for you to walk tomorrow."

After a quick peck on the lips that Dylan tries to turn into more, I hurry back behind the bar, before I don't. Sometimes I still can't believe how things turned out. I'm dating the man whose poster spent years on my bedroom wall, the rockstar who helped put Lucky's on the map. The sign behind the bar catches my eye, and I'm suddenly feeling nostalgic about so many things.

Lucky—
Twelve years earlier,
age thirteen

"Keep your eyes shut, Luciana."

Uh oh. He's using Luciana. That usually means I'm in trouble. I was named after my grandfather, Luciano Valentine. My parents thought changing the o to an a would make it a more acceptable feminine name. They'd planned to call me Luciana Alessandra Valentine, until I was born. Apparently, my auburn hair and fair skin didn't match the name, so Lucky I became.

"Where are we going?" Dad insisted I keep my eyes closed since we climbed the stairs from the subway. That had to be a whole block ago.

"We're almost there. No peeking." A door creaks and he guides me inside. I open my lids just enough for a quick peep, but wherever he's taking me is darker inside than outside, and the sun is already long gone.

Another couple of steps, the floor squeaks beneath us, and then I hear a light switch flip on.

"Okay. You can open up."

I open my eyes and look around. The big room is empty, but I know where I am. I should have guessed from the smell. He's snuck me into the back room at plenty of places like this, since the day I could walk. "A bar? You brought me to a bar?"

He smiles. "It's not just any bar." Dad's eyes meet mine. "It's ours."

"What do you mean, it's ours?"

"I mean, no more road. I know you like it here. So we're going to stay."

"Really?" The teenage I-don't-give-a-crap attitude I wear most of the time slips off, the excitement of a little kid gleaming through in its place. Of all the places we've lived, I love New York the most. The trains, the sidewalks packed with people, even the blare of the cabbies' horns sounds like urban music to my ears. And I have a best friend here. OhmyGod. I can't wait to tell Avery.

"Yep. I'm going to turn it into a karaoke bar." Dad lifts me up onto the dusty bar and points to a corner. The dimly lit room is mostly empty, with some lingering garbage strewn over the floor, but I can see the vision through Dad's excited eyes. "We're going to build a stage over there. And over here"—he waves his hand toward the other side—"we'll put little round tables for people to watch the singers."

"Can I sing on stage?"

My dad chuckles. "Once we're open, it will be over twenty-one only, squirt."

The enthusiasm I felt fades a bit. My life has been filled with places I'm not really supposed to be. Bars, clubs, festivals. I'm always stuck hiding backstage. I've heard some of the best bands play, but seen only a few perform.

Dad lifts my chin. "You will be on that stage when you're ready. If it's before you're twenty-one, we'll shut the bar down and have a private party. Think your old man will be good enough on drums to back you?"

"Do you think Mom will come?"

His face wilts a bit. "I don't know, Lucky. She's on the road a lot."

"Can I ask her?"

"Of course."

"So what's the name of this place?"

"I was thinking of naming it after my favorite woman."

"Iris sounds nice. I'm sure Mom will love it."

"Who said anything about Iris? This place is ours. I'm going to call it Lucky's."

Unlike most bars in New York City, Lucky's has been blessed with a crowd since the first night we opened. We get an eclectic mix of tourists who've read about the occasional surprise musical guest that stops in, and the local crowd that appreciates friendly service with live music. On nights like tonight, when a celebrity is in the bar, word spreads quickly.

"Hey, Avery," Dylan calls. His posse seems to have grown from ten to thirty over the last hour; they're taking up one entire end of the bar. Dylan has his phone up to his ear and he's gesturing Avery over, even though her hands are elbow-deep in the double sink.

"Sure. Don't get up," she mutters so I can hear her as she passes.

"The guy you have working the door won't let someone in who's coming to meet me."

"That's because we're at capacity. Someone needs to leave in order to let someone in."

"It's one person."

"It's a five-thousand-dollar fine, not to mention a fire hazard."

"Fine," he grumbles. "So kick someone out."

"I'm not going to kick out people. Tell someone from your entourage to leave."

"Are you fucking kidding me?" Dylan's voice rises, so I step in.

"What's wrong?"

"Rockstar here wants me to kick a customer out so he can bring another member of his tribe in."

"You know what, don't do me any favors." Dylan looks around and calls to a guy I've seen before. I think he's part of the road crew. "You." He points. "Go wait outside."

The man points to himself.

Dylan huffs, annoyed that he has to explain. "The place is at capacity. I'm meeting someone here and they won't let him in until someone leaves. Can you go outside so he can get in?"

"Sure." The guy looks put off, but finishes his beer and heads to the door.

Avery disappears to serve customers. "Who else are you meeting? It looks like you have your usual crew all here."

"The singer from the new band we signed to open the tour."

chapter four

Flynn

The place is twice as crowded as when I was here last week. The same woman is bartending, no sign of Lucky anywhere. It's not hard to find Dylan once I'm finally inside—he's got an entourage the size of his ego.

"What's up, Foreplay?" Dylan shakes my hand. He motions to the men around him, some of whom I recognize from Easy Ryder. "Guys…this is Flynn Beckham from In Like Flynn. His band is going to replace Resin for the second half of the tour. Get the audience all worked up so we can slide in and finish the job."

I smile, even though everything about this guy rubs me the wrong way.

"You want a beer, Flynn?" Avery yells from behind the bar with a warm smile.

"Absolutely."

"Guinness?"

"Sure."

"You've been here before?" Dylan asks.

"Last week. I was already here when you had to cancel."

"Yeah, sorry about that, man. Got a last-minute proposition that was too good to pass up. You know how that is." Dylan winks. "Had to miss my flight."

"No worries. Worked out pretty good. Actually came back twice this week." Avery delivers my beer with a smile. "The owner is smokin' and pretty cool too."

Dylan chuckles. "I know her well. She's actually a cunt." He takes a swig from his beer. "But I bet she's a hot lay. She's tight with my girl. Wonder if I can talk her into a little two-on-one action."

If I thought the guy was a dick before, hearing him call Lucky a cunt makes me want to knock him on his ass. But I keep my mouth shut and drink my beer instead. "This place is great. It has a sixties vibe to it."

"It's not bad. The singing can be fucking torture though. You ready to start practicing soon?"

"Looking forward to it. Doc's had my voice on strict bed rest the last two months to bring down the swelling on the nodule I flared from the forty-shows-in-forty-days gig I did for that reality TV show."

"But you're good now?"

"Voice has never been stronger. Last follow-up scheduled for the day after tomorrow."

"Good. Because I don't want your voice breaking and sounding like shit when you're warming up my fans."

"Wouldn't sign on unless I was good to go."

"Here comes my girl. Maybe she can hook you up with her friend."

I prefer to arrange my own hookups, but I nod and smile nonetheless. Dylan raises his hand and yells over a crowd of people, "Babe, come here. I want you to meet someone."

Following the lead of his voice, I turn to check out the woman walking toward us and my heart wrenches in my chest. *You have got to be kidding me. There are eight million people in New York City. Her?*

I blink a few times. The dimly lit bar is mobbed. Maybe it's not her. Or maybe he's calling to someone else. She takes a few steps closer. Fuck. There's no mistaking it's her now. That auburn hair, pale skin and green eyes—I've been seeing her face in my head for a week. She looks even better than I remember too. Green sleeveless blouse that dips to show a hint of cleavage, dozens of bracelets sparkling their way up her flawless skin. Tight jeans and leather boots that run halfway up her legs.

I'm staring, mesmerized by her every step as she makes her way through the crowd and over to us. My pulse quickens and there's a primal urge inside me to reach out and grab her as she comes within my grasp. Wrap her into my arms so no one else can touch her. Certainly not Dylan douchebag Ryder.

But then, before I start breathing again, he's reaching for her arm and pulling her close to him.

"Lucky, this is Flynn. He's the new opening act for the Wylde Ryde tour."

Seeing me for the first time, Lucky's eyes flare. A lump forms in my throat, and I'm forced to swallow it down. I take a long pull from my beer to help wash away the bad taste.

"Nice to meet you, Lucky." I extend my hand. I'm naturally a flirt; the last woman whose hand I shook was probably a teacher in high school. Actually, scratch that, Miss Cleary was hot, pretty sure I kissed her on the last day of school.

Lucky's hesitant, but places her hand in mine. The feel of her soft skin makes me wish I'd taken a chance and run my lips over the silky smoothness of her cheek. Only, I know the cheek wouldn't be enough. "Nice to meet you too."

Dylan pulls her against his body possessively and wraps his hand around her waist before delivering more than a friendly kiss.

"Flynn here has a thing for Avery," Dylan announces, looking at me.

Lucky flushes and I think I see what might be a hint of disappointment.

"Is that so? Well, don't listen to anything Dylan has to say about my best friend. These two don't get along. She's a great catch."

"Sure she is, if you're into sadistic ball-breakers," Dylan comments. "Me, I prefer sweet on the outside, with a side order of slut in the bedroom."

Lucky elbows him in the ribs. "Dylan! What the hell is wrong with you?" She turns to me. "Avery is *not* a sadistic ball-breaker. I need to go give her a hand. She's swamped again."

For the next few hours, I try not to let my eyes wander to Lucky. But I'm fighting a losing battle. The smile on her face, the way she tilts her head to the side when she's listening to someone, her body constantly moving in some small way to the music. Watching her is like watching a butterfly. It's beautiful on the outside, its wings decorated with color that captures your eye, but it's the way the butterfly flutters around, always seemingly out of reach, that makes you follow it with your eyes.

When Lucky starts dancing with Avery behind the bar, and I don't even notice the woman standing at my side vying for my attention, I decide it's time to get some air. I head toward the bathrooms and escape out the back door, a place I discovered this week that all the smokers seem to know about.

The fresh air feels good. It's a warm spring night that reminds me of what's right around the corner. Long days filled with sunlight, nights filled with women who finally have an excuse to wear little clothing. I should be looking forward to it, to getting back on tour. A different city, a different woman every night if I want it. Hell, on the road, one a night is by no means the daily limit. Yet the only thing I'm looking forward to is getting back on stage and playing my music.

"I should've known you were a smoker," Avery says as she slips outside and joins me.

"Oh yeah, why is that?"

"Oral fixation. Explains why you've been staring at Lucky's mouth all night."

"I actually quit." I inhale a long drag.

"Me too." She pulls a cigarette from her cleavage and brings it to her lips. I light it for her.

"I only smoke one every now and then. I just bummed this one."

"Then you haven't quit yet, have you?"

"Close enough." I pause. "Thanks for the heads-up that Lucky was meeting her boyfriend here tonight, by the way."

"No problem." Avery smiles and takes a puff of her cigarette. "I'm hoping Doucheluck doesn't last as long as TomKat."

"You lost me?"

"Katie Holmes and Tom Cruise. That disaster took six years to unravel. Dylan was Lucky's teenage crush. He's also a douche. He doesn't deserve my best friend. She needs a new boyfriend."

"Yeah, well. I tend to keep away from women with boyfriends. Too many problems."

"Sounds like you've been there before?"

"Not intentionally. Only when they fail to mention it before it's too late."

"Well, Lucky is worth breaking your rule."

"She's also the girlfriend of the lead singer of the band I'm going to spend six months traveling with."

"I heard. Sounds like fate to me."

"I think you're confusing fate with fatal."

Nolan Blake taught me how to smoke. How to hold a cigarette so I didn't look like a chick, how to ditch it out with my bare foot so I looked cool yet didn't burn the sole of my foot and, most importantly, how to smoke the whole thing between my lips without using my hands. The last lesson came naturally to him, considering he needed both hands free to strum his guitar twelve out of twenty-four hours of the day for as far back as I can remember.

"You know, this shit's your fault."

"What are you talking about?"

"If you hadn't taught me to smoke in sixth grade, I probably wouldn't have developed the nodule on my throat that's keeping us sitting in this waiting room looking like two gay guys."

"If I hadn't taught you to smoke, you wouldn't have ever turned cool, and you wouldn't have gotten to feel up Ellie Martin that summer."

Ellie Martin. Now that's a name I haven't heard in fifteen years. That girl had double-Ds in sixth grade. Perfectly round, like two giant cantaloupes. I sigh, thinking back to that day. "Totally worth a nodule."

Nolan chuckles. "By the way, if we were gay, you'd be the catcher taking it up the ass. I'd be pitching."

"I *definitely* would not be taking your skinny little prick. My anaconda would be splitting your ass in two." I pause. "And why are we even having this fucking conversation anyway?" We both laugh.

"Mr. Beckham," the nurse calls.

"You want me to come with you, honey?" Nolan says, loudly enough for the entire waiting room to hear. Then, with his hand adorned with a half dozen gaudy rings, he blows me a kiss.

After an hour with the otolaryngologist and a forty-five minute cab ride back downtown, Nolan and I are finally heading to Pulse Records to sign the tour contracts. Opening for Easy Ryder is an ideal gig for us— their audience looks a lot like our audience, our play time is only a little shorter than theirs, and since we have the same record label, we were able to arrange studio time to work on our next album during the tour. Yet I have a nagging feeling that I'm about to make a huge mistake. With no real tangible evidence to support my gut, I keep the feeling to myself and just try to ignore it.

The Pulse offices are impressive: walls lined with platinum album covers, framed *Billboard* charts—a literal hall of fame that leads us to a large conference room that could easily seat fifty. The pretty woman with the short skirt and high heels who steered us into the inner sanctum is replaced by an even prettier woman with an even shorter skirt and even taller heels.

"I'm Heidi, Mr. Simon's personal assistant. Welcome, Mr. Beckham, Mr. Blake." She nods. "Mr. Simon apologizes. He's running twenty minutes late. He asks that you please make yourselves at home. There is a green room down the hall to the left. Van Mars is recording if you'd like to pop in and listen. Or there is a cafeteria downstairs. If you tell them you're a guest of Mr. Simon's, everything will be on the house."

"Which one will you join me at?" Nolan asks with his usual cocky swagger. I roll my eyes; Heidi licks her lips.

"I'm going to head downstairs and get some coffee. The guy I bunked with last night doesn't even have a coffee pot," I goad Nolan.

"I don't drink coffee...why the fuck do I need a coffee pot?"

"For when I stay over, asswipe."

"Go back to your own place in Jersey. I'm not buying a damn coffee pot for you. If I keep you happy, you might stay over more often." Nolan turns his attention back to Mr. Simon's assistant. "Now if Heidi likes coffee, I might have to stop and get a pot."

I chuckle, shake my head, and leave Nolan to his morning conquest.

The cafeteria is crowded, even though it's somewhere between breakfast and lunchtime. But I suppose most people visiting Pulse generally consider morning to begin around noon.

I came in looking for coffee, but the smell of bacon wafts through the air and my body follows on its own. Coffee turns into two eggs, bacon and cheese on a roll, an orange juice and a chocolate pudding. Actually, *two* chocolate puddings. Because people who pass by fresh chocolate pudding without grabbing one just can't be trusted.

Finally at the front of the long register line, I realize I've forgotten to grab the damn coffee. I leave my tray and tell the cashier to take the next person. I seriously shouldn't walk around at only eleven in the morning with no coffee and Stevie Ray Vaughan ripping in my ear buds.

The sinuous riffs of "Texas Flood" have me lost to the music and it takes me five minutes to prep my coffee because of the constant need to stop and accompany Stevie on air guitar. Oblivious, I make my way back to the register to collect my tray and pay, when a woman's voice shakes me out of my musical coma.

"Cutting the line?" she says.

I pull the bud from my ear and turn. "Lucky? What are you doing here?" For a quick second, I actually think I might be dreaming.

She smiles. "Apparently, getting cut in line by a guy who is going to lose his hearing from playing his music so loud."

"Sorry. I was on line, but I forgot my coffee." I hold up my cup as if evidence is needed. The cashier apparently isn't as in awe of Lucky as I am; her face tells me to pay and move along. I take a bill from my wallet and motion to my tray and Lucky's. "For both."

"You don't have to buy my breakfast."

"I want to." *I'd rather buy you dinner and make your breakfast the next morning.* I look down and smile seeing the contents of her tray. Chocolate pudding and coffee.

"Breakfast of champions." She shrugs.

I know I probably shouldn't, but I just can't help myself. "Eat with me."

She looks at the time on her phone, then back to me, and bites her bottom lip. Without thinking, I reach up and tug the flesh from between her teeth. "You're going to bruise this pretty mouth."

She flushes but agrees to have breakfast. I direct her to a quiet corner of the room. "What are you doing here?" The minute the words leave my mouth, I realize she must be here with Dylan. Fuck. I'm an idiot. Any second, he'll be joining our table. Great.

"I work here."

"You work here? I thought you owned Lucky's."

"I did. I mean, I do. Avery and I are partners now and she runs it. My last night managing it was actually the night you first came in."

"What do you do here?"

"I'm a vocal coach."

"I thought you said you don't sing?"

"I don't...not in public anyway, anymore."

"You used to sing?"

"A little." She seems anxious to move the conversation from her. "What brings you here today?" Her spoon dips into the chocolate pudding and rises to her mouth and I follow it with rapt attention.

"We're signing the contract for the Wylde Ryde tour."

"Oh."

"Yeah. About that. Sorry about the other night. I didn't know you were with Dylan."

She shrugs. "You didn't do anything wrong."

"Maybe not, but I wanted to."

Her cheeks pink up again. God, I love the color of her skin. The way it doesn't allow her to mask any of her emotions, even if she tries.

"Well. It all worked out anyway. Avery is incredible."

"Avery?"

"I thought you were interested in her."

"I actually said I was into the bar's owner."

She looks confused, and then her mouth forms an O. Right before her cheeks flush again.

"Don't worry...Dylan just assumed I meant your friend." An awkward silence falls. "So how long have you two been together?"

"A little less than a year."

I nod. "You eat chocolate pudding and coffee for breakfast often?"

She giggles. "I have every day since I started here. I just can't seem to pass the damn display."

"I know what you mean."

"I better watch myself. I have no self-control around chocolate, and between not running around the bar all night and having a cafeteria with good food in the building, my ass is going to bear the brunt."

"I'll watch your ass for you. Make sure it stays in top form." I wink.

"How chivalrous of you."

"I'm good like that."

She shakes her head. "So are you excited to go on tour?"

"I'm excited to play in front of an audience again."

"You took a break?"

I nod. "Not by choice. Nodule on my throat."

"Sorry. Strained from too much singing?"

"That's what the doctor said."

"Well, there're a lot of things you can do to keep it from flaring up. Have you been to a voice coach?"

"No."

"I'll give you my number. Call me if your voice starts to show signs of strain. I might be able to help."

I nod, lift my phone, and snap a picture.

"Hey. I'm eating. Why did you take a picture?"

"To go with your number in my phone."

"And you needed it to identify me because you know a lot of Luckys?"

She has a point. "What's your number?" I ask.

"Let me see the picture or I'm not giving it to you."

I arch an eyebrow. "You're going to injure my voice and most likely ruin my career because of one bad picture of you with chocolate pudding on your lip?"

Her eyes flash. "I have chocolate pudding on my lip in the picture?"

"Maybe." I smile.

Lucky grabs for my phone, but I pull my hand back just as quickly.

"Let me see the picture!"

"Okay. But only if you give me your phone number first."

"Is there really even chocolate on my face in the picture?" She licks her lips.

My eyes fall to watch her tongue. There's a drop at the corner of her mouth. I lean forward and swipe it with my finger. Her lips part. Then I lift my finger to show her the tiniest of smudges…right before I bring it to my mouth and lick off the pudding. "Delicious." *Chocolate pudding and Lucky. My new favorite flavor.*

"I shouldn't even give you my phone number now."

"Why, because I gave you a compliment?"

"What was the compliment?"

"I said you were delicious."

"I thought you were talking about the pudding."

A wicked grin on my face, I slowly shake my head back and forth.

"You're dangerous."

"Thank you."

"That wasn't a compliment."

"Think you need to work on the difference between compliments and insults."

Time flies, both our trays are long empty, and I've been gone for close to an hour, even though Heidi told us Simon would be only twenty minutes late. But I just can't bring myself to walk away from her. She tells me a little about Lucky's and her new job, and I'm actually enjoying the conversation—maybe even as much as I enjoy looking at her. There's an odd familiar feeling that I get when we talk. It was there the first time we spoke, even more so today. It feels like I can finish her sentences, yet I don't want to interrupt her because the sound of her voice slides over me in a way that I can't describe. I just know that I like it. A lot. I like *her*. I like the way I feel when I'm around her.

"Shoot. I didn't realize how much time has gone by. My next session is probably waiting." She stands, but it looks like she doesn't really feel like leaving yet either. "Umm...let me give you my phone number. In case you have any problems with your voice."

"That would be great."

I hand her my phone and she punches in her number. "That's an awful picture of me." She hands back my phone.

"There's no such thing."

She smiles and shakes her head. "Maybe I'll see you around."

My brain has every intention of giving her my hand. But it doesn't catch up to my body before I have one hand cupped behind her head and my mouth is closing in on her cheek. I suppose I should be grateful my body compromised and went for the cheek, rather than the mouth. Feeling the softness of her skin under my lips makes me want to run my lips along *other* places on her body. *Every* place on her body. "You know, I've been thinking a lot about something you said the first night we met."

"Oh yeah. What's that?"

"You said if you strip a woman down to her underwear, you can learn a lot about her. Since you have a boyfriend and I can't do that, I think it's only fair you tell me what kind you wear."

The pink on her cheeks is definitely my new favorite color. She shakes her head and I think she isn't going to give me an answer. But then she surprises me by leaning in and whispering, "Lacy boy shorts...unless I'm wearing leather pants."

"What if you're wearing leather pants?"

She smirks. "Commando." Then leaves me standing there with my mouth open, staring at her ass as she walks away.

chapter five

Lucky—
Twelve years earlier,
age thirteen

The green neon script sign behind the bar makes me feel like what Dad keeps telling me is true—Lucky's is *ours*.

"Get used to it, princess. Your name is going to be in lights much bigger than just our little sign." Dad pulls me close to him and kisses the top of my head.

"Don't you think someone whose name is important enough to be lit behind the bar should be able to watch the show tonight, Daddy?"

"She is pretty important, you know," my friend Avery chimes in.

My father groans. "Girls. You're going to get us shut down before we even get through opening night."

"Please, Daddy!"

"Please, Daddy!" Avery follows my lead, her hands steepled like a communion girl's. "We'll stay off to the side of the stage near the hallway to the back. And if the man walks in, we'll run into the back room before he sees us. I promise."

"The man?" Dad asks.

"Yeah, you know. Five-oh. The fuzz. Flatfoot. Smokey. Doughnut disciples, the po-po," Avery offers.

Dad shakes his head, but smiles. "I know I'm going to regret this, but fine. You girls can watch. But only the first show. You are not staying in the bar all night."

I still can't believe my mom scored us one of the hottest bands around. The lead singer is gorgeous. His poster hangs on my wall, perfectly positioned so I fall asleep every night with his sky blue eyes staring at me.

And now he's about to be ten feet away. I really hope I don't pass out. The lights dim and my dad hops up onto the small stage and delivers a quick introduction, not that any introduction is needed. Then the room, which is filled to capacity—a line of hopefuls running all the way around the block—erupts in screaming, and the guy who makes my knees weak appears from the parting crowd.

A black tee shirt, worn jeans, black boots—both his arms already covered in tattoos at age twenty-three. Simple, yet simply perfection. He stands on the stage like he owns the place, looking like the rockstar that he is. Then he smiles and every woman in the place goes wild.

The shirtless drummer pounds his sticks on the drums a few times to start the song. He's good-looking, but not in the same league as the lead singer. And then I hear that voice. It's beautiful—filled with an intensity so hot, I fear I'll melt standing this close. Is it possible to fall in love with a man who doesn't even know I exist? In that moment, I'd swear it is. Because I'm head over heels in love with Dylan Ryder.

chapter six

Lucky

My phone buzzes on the nightstand while I tear off yet another rejected outfit and toss it onto the bed. The pile of discarded clothes is growing into a mound—I'm usually not so indecisive. Standing in my bra and panties, I reach for my phone and swipe my finger to read the incoming text.

Something came up and I'm running late. Sorry, babe. I'll meet you at the party.

Not having to rush for Dylan's arrival, I spend another thirty minutes deciding on just the right thing to wear. I settle on super-skintight black leather pants, a simple black body-hugging blouse that shows off my well-endowed anatomy and dangerously high leather boots with an open peep-toe. A silver cuff bracelet on one upper arm, a few dozen bangles on the other, and I finally like what I see. It's understated, rockstar chic. If only it were the truth.

I make it to the party fashionably late. Dylan makes a big production over my arrival, whistling a catcall and taking me in his arms for a passionate kiss that wouldn't be considered appropriate in most crowds. Although this group doesn't look twice. Not when half-naked groupies backstage are the norm. The first time I went to see Dylan play, a woman was giving the drummer a blowjob on the couch in the back lounge area, while the rest of the band was arguing over the set list only ten feet away. No one batted an eye.

Dylan orders me a drink and the waitress delivers it with a look of annoyance for me and a groupie-quality smile for Dylan. I take a few sips, unsure what the contents of the glass consist of, although I'm positive it is *not* the Cosmo I ordered.

I stand dutifully by Dylan's side as he holds court, entertaining his ever-expanding circle with stories about all the gigs they've played in different cities. My gaze wanders around the room, taking in famous faces, leaders in the music industry and a bevy of beautiful women. Then it falls on a set of startling blue eyes that are already trained on me.

Flynn cocks his head to the side and raises his glass from across the room. His grin is absolutely…adorable is the only way I can describe it. I can't imagine men appreciate being called adorable, but there's just no other way to explain it. It's the dimpled grin of an eight-year-old boy standing in front of his first crush with a bouquet of dandelions proudly clutched behind his back. Only this grin is attached to the chiseled face and body of a mouthwateringly sexy man. He's wearing just a pair of dark jeans, black boots, a skin hugging henley and a well-worn black leather jacket. His right ear has one earring, his left three or four. Tonight his shoulder length hair is pulled back, only accentuating his incredible blue eyes and dark lashes. *Damn.*

I nod and tilt my glass back at him, but he doesn't turn away. Even when the blonde I hadn't noticed standing next to him wraps her arm around his waist possessively.

The next two hours go pretty much the same way—Dylan soaks up the limelight, the waitress serves me dirty looks and the wrong drinks, and my eyes wander, always seeming to land on Flynn. Each time, I'm met with his blues already fixated on me.

"I'm going to find the ladies' room and get some air for a few minutes," I say to Dylan, who's busy entertaining the crowd that surrounds him. It's his night, and he knows how to hold court like a pro.

I spend a few minutes in the bathroom and then go in search of some fresh air. We're on the third floor, but I noticed a breeze coming through a heavily draped set of doors as, every once in a while, people disappeared behind the curtain. Finding an empty balcony, I slip outside into the clear night. From inside, the muffled sound of Christina Aguilera's "I'm Okay" plays, and I close my eyes and quietly sing along.

Enjoying the solace, I don't hear the door open behind me. "Your voice is beautiful." I know that soulful sound before I even turn to take in the man it belongs to.

"Thank you." Both of Flynn's hands are full. His left holds a beer bottle, his right extends a martini glass in my direction.

"This one is made right."

I furrow my brow.

"The drink," he clarifies.

"How did you know the others weren't made right?"

He holds my eyes for a moment, almost as if he's searching for something, before he responds. "Your nose scrunched up each time you took a sip." He shrugs and takes a draw on his beer, eyes watching me over the tipped-up bottle.

I squint at him and lift the drink to my lips.

"Better?" he asks.

"It is. But how did you know what I was drinking?"

"Asked the waitress who kept bringing you the wrong ones."

"And she suddenly found the recipe to make it right when *you* asked?" I arch one eyebrow suspiciously. I knew that woman was doing it on purpose.

Flynn looks a bit embarrassed.

"Well, thank you for noticing and coming to my rescue. You're quite observant."

He chuckles. "Women tend to call me the other O word."

My brain jumps to *orgasm*, even though I know it makes no sense that a woman would call him an orgasm. "What other O word is that?"

"Oblivious." He drains half of his beer. "So what brings you out here?"

"Just needed some fresh air. You?"

He averts his eyes, looking down almost shyly. Then he shrugs, and the crooked smile that I imagine has charmed the pants off droves of women is back. "I saw you come out here."

"Won't your date be looking for you?"

"Didn't bring a date. Won't yours?"

"Dylan's busy. Not even sure he noticed I'm gone."

He looks at me thoughtfully for a minute, and I think he's going to say something, but then he seems to think better of it and just nods.

"So you have some pretty legendary parents, huh?"

I quirk an eyebrow. "Stalk much?"

"I prefer to call it industry research."

"Hmmm. So you know who Avery's mom is?"

"Avery?"

"My best friend. The new co-owner of Lucky's."

"Her parents are in the business too?"

"Nope." We both laugh. "How's your voice holding up?"

"It's hanging in there."

"You should rest it between the shows on the Wylde Ryde tour. Forty shows in forty days is too much for any set of vocal cords."

Flynn grins, but says nothing.

"What?" I ask, confused at what I've said that's put the sexy-as-hell smirk on his face.

"Stalk much?"

Damn it. So maybe I learned a little from Google the night after we had breakfast. My cheeks heat, but I pull a play card from his deck. "I prefer to call it industry research."

He throws his head back and laughs. Innocently closing the small distance between us, Flynn moves to stand next to me at the rail. When his arm brushes against mine, every hair on my body stands up and welcomes the close proximity.

"Leather pants," he murmurs, then sips his drink. "I hope you know you're killing me."

Somehow, I knew he'd remember the conversation we had. I change the subject before he asks if I wore them on purpose. My skin isn't good at lying. "You know, if you spend too much time out here with me, the blonde who was hanging on you might find another rockstar inside."

"Oh yeah. Does that work both ways? If I spend too much time out here, is it possible you'll find a new rockstar, too?" The shy, yet completely irresistible boyish smirk is back. Lord, it's even more dangerous up close. I need to get out of here before I forget which rockstar I came with. Actually, now that I remember, I came here alone.

"There you are!" The curtain parts and the blonde who was wrapped around Flynn shrieks. She eyes me up and then snuggles close to him, her hands possessively attaching themselves to him from behind.

Suddenly, I feel like a third wheel. And yet I have the urge to peel the woman's hands off him at the same time. "I should get back. Thank you for the drink." I force a smile and turn toward the curtain-clad set of double doors.

"Wait." He reaches for my arm and I turn back. A few awkward heartbeats pass and then a goofy smile lights up his face. He stopped me from leaving as if he had something to say, but now is drawing a blank. "Umm," he fishes for something. "This is Lucky," he introduces me to the blonde. "Lucky, this is…" He totally has no idea what her name is, even though she's been hanging on him for the last few hours.

Blondie takes his cue, not looking even remotely offended. "Kylie."

Figures.

"Nice to meet you, Kylie," I say.

Ignoring me completely now, she focuses her attention on Flynn, who has turned his body in my direction. Not garnering the response she seeks, she walks around to face him, effectively standing between the two of us, her back to me. "I was hoping for just me and you. But if you want a three-way, can we make it a four-way? My friend would love to join, too."

My eyes flash with irritation at her assumption. Yet Flynn takes her offer in perfect stride—as if an offer for a threesome, or foursome for that matter, is an everyday occurrence. He rubs his hands up and down Blondie's arms, more soothing than enticing. "Thanks, maybe another time." He looks to me apologetically.

With only a roll of my eyes as a parting gesture, I turn to make my way back into the party. I don't belong out here with Flynn anyway. Not when the man I've dreamed about for half my life is waiting for me inside, and he's leaving to go back on tour tomorrow.

chapter

seven

Flynn

"**F**ucker needs to get a damn coffee pot," I grumble, grabbing a container of orange juice from the top shelf of the fridge. I lift, expecting weight, but it's light as air. Shaking it up and down, there's no swish of juice inside. Of course.

A warm hand on my bare back surprises me. "Morning," a come-hither voice purrs. I turn to find a naked woman. She's tall, only an inch or two shorter than me, probably almost six feet, with bleached blond spiky hair and tan skin. Her body is toned and sinewy, not generally my type, but damn if she isn't sexy as hell.

"Morning. Nolan still sleeping?"

"He snores."

I chuckle. "No shit. Try sleeping on a bus with him. The shake from his snore is worse than the vibration of the engine. He also doesn't have a coffee pot."

"You're Flynn, right?"

"I am."

Naked Woman pours herself a glass of water and drinks it, then refills it and offers the glass to me. I take it and guzzle down half of it.

"I like the rain, Flynn," she says in a husky voice as she presses her palms against my bare chest. I'm wearing boxer briefs, didn't bother to slip on the pants I left next to the couch when I crashed last night. It was quiet when I let myself in; I assumed Nolan was alone or not home yet.

"Don't think it's supposed to rain today."

She reaches down and squeezes a handful of my morning wood. "You can make it rain. Golden showers in the morning bring sunshine the rest of the day."

I choke on the last mouthful of water. "Ummm…thanks, but I have to run." As in, run the fuck out of this place. I take a few steps toward the couch to collect my things, and can't help myself. "You know, Nolan loves to be woken up with a heavy rain."

The woman's eyes glimmer with excitement and she hurriedly retreats toward the bedroom. Nolan knows how to pick 'em. I'd better disappear quickly; he's going to kick my ass after getting woken up by a warm stream of yellow on his face that isn't sunshine.

I stop by Becca's and hang with Laney for a few hours before grabbing a quick shower. I trade my usual coffee in for hot tea in an attempt to soothe my raw throat. It's on fire from the smoky after-party that made the label's Easy Ryder album release party seem like a party full of priests.

Unlike most nights lately, I went home alone at the end of the party. Although it definitely wasn't for lack of opportunity. The Easy Ryder guys may have ten years on us, their groupies are older, but it doesn't mean things have slowed for them by any means. Just the opposite, in fact. The smokin' hot thirty-somethings are more aggressive than the barely legal women who tend to follow In Like Flynn around.

I walk into Pulse Records right at three. Afternoon appointments for musicians tend to be a given. Today Nolan and I are being introduced to our practice manager—the person assigned to keep our asses in line as we get ready to join the Wylde Ryde tour. She won't have any problem with In Like Flynn showing up for the practice schedule she sets, but I hope she's got thick skin with Nolan and the rest of the guys.

Nolan strides in looking like what he is—severely hung over, maybe even still drunk. Tabby, the practice manager, takes one look at him and tells him she's going to get him a protein shake.

"How was your morning?" Lounging back in my chair, I link my fingers together behind my head and settle in to enjoy the entertainment.

Nolan groans. "I'm not sure if night ended and morning actually began yet."

"Usually, I call morning anything after I take a *shower.* I feel like my morning *shower* is a rebirth of sorts. Almost like a *christening.*"

Nolan shoots me a look that tells me he knows I'm up to something, yet he's still in the dark about what the hell it is. "What the fuck is up with you today?"

"Nothing." My face gives away that I'm full of shit.

A few minutes, later Tabby comes back in with Nolan's shake. "Ready to get started?"

"I'm sorry. I need to hit the restroom before we get started. Can you just give me a minute, Tabby?"

"Sure, of course. No problem. Nolan and I will get to know each other."

"You sure you don't have to go, Nolan?" I ask as I unfold from my chair.

"What the hell is wrong with you? You can't take a piss on your own now?" Hung over and suspicious equates to a short fuse for my longtime friend and bass player.

I pat him on the back as I pass by the seat he's slumped in and lean down so only he can hear. "Thought maybe you'd want to stand in front of the urinal. Heard you like golden showers these days."

Sick, hung over, drunk or not, Nolan tears ass and chases me around the entire floor. I'm going to guess Tabby got a fair sample of what she's in for over the next few months.

I told myself I was going to the meeting and leaving. I wasn't going to hang around like a puppy looking for scraps of something he has no business sniffing around. Yet here I am, for the fourth time, passing by the studio where I know she works. I grumble at myself and set off to grab the coffee I avoided earlier before traveling back downtown.

Deciding some fresh air will do me good, help clear my head, I stroll to the main entrance. In the reflection on the glass lobby doors, a set of legs catches my attention. I've never seen them before, yet I know who they belong to before I raise my eyes to take in her beautiful face.

I hold the door open and wait for Lucky to pass. She's busy messing with her phone and doesn't look up until she's about to cross the threshold. "Thank you," she says, and then her eyes focus on my face and surprise registers on hers.

"Flynn?"

"At your service." I bow my head and pull the door wider, sweeping my hand for her to walk through.

She smiles, but squints to assess me. "Are you following me, Mr. Beckham?"

The way my last name falls from her lips has me momentarily glad she knows I'm Mr. Beckham, because I could definitely get lost in this woman and forget my own name. "Wouldn't I be behind you if I was following you?"

"I suppose..." she trails off suspiciously.

"You're following me, aren't you?" I deadpan.

"What? No! I am not. I was just leaving. I didn't—"

"Relax. I'm kidding."

"Oh."

Without thinking, I rest my hand on the small of her back and guide her the rest of the way out of the building. It feels natural—right—so I don't let go even when we're outside.

"Your voice sounds hoarse, is it bothering you?"

It's not. "Maybe a little."

With concern in her eyes, Lucky stops and lifts her hands to my throat. "Is it sensitive to my touch?"

No. Although some other parts of my body feel your touch. "A little."

"You need to retrain your voice or you're going to wind up without one. Come by the studio. At least let me teach you some new techniques to help keep the strain off your cords."

If she were any other woman, with the way my body reacts around her, I'd be detailing the techniques I'd like to show her in return. But I don't. She's not just any woman…she's *Dylan freaking Ryder's* woman. I should walk away, not even go near the temptation. But living life without temptation is like having a heart that doesn't beat. And I'm a musician. I need a good strong beat.

chapter eight

Lucky

I peer at the clock through sleepy eyes and want nothing more than to turn over and pretend today isn't today. But it is. Cheery sunlight flitters into the room through the open blinds and lands straight on my face. Dark clouds and rain would be more appropriate to match my temperament for the day I'm facing.

The life we want does not often come easy. It was one of my dad's favorite dadisms. I used to ignore most of them, sometimes even roll my eyes when I heard them spoken. I listened to the words a hundred times, yet I never really *heard* him. Not until I woke up one day and realized I'm twenty-five years old, and I'm frozen in place. And it isn't just the singing.

Settled into a comfortable life, I resist most change. My career, my friends—even my relationship with Dylan. He's older, and moves at a faster pace than me. I don't want to leave another one of my dreams behind. So I started seeing Dr. Curtis again. We worked together on my stage fright for almost four years, before I finally gave up. Six months ago, I decided it was time to try again. I realized I was more afraid of regret than I was of making changes.

When Dr. Curtis and I came up with the twelve-step-like program to combat my fear of singing on stage, it seemed so easy. The plans were all in the future, not the here and now. Now the day of reckoning is staring me in my face.

Step one: Admit you have a problem. That was a piece of cake.

Step two: Let go of the past. And so I sold half of Lucky's to Avery. Became a silent partner only. Check.

Step three: Get a job that involves music. Pulse Records voice coach. Check. I'm making progress. On a roll now.

Step four: Sing for a small crowd of friends on a small stage.

The needle of progress makes a loud screeching sound as it halts. Herein lies the reason for my racing pulse this morning. I've already spent hours debating the definition of "a small crowd." My definition was Avery and Jase. Somehow, I let Avery talk me into three more. Five is most definitely a small crowd. The idea of singing in front of one person makes my palms sweat. Two makes me lightheaded. I can't even imagine what five will bring.

To make matters worse, I have to get through a packed day at work, which includes an hour of one-on-one coaching with Flynn. It's not that I don't want to help Flynn…it's that I *really* want to help Flynn. Perhaps I'm a little too eager.

My entire life has been spent around musicians. Famous, infamous—legends, even—I stopped getting anxious around them years ago. But something about Flynn Beckham makes me nervous. He's different. Sure, from the outside he's a rockstar, all gorgeous and self-confident, with that laid-back swagger that comes with years of being praised for a multitude of talents. Yet somehow he still feels unaffected by fame. He's playful. And comforting. Oddly, I find myself thinking my dad would have liked him.

The first step in assessing a singer's vocal health is to observe. I ask the artist to recite the words to the song they last sang so I can examine their vocal posture during normal speech and inflection.

"Just a verse is fine. I want to see how you're filtering laryngeally generated sound up through your vocal tract."

Flynn shrugs. "If you say so." Then he proceeds to recite some lyrics, "'When life gets rough, I like to hold on to my dream of relaxing in the summer sun, just lettin' off steam.'"

The words are vaguely familiar. "Is that from one of your songs?"

"Nope." He offers nothing more.

"It's familiar, but I can't place it. Who sings it?"

"Olaf."

"Olaf?"

He smiles. "It's from the *Frozen* soundtrack."

"That's the last song you sang?"

"Sang it three times just this morning."

"Disney fanatic?"

"My niece, Laney, loves it."

Earrings, rings, leather tied around his wrists, tatted skin, scruff on his face, hair a sexy mess—and sings Disney songs to his niece. The inside of this man may just be as beautiful as the outside.

"That's the sweetest thing I've ever heard. How old is she?"

"Four."

"Does she know her uncle is a rockstar?"

"Definitely not. Did you know your parents were rockstars?"

I laugh at the notion. "Definitely not. My dad was a total goofball."

"Well, I'm sure that's how Laney feels. I'm the uncle who lets her eat crap and go out in her pajamas. She jumps up and down when I enter a room, but it's basically because I bribe her to think I'm cool."

"Sounds more like she thinks you're cool because she knows the real you."

"Did you think your dad was cool?"

"Not until I was an adult. I remember this one time, I must have been about twelve, we were walking down the street and this woman ran up to him and asked him for his autograph. She whipped open her shirt, right there on the street, for him to sign her boob and she wasn't wearing a bra."

"What did your dad do?"

"He pulled her shirt closed and told her to have some respect for his daughter. I thought the woman had to have escaped from a mental institution to do that to my dad. I mean, he was just Dad."

"You saw him for who he really was. Everyone else saw the image they wanted to see. The hard part of fame is remembering which expectation you need to live up to. It's easier to do what the fans expect. Living up to the Laney standard is much harder."

"Legions of women would be devastated if they knew your heart was already taken. Laney is a lucky girl."

"I'm saving room for one more in there, don't worry." He winks. And all I can think is that that girl is damn lucky, and part of me wishes it was with a capital L.

Getting through Flynn singing is incredibly hard. Who knew the songs from *Frozen* could be so unbelievably sexy? The way his throat moves, the way his mouth caresses each syllable of the low, raspy sound that falls from his lips. I should be watching his posture, his breathing, the way his larynx forces out the words—but instead I'm focused on the beauty of his mouth and how the sound of his voice glides over my body, making it feel both warm and tingly at the same time. I'm lost when the song finishes, yet I haven't really observed him yet.

"So. Give it to me straight. What am I doing wrong?"

Ummm…absolutely nothing from what I can see. Everything was perfect. Don't change a thing. Shit. "Could you do it again? Maybe a different song, one you haven't sung in a while. So the sounds are less familiar to your body. Sometimes that can give me a different view." At least I make it sound like a real thing when the words come out.

He sings again, and this time I force myself to observe. "Hmm…your posture is great. Most people have a tendency to favor one side of their neck, which makes them tilt a bit when they speak, and it becomes magnified when they sing, which puts strain on the muscles around the vocal cords. Your alignment is perfect."

"Thank you, it goes with the rest of my perfectness," he says with a teasing arrogance that, from the little I know about him, I know isn't real.

"You didn't let me finish."

"You can't now tell me I'm not perfect. I was already basking in the glow."

"Actually, it was perfect…but almost a little too perfect. Which makes me think you don't usually stand this way when you sing."

"It isn't the way I normally sing. On stage, I usually have a guitar over my shoulder. Even if I'm not playing it, it's there."

"Well, I need to see you holding your instrument to assess you fully, then."

Flynn's eyebrows quirk up and the dirty grin on his face is unmistakable.

"The *guitar*. I'd need to see you holding the *guitar*."

"That's a shame." He shrugs, the playful smile still on his face. "But okay. It's your call. Whatever instrument you want to see me hold is fine with me."

"How big of you."

"So now we're talking about the other instrument again?"

I roll my eyes, although this conversation is having more of an effect on me than I let on.

It's after six when we finish, yet it feels more like fifteen minutes and not two hours that have passed. "I have to run. I'm helping out Avery at Lucky's tonight. She's not having much success finding a waitress."

"Maybe I'll stop by tonight with some of the guys from the band. If that's all right?"

"I'm sure Avery would be excited if you came. The place will be buzzing with In Like Flynn making an appearance."

Flynn leans in to me, the scruff on his jaw rubbing against my cheek. "Isn't Avery I want excited when I come." He kisses my cheek and disappears, as if his words aren't going to leave me flustered for hours.

chapter nine

Lucky—
Nine years earlier,
age sixteen

"**Y**ou excited, princess?" Dad pops a square of the Hershey's Special Dark we share every day into his mouth.

"I can't wait. I haven't seen her in six months."

Dad's face falters for a fraction of a second, but then he smiles. "I was talking about getting on stage this afternoon."

"Oh. Yeah. That too, Dad."

"You nervous?"

I'm not really sure if he's asking about Mom or singing this time, so I give an answer that I think will satisfy him for both. "A little." The truth is, I'm nervous about seeing Mom again. I'm not sure why. I wasn't even nervous about singing on stage at Lucky's for the first time, until Dad told me Mom was coming to watch. Then my palms started to sweat when I thought about performing—in front of Iris Nicks.

"You're going to be great. You were born to be on a stage. I wish I had half the talent you do." Dad kisses my forehead.

I've sung in front of crowds before. A few months ago, the school talent show was sold out when I sang—every seat filled with kids I'd have to see at school the next day, yet I didn't hesitate when I walked out on stage. I remember standing behind the curtain, watching the Massey twins do their gymnastics routine while I waited for my turn. My eyes scanned the crowd, a feeling of anticipation beginning to creep up from the pit of my stomach as the audience roared with applause when the twins landed their final flips. I was next. Then, right before I got on stage, I caught sight of the man standing in the back corner of the audience. Arms folded, standing tall, a proud look on his smiling face. Dad. The announcer called my name and I took a deep breath and walked slowly to the center of the stage. The lights blinded my vision to everything below. But I still knew he was there. I sang my heart out as if he was the only one watching. Somehow, it was all I needed.

Today, Mom arrives a half hour before my scheduled show time. A flurry of activity surrounds her entrance, as it always does. She's never alone. I watch from the corner of the room as she kisses Dad hello. *On the lips.* He smiles and rubs his hands up and down her arms. My parents definitely have a strange relationship. Half of my friends have parents that are divorced, but most of them can't stand the sight of each other. Maybe it's because my parents never married that their uncoupling when I was five was so much more harmonious.

Mom looks around the room and her smile brightens when her eyes land on me. She walks toward me with her arms open wide, and it takes every bit of my sixteen-year-old cool self not to run to her. Don't get me wrong, I love living with my dad, I just wish I got to see Iris more.

An hour later, it's show time. Lucky's is packed, even though it's a Sunday afternoon. It's an odd mix of my parents' music friends, industry people and a handful of kids from school. Avery stands next to me on the side of the stage as the MC introduces me. With a nudge from her, I walk the few steps until I'm standing front and center. My eyes roam the audience. Unlike the time I sang at school, there are no blinding lights to restrict my view. Instead, I see every face—every face watching me.

Eyes connect with mine. Expecting. Waiting. Watching. I just stand there. A deer frozen in the headlights. Mom sits front and center. She nods. As if to say, *go on, start singing already*, but I don't. Instead, I frantically search for Dad. He's standing in the back of the room. Our eyes lock and I ease a bit just finding him. I look down at his feet and nod to the small band standing behind me and they begin to play. Thirty seconds later, I'm singing my heart out and can't see a single person, even though nothing has changed.

chapter

ten

Lucky

It's been two days since I heard from Dylan. The sound of his sexy voice does what it's done to me since I was fourteen years old—I grin like a teenager when he says he misses me.

"I miss you, too."

"What have you got planned for tonight?"

"I'm actually on my way to Lucky's now. Avery's still down a waitress, so I'm filling in."

"Why is it that you're always there when she needs you, but not when I need you?"

"When did you need me?"

"I need you now." Dylan wanted me to go with him on tour. Sell Lucky's entirely and travel with Easy Ryder. It's been a source of contention between us lately, and part of the reason I decided it was time to start seeing Dr. Curtis again.

"You don't *need* me. You want me. There's a difference."

"You keep saying that, but you're disregarding my *needs*."

"Really? I thought I did pretty good fulfilling your needs."

"When you're actually around, you do."

"We'll see each other in less than two weeks. I'm coming to the Atlanta show. Remember?"

"Two weeks is a long time."

"Absence makes the heart grow fonder, you know."

"That's bullshit. I still don't see why you couldn't come with me."

"You know why." We've been through this a dozen times and the place to rehash it is not on the phone while I'm walking into Lucky's. He doesn't get why I need to keep with my plan. Why not being on stage is holding back more than just my singing career. I need to break through to move forward. "Tonight I'm going to get up on stage after Lucky's closes." Saying the words out loud brings a new wave of nausea.

"You'll do great. Although that little stage is beneath you."

"*You* sang on this stage once."

There are some gargled voices in the background. Dylan covers the phone and then returns. "I gotta run. I need to do a sound check."

"Okay. Good luck with tonight's show."

The bar is busy, but that doesn't stop me from checking the time on my phone every three minutes. The way I'm watching the minutes tick down with dread, you'd think a bomb was due to explode. Actually, with how terrified I feel, waiting for detonation might be easier.

I clear a table and head toward the bar with new drink orders completely oblivious to my surroundings, when a familiar voice greets me. I jump, the simple sound startles me from my obsessive preoccupation with how many minutes remain until I'm facing the firing squad. My full tray wobbles on my unsteady hands and then tips, sending a half dozen empty glasses smashing to the wooden floor, where they shatter into a million tiny pieces.

"Shit!" I drop to my knees and attempt to rake the glass with my hands, but all it does is slice small shards into my fingers.

"Are you okay?" Flynn says. "Sorry. I didn't mean to sneak up on you. I thought you saw me." He's down on his knees attempting to help me gather the mess I've made.

"It's not your fault. I'm…just a little preoccupied tonight."

"A little? My uncle Nathan with Parkinson's has more stable hands than you tonight." I look up at Avery and she points in the direction of the back. "Go! You need a break. Jase and I got this. Take as long as you need."

"You sure?"

"I insist." She jabs her finger at the man next to me. "You. Flynn. Go with her," Avery orders. She hands him a bottle. "Take this. She needs it."

A minute later, we're outside. The fresh air hits me and suddenly I'm bent over, hands on my knees, gulping air like I've been deprived.

Flynn wraps his arms around my waist and grabs me tight—he's afraid I might fall. "You okay?"

I take a few shallow breaths before I respond. "I'm good. Sorry. Panic attack. It's been a while since I've had one. I forgot what they can do to me."

We're in the alley behind the bar. Surprisingly, it's empty—usually there are a few smokers polluting the air back here. Flynn rubs my back as I attempt to regain my composure.

"You wanna talk about it?" he asks as my breathing returns to normal.

Two guys stumble loudly into the alley, lighting cigarettes before they're even fully out the door. Flynn looks at them, then me, and grabs my hand. "Come on. Let's go for a walk."

Fingers linked, we walk silently from the alley and make our way around the corner to a bench just outside Bryant Park. It's after midnight and the street is quiet, especially for New York.

"So, I'd like to think you were so happy to see me, you couldn't contain your excitement. But something tells me that isn't it." Flynn uncaps the bottle of Jack Daniels that Avery handed him and offers it to me.

I take a swig. My face scrunches up from the taste. "Thank you for walking with me. I actually feel better already." I extend the uncapped bottle back to him.

He lifts the bottle to his lips, and then stops. "Glad I can help. Hope it's my company and not the alcohol." He gulps a shot from the bottle and smiles. "So tell me what's going on? What's got you so anxious?"

"It's just...anticipation of something I need to do."

"You breaking up with Dylan?" His voice sounds hopeful.

"No. Nothing like that."

He brings the bottle to his mouth a second time, mumbling before he drinks, "That's too bad."

The first real smile of the day threatens my lips. "You're ridiculously charming, Mr. Beckham. Women must fall at your feet."

"Not the right ones," he says and offers me the bottle, but I decline. "So talk to me. What's got your sexy self all twisted up tonight?"

"It's nothing, really. I..." It's difficult to admit my fears to anyone, let alone a guy who does what I fear most on a regular basis and makes it look as easy as breathing. "I sort of have stage fright."

"Okay..." he says, waiting for more.

"And I'm supposed to sing tonight at the bar."

"When was the last time you got up on stage?"

"Eight years ago."

"Wow. It's been a while. Have you tried before tonight?"

"No." I chuckle, knowing how ridiculous I must sound. "I've been working up my courage."

I expect him to laugh at my admission, but he doesn't. "Did you always have a fear, or did something happen that scared you?"

"A little of both." It's the truth. Well, sort of. I was always nervous when I got on stage, but then...one day...everything changed.

"When you used to go on stage, what calmed you when your nerves got the best of you?"

I don't have to think about the answer, yet I take a minute to steady myself before I speak. "My dad." It's ironic how the man could be the source of my strength and now, a big part of my fear.

Flynn takes my hand and squeezes. There is something so comforting about the way he looks at me, waits for me to continue. It makes me feel like he really wants to hear whatever I have to say—like each conversation is a layer he peels back, yet his goal isn't to strip me bare. Instead, he leaves me feeling blanketed.

"The first time I went on stage, other than at school, was here at Lucky's. I was nervous. The crowd was pretty much filled with faces that I'd already won over before singing my first note—my friends, my mom's friends, my dad's buddies. It wasn't a tough crowd. But I got up there and froze anyway. I looked around the room. Every smiling face my eyes landed on made my heart thump louder in my chest. Until I found my dad in the crowd. He was beaming proudly. It helped to take the edge off, although I still wasn't sure I could go through with it. But then I looked down and saw he was barefoot."

"Barefoot in the bar?"

I smile, remembering back to that exact moment. Looking down at his wiggling toes, the spirit of who my father was somehow cracked through all of my tension and brought me relief. "My dad always played barefoot. He liked the feel of the drum pedal under his foot and the vibration that caught on the floorboards and seeped up into his legs. But it was more than that. He said the earth under his feet made him feel grounded…somehow balanced. It helped him forget everything else and give everything over to the sound." My voice breaks as I finish.

Flynn wraps his arm around me and pulls me close. It feels good, comforting, I close my eyes, but it doesn't stop a few wayward tears from falling. My dad was everything to me.

Although he keeps me physically close at his side, Flynn gives me the mental space I need for a few minutes before he speaks. "He's going to be watching you tonight. With a big smile and bare feet. He may not be in the audience anymore, but that doesn't mean he can't see you. You just need to close your eyes and see him."

I look up into Flynn's beautiful blue eyes. "He'd want me to sing."

"So that's what you need to do, then," he declares with unerring confidence. "You want to know my secret for calming my nerves on stage?"

"*You* still get nervous?"

"Sure." He shrugs. "Sometimes it's worse than others. I can't even figure out what makes it easier for one show than the next. You'd think it was the venue or size of the audience…but it's just random for me."

"Well, tell me your secrets, rockstar."

"I'll tell you. But if word gets out, it might tarnish my rockstar status. So you have to keep it to yourself."

I make an X across my chest. "You have my word."

"I recite the words to a song in my head and take a walk around the stage."

"That doesn't sound so bad."

"The song is 'Twinkle, Twinkle, Little Star.'"

"Oh." I chuckle. "Guess that might soften the bad-boy rockstar image just a bit."

"Did you know it has five verses?"

"'Twinkle, Twinkle'? You mean there's more to it than just, 'how I wonder what you are. Up above the world so high, like a diamond in the sky'?"

"Yep. A lot more. Most of the world doesn't know the best parts."

I shake my head, amused, yet intrigued by his enthusiasm. "Why did we only learn two verses as kids if there are five? And more importantly, why do *you* know the five?"

"I don't know why we've been deprived of the other three. But I found out about them in college. Astronomy major. Did a paper on what makes stars appear to twinkle and titled it 'Twinkle, Twinkle, Little Star, How I Wonder What You Are.' I looked up the lyrics to make sure I had them right, since half of us sing things we learned as a kid wrong, and found the whole song."

"Astronomy major, huh? The more I get to know you, the more I find you're a complete enigma, Flynn Beckham."

"Are you into enigmas?"

I laugh his harmless flirtation off, but all I can think is…shit, I'm into enigmas.

I sat around talking to Flynn on that park bench for almost another half an hour. He told me one of the lost 'Twinkle Twinkle' verses, but refused to tell me the others. He promised I'd get the remainder of the classic song when I was done with my performance. My reward—which he'd grace me with after I sang. It meant he was planning on staying for my performance, monumentally increasing my crowd by twenty percent, from five to six. Oddly, it gave me more comfort than stress to know he'd be there.

That didn't mean I spent the remainder of the night in a calm state—not by any means. I dropped another tray, screwed up half my orders and gave my last customer twenty-six dollars change from his eight-dollar drink…that he paid for with a twenty.

But I made it through without running away, at least. And now, as I stand here locking the door while the last patron stumbles from Lucky's, I feel my nerves fraying at their ends. A body comes up close behind me in the narrow hallway. I know who it is without turning around, yet I'm so jittery it doesn't stop me from jumping.

"Sorry. Didn't mean to scare you again." Flynn's voice is low, soothing.

"I'm just a—"

"I know. That's why I followed you out here. Figured you might either sneak out the door behind the drunk guy who just left, or could use some calming."

"I'm still here."

"I noticed. So I figured I'd give you a small reward now."

Umm…yes, please.

"Oh yeah?" I turn around and face him. "And what is my reward for not ditching out?"

Flynn leans in, every hair on my body standing to welcome him into my personal space. Traitors. I feel his breath on my neck as he whisper-sings into my ear.

Then the traveler in the dark,
Thanks you for your tiny spark,
He could not see which way to go,
If you did not twinkle so.

Verse four. He'd given me verse three on the park bench.

A minute ago I was on edge at the thought of getting up on stage. Now I'm on edge for a totally different reason.

"It's beautiful. Such a shame I didn't know about it all these years."

Flynn's eyes wander to my mouth. "It sure is."

Before I get on the stage, I think back to when I was seven. My dad took me to a public pool out on Long Island. He was busy laying drum tracks for a studio album with his band. We'd passed the pool for three days before he got to take me. I stared longingly at the high diving board each time we drove by. I was a good swimmer—hotel pools were one of my favorite parts of traveling with the band—but I'd never been on a high dive board before. I was an anxious mix of excitement and nerves. By the time we walked into the fenced-off pool area, I could barely breathe. I wanted to back out. But Dad was excited to take me, and I didn't want to disappoint him. So I sashayed right over to the long line and forced a smile back at him as he waited by the edge of the pool. When it was my turn, I quickly climbed the stairs. Even more quickly, I walked toward the end of the board, telling myself I was just going to keep walking. Rip off the Band-Aid of fear I wore with one quick tear, and walk right off the end of the board. I made it three steps from the edge. Then my knees froze and crippled me. I couldn't take another step.

This time is no different. My audience of six sits patiently in their seats while I stride confidently toward the stage. Of course it's false confidence, but I work it anyway. Reaching the edge of the stage, which is only three steps off the ground, I actually climb the stairs with spring in my step. I make it two steps toward the center of the stage. And my knees freeze. I'm seven years old all over again.

I take a few deep, cleansing breaths.

They don't help.

I close my eyes and try again.

Breathe in.

Breathe out.

I need to do this. *Eight years.* It's been eight long years. I love to sing. Picture having the one thing that you love more than anything in the world right in front of your face every day. Only it's behind a wall of impenetrable glass and you can see it, but you can never reach it. Never touch it. That's how I've felt the last eight years. But my knees…they just won't move.

I close my eyes and try again. I want this.

Breathe in.

Breathe out.

The pounding in my chest gets louder. It feels like my heart might really explode. I reach up and rub at the tightness.

I start to sweat.

The room is eerily quiet, yet I know there are six people sitting only feet away.

"Lucky," Avery says in a soft voice. She's testing the waters, unsure of how I might react.

Hearing her voice doesn't pull me out of my panic, but it does calm me a bit. I swallow and force my eyes to look out at the room, without giving myself time to mull it over.

Avery is cautiously watching me. She attempts a smile over her worried face.

Through a fog, my eyes drift to the others in the room. There's Jase; Levi, the DJ from tonight; and two of our friends. They're all sitting together around a table, trying their hardest not to look disturbed by my display, but their faces can't hide their concern. Then I look over their heads and my eyes fall on Flynn. He's leaning casually against the back wall and he smiles at me. I try to smile back, but fail miserably.

Thinking I could use a major distraction, my eyes trail lower. Down Flynn's neck to his tatted arms folded casually over his lean, masculine chest. I skim his narrow waist and my eyes linger on his jean clad thighs.

And then I see it.

He's barefoot.

I can't remember any man ever doing anything so sweet for me in my entire life. Except maybe the man he's channeling.

Staring down at his feet, my focus shifts—I'm not thinking about being on stage...about *that last day* on stage. Instead, I'm staring at Flynn's wiggling toes and thinking, *Damn...even his toes are sexy.*

The corners of my mouth tilt upward and my eyes follow their lead. Flynn's beautiful blue eyes dance with triumph—he knows he's gotten to me.

A minute later, I sing for my audience of six. Four verses of "Twinkle, Twinkle, Little Star."

The elation we all feel when I'm done morphs into three hours of celebration. The sun is coming up by the time we all stumble onto the street from Lucky's. I throw my arms around Flynn's neck and hug him tight, thanking him for the twentieth time. He hugs me back just as tight, I notice. I'm not sure if it's the alcohol, the emotions of the night, or just the man I'm clinging to, but for some reason, I don't want to let go. Being in his arms soothes me, makes me feel something I haven't in a long time. I can't put my finger on what that something is, I just know I like it. Maybe a lot.

Too soon, Flynn hails Avery and me a cab and kisses me sweetly on the cheek before helping my swaying body into the car. I'm disappointed he doesn't join us—I'm not ready for the night to end. Not ready for whatever is going on between Flynn and me to end. Halfway home, I realize he never told me the fifth verse.

I don't have to wait long. Just until the text comes the next day.

chapter

eleven

Flynn

I walk the short distance to Becca's rather than back to Nolan's place to crash. No doubt there's a party at Nolan's that will still be in full swing, with the ratio of men to women heavily tilted in the band's favor. But I'm just not in the mood to continue the festivities with a bed full of groupies tonight.

I use my key to slip into the apartment quietly, careful not to wake anyone. On my way to the guestroom, I pass by Laney's room. The door is open, so I peek my head inside. She's sound asleep, snuggled up to the giant Elsa she suckered me into buying last time I was here. Damn, she's adorable even when she sleeps.

Blinds drawn, the guestroom is pitch dark, even though the sun is already crossing the horizon outside. I don't bother to pull back the covers, instead lying diagonally across the plush comforter my sister keeps ready for my unannounced arrivals. I inhale a deep breath—I'm tired, ready to let my body slumber until my niece realizes I'm in here and pounces on me bright and early.

Without standing, I strip to my boxers and toss everything to the floor except my phone. I thumb off a quick text before powering my iPhone down.

> *In the dark blue sky you keep,*
> *And often through my curtains peep,*

For you never shut your eye,
Till the sun is in the sky.

The sound of Laney's giggle is almost always how I wake when I sleep at my sister's. But not today. Instead, it's the constant buzz of the high-pitched doorbell. Someone is either standing in the hallway pressing the button insistently every two seconds, or the thing is broken, with the sound on the fritz. Covering my face with a pillow doesn't drown out the noise enough to let me ignore it. For the sake of whoever is on the other side of the door, the damn thing better turn out to be broken.

"God damn it," I grumble. Without even bothering to look through the peephole, I whip the door open. The anger I was feeling from being woken only gets worse when I see the asshole who was pushing the damn buzzer.

My brother-in-law.

Or, more correctly, my ex-brother-in-law. What Becca ever saw in this douchebag is beyond me.

"What the fuck?"

"Nobody answered."

"Maybe that means no one is home. So leave, asshole." I begin to push the door closed, but Douchebag sticks his foot in the door.

"Are they home? Rebecca and Helaine."

"Bec and Laney." God, this guy is such an uptight prick. Professor Douchebag. "I don't know."

"How can you not know? The place isn't that big."

"I was sleeping. And yeah, the place is pretty small…compared to the palace you live in with your twenty-two-year-old student. Or did you already cheat on that one and move on to a new crop of freshmen?"

He ignores most of my rant. "It's four in the afternoon and you're still sleeping?"

"I work nights."

He guffaws. "Work? You sing a few songs and screw the swooning teenyboppers when you're done. I'd hardly call that real work."

I smile. And take a step into his private space, craning my neck down six inches to look him in the eye. "Why don't you bring that new young wife down to the show so she can swoon over someone closer to her own age?"

"Fuck you."

"Move your foot, or you're going to have some broken toes when I slam this door shut."

"Just get Rebecca."

I take a step back inside the apartment and slam the door shut. I know Becca isn't home, or she would have been at the door getting between us in two seconds flat. But I stroll through the apartment to double check anyway. Beds are made, no sign of Bec or Laney. The asshole is ringing the bell again before I even make it back to the door.

I enjoy the little pansy professor's nervous jump when I whip the door open again. "They're not here. Leave."

"Where are they?"

"Out." I attempt to slam the door again, but he sticks his damn foot in it again. That thing is definitely going to be swollen later. Who the hell wears loafers anymore, anyway?

"Can you give Rebecca this?" He offers an envelope.

"What is it?"

"It's none of your business."

"Then give it to her yourself."

"Just take it. It's a check. For Helaine's birthday party."

"Not showing up again?"

"We have—"

I snatch the envelope and slam the door in his face. Luckily, this time it closes.

After a quick shower, and forgoing a shave in favor of two-day-old stubble, I power on my phone to find a response to the "Twinkle, Twinkle" lyrics I sent last night.

I might have hummed myself to sleep with a certain nursery rhyme last night.

The anger from Douchebag's visit dissipates surprisingly easily. Before I can text back, my phone chimes again.

Thank you for last night. I wouldn't have gone through with it if you hadn't been there for me.

Glad I could help. Your voice is incredible. You belong on a stage.

You're good for my confidence. ? I owe you one. Another voice coach session maybe?

You owe me one, huh?

I do.

Doing anything right now?

What did you have in mind?

I leave a note next to Douchebag's check and an hour later I'm at her door.

"So how old is she going to be?"

"Five."

"Five, huh. What types of things is she into?"

"*Frozen*. She's pretty much obsessed with anything *Frozen*."

Lucky pulls the front door closed and locks it. She drops her keys into her purse and smiles at me. "Well, I'm all yours. Where should we go first?"

All mine. I like the sound of that. "I was sort of hoping you'd tell me where we should go. I've never been a five-year-old girl."

She leads me to a stairwell and I open the door for her to walk in front of me. It's the first time I've seen her dressed casually. She has on those low-on-the-hip, tight black yoga pants that fit like a second skin, hugging the curves of her shapely ass. A white tank top and a three-quarter-sleeve denim jacket. Her feet are clad in aqua Chucks. I'm quite enjoying the view as we reach the landing three stories down.

She turns to speak to me, catching my eyes glued to her ass. At first I think she's going to call me on it, but she lets me slide, opening the door that leads to the street instead. "How about FAO Schwarz?"

We're stopped just outside on the sidewalk. People are coming and going in different directions. "Never been. Sounds good to me."

"It's probably about a mile and a half. Subway or walk?"

"I like to walk. But whatever you prefer."

"Walk it is, then."

Our conversation flows easily the first mile. We cover everything from her friendship with Avery to my starting the band in middle school. When we pass a CVS, she asks if we can stop.

"Hungry?" She empties the shelf of Hershey's Special Dark bars and puts them on the counter. The cashier counts out nine.

"They're hard to find. I was almost out. This chain is one of the few that stocks them."

"And you need that many because…"

She shrugs. "I eat half a bar for breakfast every morning. I totally blame Mr. Hershey entirely for the size of my ass."

"Remind me to send him a thank-you note."

She shakes her head and tosses the bars into her purse. We're two blocks away from the toy store, stopped at a red light, when we're interrupted by a girl. Or maybe she's a woman. Her body is all woman, I can tell, since most of it is on display, but her face looks young still.

"Excuse me. Aren't you Flynn Beckham?"

It's been happening more and more lately. After the reality TV show, I was mobbed for a while, but then things died down. Now, with the announcement of In Like Flynn joining the Easy Ryder tour, and the upcoming release of our next album, I've been getting a lot more attention from the tabloids. Which means street recognition.

"I am."

Her eyes light up. "Could I take a picture of us? The girls in my dorm will never believe I ran into you on the street without proof."

I look at Lucky and she smiles. I suppose she's used to the attention more than I am. With her parents and…her boyfriend.

"Sure."

The girl snuggles close to me, pressing her chest up against mine, and smiles as she holds out her iPhone and shoots off a dozen pictures.

"Is she your wife?" She glances at Lucky with a look of annoyance and then back to me expectedly.

"Umm…no."

"Can I buy you a drink later?"

I'm pretty sure I'll never get used to being asked out. Lucky sees the discomfort written on my face and grabs my hand, weaving our fingers together before addressing the girl. "We may not be married, but we're exclusive, sweetheart."

Then she turns her attention to me. "Light's green, honey."

I grin and follow my woman's lead, hand in hand.

"Thank you for that."

"No problem." She smiles. "You saved me yesterday. It's the least I can do. But I think you might need to start wearing a hat and sunglasses."

The rest of the way to FAO Schwarz, I never let go of her hand and she never attempts to pull it away. I open the door lefty, even though it's an awkward, totally unnatural movement, just so I don't have to give up the contact.

"After you," I say. She walks through the door and then unexpectedly turns and starts speaking. She stops midsentence when she again catches my eyes glued to her ass. This time she doesn't let me off the hook so easily.

"See something you like?" She arches an eyebrow.

"You have no idea," I reply with a wry grin. "Is it wrong to say that you have an amazing ass?"

Smiling, she cocks her head to the side. "I'm not sure. Last week I was wearing those leather pants I just bought and I asked Avery how I looked. She made me do the spin move and then she told me my ass looked great. So I suppose it's acceptable to give your honest opinion on body parts to friends."

"Good to know." Then I make a slow inspection of her—starting at the bottom and leisurely working my way up. My eyes linger at the sliver of skin showing between her yoga pants and the tank top she's wearing. Traveling further, I openly steal what can only be considered a leering look at her full breasts and then, eventually, my eyes lock with hers.

She raises her eyebrows in question, but says nothing.

"I'm a good friend. Just wanted to make sure I was ready to give you more honest opinions on your body parts."

She shakes her head. "Come on, *pal.*"

We spend more than two hours roaming through FAO Schwarz, yet I haven't even picked out a gift for Laney's birthday party tomorrow yet. The giant piano floor mat that I've seen in movies like *Big* kept us occupied for more than an hour. The two of us jumping around and playing real songs with our feet eventually attracted a crowd. Lucky grabbed my hand and whisked me away when she noticed some of the moms were whispering and taking out their cellphones.

We're almost through the entire store when we stop in front of a display. There's no deliberation or discussion, we both just smile at each other and I pick the box up and head to the cash register—even though I know my sister is going to kill me.

I walk Lucky back to her apartment, not ready to leave her yet. We stroll casually, laughing the entire time. Until we reach her building. She fidgets for a minute, playing with her keys before looking up at me.

"Do you want to come up? I could wrap that for you. I have a stash of wrapping paper and I'm guessing you don't."

I know I shouldn't. Because, let's face it, *I really want to*. I'm just about to accept her offer when her phone goes off. The ring tone leaves no doubt who is calling. "Betrayed." Easy Ryder's most popular song blares from her hand. She stares at the picture flashing on her phone.

"Sorry. I can call him back later."

"No. It's okay. I should probably get going anyway."

Her face falls a little, but she recovers quickly with a conciliatory smile. I lean down and kiss her cheek. It's innocent enough, my lips don't linger, but when I start to pull back, Lucky wraps her arms around me and hugs. Tight. I've never been one to put my private life on display, but the urge to kiss the hell out of her in public is almost primal.

"Thank you again for last night, Flynn. It meant a lot."

Pulling back, our eyes meet just as the song abruptly stops midverse. Dylan Ryder may have stopped singing, but he's standing right between us now. And damn if I don't want to push him out of my way.

chapter twelve

Lucky

I thought about contacting Flynn all week, but in the end, I didn't. On Tuesday, I went as far as typing out a text, although my finger ultimately hit Delete after hovering over Send for a long time. *How did Laney like her gift?* The text was innocent enough. Yet, the reality is, anything related to Flynn Beckham stopped feeling innocent about ten minutes after I met him.

I disembark from the plane to Atlanta in a daze. Dylan is picking me up at the airport. We haven't seen each other in two weeks. I'm looking forward to it. Well, mostly I'm looking forward to it. But there's something churning inside my belly that also makes me nervous about our reunion, although I'm not completely sure why.

Riding the escalator down to baggage claim, I'm surprised when I see Dylan at the bottom. I assumed he would be in the car and one of his security guys would be meeting me. He's wearing a baseball hat, sunglasses and a grey hooded sweatshirt with the hood pulled over the hat, masking some of his face. Couple the look with a pair of faded jeans and sneakers and he actually blends into the crowd. Easy Ryder has had seven platinum albums in ten years, five consecutive sold-out tours, and most people have at least one of their songs on their iPod—even men. Blending into the crowd is definitely not the norm for Dylan Ryder.

He's playing with his phone but looks up just when I hit the bottom. The sunglasses he's wearing shield his eyes, but I know from the curl at the corner of his mouth that he's looking at me. He doesn't step forward; instead he waits for me to come to him.

Neither of us says a word, but when I reach where he's standing, he wraps his hand around my waist and pulls me to him, his mouth sealing possessively over mine. It's more a welcome-home-from-the-military kiss than the greeting of a man who is attempting not to call attention to himself.

"Well, this is a surprise," I breathe when he releases me.

"That I'm standing here or the kiss?"

"Both, I suppose."

"Well, it shouldn't be. I told you I would pick you up."

"I know, but I guess I expected you to wait outside."

"Guess I missed my girl." He gives me a chaste kiss. "I have more surprises for you later." He winks.

Trying to avoid any more attention than he's already garnered, Dylan looks down as we make our way to baggage claim and, lucky for us, my suitcase is one of the first to come out. A few women on the other side of the conveyor belt are already whispering and pointing in our direction by the time we're heading to the car.

"Hi, Johnny," I say to the Hulk-like man in the dark suit who steps out of the car to open the back door of the Escalade for us.

"Miss Valentine." He nods. Dylan's security team are their usual friendly selves, I see.

Before Johnny pulls away from the curb, Dylan's hand is already slipping under my skirt.

"Stop," I whisper a warning and glare at him.

"Why?" He tugs me closer and his lips find my neck.

I pull back. "Umm…because we're not alone."

"He's seen a lot worse."

I'm dating a rockstar, it's not like I think he's a virgin. Far from it. But the reminder of the carefree things that have happened in the presence of others still stings. "Thanks for the reminder."

"Come on, Lucky. I didn't mean it like that. You know what I meant."

I try to shrug it off. I haven't seen him in two weeks, and I should be excited he's so eager to get his hands on me. "I know. Just…not here."

"But I have to go straight to sound check," he pouts.

"Then it sounds like you may have to wait until tonight."

Dylan groans. "I hate waiting."

I lean in and whisper in his ear, "But good things come to those who wait."

I may have spent half my life in a bar, but I've never been good at drinking. Perhaps it was the years of watching drunks make fools of themselves at Lucky's that soured me against public intoxication. It's not that I don't drink…Lord knows Avery and I have had some nights that turned into morning-afters I'd like to forget. My drinking just tends to be limited to when I'm not at a public event. Tonight I make an exception to my normal sober policy—my nerves getting the best of me for some reason.

Dylan was supposed to take me back to the hotel after the sound check this afternoon. Instead, equipment problems and an issue with the acoustics in the arena kept us here straight through to tonight's show. Apparently, the amphitheater had recently undergone some construction that was supposed to be completed, but defective materials caused a delay. The contractor tried to put a Band-Aid on a bullet wound, temporarily sealing up the ceiling with wood, but it isn't absorbing the sound correctly, instead sending unbalanced reverberations scattering all over the room.

"Sorry, babe." Dylan comes up from behind me in the lounge backstage. "I'll make it up to you later."

"It's fine. Jack kept me company." I turn and wrap my arms around his neck. My speech might be slightly impaired.

"Who's Jack?" There's an edge to his voice.

I squint at him. It might also help me focus in my intoxicated state. "Do I detect a hint of jealousy from the man who has panties thrown at him every night?"

"You know I don't share, Lucky."

"Relax. Jack isn't a man, silly. But if he was, you'd certainly have some competition. He makes me feel warm all over."

"How much did you drink?"

I hold up my pointer finger and thumb to demonstrate a small amount. "Just a smidgen."

"A smidgen, huh? I think you and Mr. Daniels may have gotten a bit more intimate than a quickie. Fuck," he groans. "I might be jealous of a bottle of Jack."

I giggle, even though I tend to not be the giggly type. It's the alcohol making everything seem funnier than it is.

Dylan pushes my hair behind my ear. "I have to drop by the after-party tonight. The label has some of our bigger sponsors going. But we don't have to stay long. Then I'm all yours for twenty-four hours."

"Not quite twenty-four. My flight is at four tomorrow." Since I just started a new job, it's a very short visit. I can't miss work on Monday.

"We'll see about that," Dylan says cryptically as he leans in, his mouth finding my neck. We already argued on the phone about my leaving on Sunday afternoon. He wanted me to stay until the band pulled out of Atlanta on Monday night, but my new job is important to me. I've got a happy buzz going and have no desire to ruin it by rekindling the fight we already had, so I save it for tomorrow. Plus, Dylan's mouth at my neck is leaving me with little resolve.

Dylan and I watch the opening act from the side of the stage. Resin is a British band that has gained popularity since the beginning of this tour. They're huge in Europe already, and the US radio stations are starting to give them more and more play time. It's no surprise they're choosing to leave when the Wylde Ryde tour begins six months of additional show dates. At least this time when Flynn pops into my head, there's a reason he should. In Like Flynn is taking over for Resin in less than two months. My eyes fly up toward Dylan at the thought...as if he could see me thinking that I'm looking forward to those show dates.

Dylan Ryder puts on a pretty amazing show. Normally, I can't help but watch in awe. When he sings on stage, a little piece of me still feels like the fourteen-year-old girl who idolized him from afar. The girl who lay in bed at night, staring at his poster. But tonight I only last two songs. The music is piped in all throughout the backstage, so I don't miss that—but I opt not to watch him sing.

I fix myself another Jack and Coke and take a seat on the couch in the band's lounge. All the band members except Dylan share one big room backstage. Dylan, of course, has his own.

A handful of groupies mill around, waiting for the guys to finish. It makes me wonder whose job it is to pick the women who are allowed backstage. Does a security guard wander through the audience with a list of requirements? *36D, check. Short skirt, check. How's your gag reflex, honey? Check.*

I swallow the thought along with half the contents of my glass. I'm definitely feeling no pain. My mind again wanders to Flynn. The alcohol clouds my judgment and I shoot off a text before I can think better of it.

How did Laney like her gift? At least my text doesn't come out slurred.

He responds within a minute. *She loved it. My sister...not so much.*

You can't make all the girls happy.

Now that's a shame. Bet I know one girl I can make smile?

He doesn't know I've been smiling since his first response. *Long distance smile promises. You must be pretty confident, Mr. Beckham.*

Oh. I am. You ready?

A huge smile hasn't left my face. *Can't wait.*

My phone is quiet for a minute. I'm growing anxious he might not respond again. Finally, my phone pings. But it's not a text, it's a video. I press play. The camera focuses on a little girl holding a microphone. She's wearing a princess tiara, plastic high-heel shoes and a skirt made of purple tulle. A half dozen strands of beads hang from around her neck all the way down to her tummy.

Flynn's voice prompts her from behind the camera. "Who are you dedicating the song I taught you today to, Laney?"

"This song is dedicated to..." She scrunches up her face and takes a step toward the camera, whispering loudly. "I forgot her name, Uncle Sinn."

Flynn chuckles off-camera. "Lucky," he whispers.

Excited, Laney steps back in place and holds up the microphone. "This song is dedicated to Lucky." Then she lowers the microphone and says, "That's a funny name, Uncle Sinn."

Flynn laughs. "It's no funnier than Laney."

"Yes. But my real name is Helaine. What's Lucky's real name?"

Even though I can't see him, I know he's smiling. "I don't know, Laney. I'll have to ask her. Can I get back to you on that?"

She nods with exuberance.

"You ready now?"

She nods again.

Flynn leans forward and pushes play on the Disney *Frozen* karaoke machine. The machine he carried for more than a mile on the walk from FAO Schwarz to my apartment. Warmth spreads through me when I hear the first note. I'm smiling ear to ear while Laney sings "Twinkle, Twinkle, Little Star."

All. Five. Verses.

I think of the little princess sitting on her tatted rockstar uncle's lap while he teaches her the song. My ovaries might just explode.

The video ends. I really want to watch it again, but I can't wait to respond to his last text.

> *My smile is HUGE.*
>
> *I might have cheated. She's sort of irresistible.*
>
> *She takes after her uncle.*
>
> *I'll have to take you over to meet her when I get back into town.*

My stomach does a little drop. He's leaving? For how long? I didn't have any plans to see him, yet knowing he won't be in the same city disappoints me for some reason. *Going away?*

> *Hitting the road. Gone for a month.*

A month? Why does that bother me? We exchange a few more texts and then Easy Ryder has finished their show, and the entire lounge swirls with excitement.

Dylan finds me. "You disappeared halfway through the set."

"I was feeling sort of queasy," I lie.

"You spent too much time with Jack and didn't eat. Come on, there's food in my dressing room. Let me feed you before we have to go to the after-party."

It's two in the morning before we finally head back to the hotel. I left for the airport at six a.m. yesterday, so I've been awake for nearly twenty-four hours. The lack of sleep and drinking catches up to me and I fall asleep with my head on Dylan's shoulder on the car ride back. He wakes me when we reach the Gideon Hotel, but my energy level is drained…I'm flashing on empty.

"I need to take a quick shower. You want to join me?" Dylan asks hopefully when we get into his suite.

"I'm too tired." I plop down on the inviting king-size bed.

"I'll be fast." He kisses me, and strips as he heads into the bathroom.

I'm not quite asleep when he crawls into bed and I feel his naked hard body against my back. "I hate those sponsor events. Bunch of suits more interested in checking out my woman than talking business." He sweeps my hair to the side and kisses my neck while his erection pushes into me.

"You're crazy. No one even notices me when I walk into a room with you."

He reaches around and cups my breasts. "Maybe if you would cover these up a little, some of the men in the room would be able to focus more."

I turn over to face him. "Are you serious? I had barely any cleavage even showing tonight."

Dylan pushes my shirt up and the cup of my bra down. His head drops to my exposed breast. "I'd prefer to keep what's mine less on display."

"Coming from the man who sang half his set bare chested tonight?"

"That's different. I'm selling an act." His tongue flicks over the tip of one nipple.

"What if I was the one on stage? Wearing skimpy clothes as part of my act?"

He swirls his tongue around until my nipple is a taut peak, and speaks before moving to the other breast. "I don't even want to think about it. I'm just glad you're happy behind the scenes."

Dylan is still sleeping when I wake the next morning. Actually, it's more like afternoon. It's a rarity for me to sleep so late; then again, I don't usually drink so much. And I have a four o'clock flight to catch. I wasted the little time we had together yesterday with drinking copious amounts of liquor I knew I couldn't handle, and then half the next day sleeping it off. I slink out of bed, trying hard not to wake the naked man lying diagonally across the mattress, and head to the bathroom to shower.

I let the water run over me, hoping it will quell the growing throb in my head, but no such luck. I think it might actually make me feel even worse. The pulsating showerhead should feel like a tiny massage but more closely resembles little mallets hitting my skull. Not good. I finish quickly and stumble out of the shower, feeling worse than when I walked into the bathroom.

I need coffee.

And aspirin.

And more coffee to wash down the aspirin.

Luckily, I keep a mini–first aid kit in my travel case. Underneath the useless packages of gauze and suture-removal sheers—really who needs to remove their own stitches?—I find the small packet of Tylenol that I've seen there the few times I've opened the case.

Great, they expired three months ago.

I swallow them anyway, using only a handful of water from the bathroom sink. Very ladylike.

I do my best at fixing myself, pulling my hair into a ponytail, applying moisturizer, a quick coat of mascara and a few pumps of perfume. The smells make me nauseous.

Dylan's voice startles me when I tiptoe back into the bedroom.

"You took a shower without me." He's lying on his stomach, face-down still, his tight ass enticingly bare. "And you're dressed already. When I heard the water go off, I was hoping I'd used all the big towels last night and you'd have to use one of those small ones. I was looking forward to seeing you wet in a tiny towel."

I smile. His head isn't even lifted off the pillow, yet he's got a clear visual of what he was hoping to see. I walk to the bed and sit next to where he's lying. "Sorry to disappoint you, but my flight is in a few hours and I need to get going soon."

"No, you don't."

I'm not sure if he means I don't need to leave so early or he wants to have another argument about my returning tonight. "Yes, I do." I hedge. "I'm not sure about Sunday traffic, but the airport is at least half an hour away and my flight is in three hours."

"You don't need to be on this afternoon's flight." Guess I hedged wrong on what we were arguing about.

"Yes, I do."

"No, you don't."

I sigh. "I told you, Dylan. I just started my job and I don't want to ask for time off so soon."

"You don't need to ask for time off. There's been a change of plans with your new job."

I freeze. "What are you talking about?"

"You've been reassigned."

"Reassigned?"

"Yes. For the next month, you're on tour with Easy Ryder."

"What? Why?" Why would the label send a voice coach to travel with the band? No one has any issues that I'm aware of. "One of the guys is having trouble with his voice?"

"No. But Linc's girl is going to have the babies a few weeks earlier than planned and he needs to go home for a few weeks." Linc Osborne is Easy Ryder's bass player and sings a few of the songs on their new album. He's a tenor with a to-die-for falsetto and the songs he does are very popular. His girlfriend is pregnant with twins and the doctors have had her on bed rest for months, trying to hold off labor as long as they can.

"I'm missing the connection to me."

"I got someone to fill in…but the label is concerned. He's had voice issues and he's singing a few weeks earlier than he should be. It's only two songs a night. They're just being cautious."

"So they want me to work with him? While you're on the road?"

"Yep." Dylan pulls me from sitting to lying down on the bed. I'm quickly on my back beneath him. "And that means we both get what we want. I get to have you with me for a while. And you don't have to miss any work."

I'm not really sure how I feel about spending weeks on a tour bus with the band. With Dylan. I suppose a few weeks of being together might help me move forward in our relationship. Dylan's been pushing for more and I've been hesitant. Yet there's a nagging feeling in my stomach.

"Say something. I thought you'd be happy."

"I am," I say, but the hesitancy is clear in my voice. Even I don't believe me.

"I think I need to show you how much fun being my bunkmate on the bus can be." Dylan rolls us so I'm on top of him. I can feel his happiness about the arrangement pushing up against my belly.

"But…but I need my things."

"I'll buy you new things."

"What about—"

"Relax, Lucky, will ya? I thought you'd be excited to come on tour."

"I am…" *Am I?*

"I'll fly Avery out to spend the weekend when we hit Austin. There's a festival and a bunch of parties." Dylan is *not* a fan of Avery. I know he's trying.

His thumb and forefinger tip my chin up so our eyes meet. "It will give you a chance to see if our future is what you envisioned."

It suddenly dawns on me for the first time—I've never envisioned our future together.

As if dinner with the lead singer of Easy Ryder didn't attract enough attention, the full band all sitting around one large round table is the paparazzi's dream come true. And the guys certainly don't attempt to keep under the radar. Duff, the keyboard player, is in a heated exchange with Mick, the drummer, when Dylan and I approach the table. We're a bit late, but then I had a lot of things to do today since I'll be heading to Miami tomorrow with a bus full of men, rather than back home as expected.

"No fucking way. I had to listen to months of this guy's snoring." Duff jabs his thumb in Linc's direction. "I am *not* listening to your sorry ass boning every night over my head."

"Maybe if you could find a piece of ass who wanted to bone your little dick, you wouldn't notice the sound coming from my bunk."

"Accommodations dispute," Dylan leans in and whispers to me as we take our seats. The next part he says louder. "I swear to God, if they aren't fighting over which chair to sit in, it's which bunk they get."

"Fuck off, Ryder. If you didn't take the only bedroom, you'd be in these fights too, asswipe."

"That's why I'm glad I'm the king." Dylan stretches back in his chair. Duff, Linc and Mick hurl bread at his head. Dylan catches the second piece and takes a bite. "Just give the kid the bottom bunk. Duff can move to the top bunk and you can stay where you are."

"I don't want to room with the kid. What is he, like twenty-four? Dude, think of what we were like ten years ago going on our first tour." Mick looks at me apologetically. "No offense, Lucky." Then he continues with his rant to Dylan. "And that kid's prettier than you were. I'll never get any sleep with all the babes that are gonna be fuckstruck with that one."

"Fuckstruck?"

"He's gonna be a pussy machine."

"Have some manners around my girl, asswipe."

Listening to the way the guys describe the activity on the bus starts to make me think I was right for feeling unsure about things earlier. Dylan and I spent all afternoon together. His attentiveness and the simplicity of the day—shopping, walking around Atlanta incognito—had started to mollify the anxiousness I felt when Dylan first surprised me with my temporary job assignment. But now, apprehension is starting to creep up again.

"Why don't you declare the bus a guest-free zone? That's what my Dad always did."

Every mouth silences and every head turns in my direction.

"What's the point of being in a band if you don't get laid?" Duff says, aghast at the notion.

"How about for the music?" a voice I recognize says from behind me.

It couldn't be.

I turn.

Holy shit.

But how?

And Why?

Then the pieces of the puzzle all click into place and I'm able to see the whole picture. *The kid. Voice issues.*

I stare up at Flynn.

He stares back at me.

And I realize. I'm totally fuckstruck.

chapter

thirteen

Flynn

Now *this* is going to be interesting.

The label told me they were setting me up with a voice coach. Even though I feel fine, the insurance company wouldn't insure the tour unless I finished the mandated voice rest period my doctor had suggested on the physical he completed. He'd cleared me for In Like Flynn to open for Easy Ryder starting in two months, but filling in for Linc is much earlier than the doctor was comfortable signing off on. The coaching was how the label convinced my doctor and the insurance company I wasn't a risk. I must be an idiot. It never once crossed my mind that they'd assign me Lucky.

Damn, she's beautiful. It shouldn't surprise me. I've been reminded a lot of that lately with how often I find my thoughts wandering back to her.

"Only a dude that's as pretty as you can say you do it for the music." Duff snorts. "Damn. I'm glad I'm behind a drum set. I wouldn't want to stand next to you."

Dylan's jaw tenses. He nods in my general direction. "Take a seat, Flynn. You remember my girlfriend, Lucky?"

"I do. Nice to see you." I smile and tilt my head, curious about how we're going to play this.

She looks up at me, squints, assessing, and then smiles. "Nice to see you, too."

There are two open seats, one between Duff and Mick and one next to Lucky. I choose the latter. Who wouldn't?

"So, Flynn, ya snore?" Linc asks.

"Not that I'm aware of."

"What's your fucking style?" Mick says, as if he's just asked the time.

"My what?"

"You know, your fucking style? Are you loud? A slammer? Reverse cowboy? Ménage?"

"Cut the shit, Mick," Dylan snaps.

"What? I'm gonna find out soon enough anyway. It's a small sleeping area."

"Don't be so sure about that. I've had a dry spell of late."

"The way you look? You must have been hanging out in a seminary."

"Nah. Just haven't found anyone interesting *who's available.*" Lucky and I exchange fleeting glances.

"Well, one night on stage with Easy Ryder and my guess is your single ass finds someone *interesting* enough to help you ride the post-show high."

Throughout dinner, I watch the interactions between Dylan and Lucky. He's into her, there's no doubt about it. The unmistakable possessive gestures are there; a part of his body always seems to be touching hers. An arm loosely around the back of her chair, his hand on the table brushing up against hers, the way he leans into her when even the waiter comes around to fill water glasses. A lion with a soundless roar.

But after two hours, I'm still not sure what to make of how Lucky is with him. It's nothing out of the ordinary that makes me think she may not return the same level of worship...it's just that what I see is...ordinary.

After dinner, the maître d' comes to the table to tell us a crowd has formed outside. He offers the back door, but the band manager had already suggested the guys sign autographs outside before they leave. We're pulling out of Atlanta right after the last show, so tonight is a local photo op. Dylan reminds me I'm not part of the band yet, and security escorts Lucky and me to the back door. We slip outside into a dark SUV undetected.

Alone in the car, neither of us says anything for a minute. Then we both start speaking at the same time. "Did you—" We laugh.

"You had no idea either?" Lucky says.

"Nope."

"Why does our hanging out last week feel wrong to admit now?"

I know the answer—it's a simple one. "Because it felt right."

Our eyes lock, and I feel it. The shit that stirs through the air when I'm near her. Damn. And fucking A if she doesn't smell incredible too. The oversized SUV suddenly feels pretty small.

I'm actually grateful when security pulls the SUV around to the front of the restaurant and Dylan and Duff hop inside. I'm not sure how much longer I could sit next to her and not touch. I think about it the whole ride back to the hotel. And I wonder, what would she have done if I had touched?

I load my stuff onto the bus before we head to the final show in Atlanta. Unsure where I'm bunking, I toss my bag under the table and take a look around. To the right, a long desk, equipped with a large flat-screen TV, various game consoles and two laptops securely affixed, dominates the living area. The rest of the space is taken up by a leather couch, capable of holding the entire band, a wide matching recliner, two tables, and compact, but efficiently equipped, stainless steel appliances.

A door separates the living area from the sleeping quarters in the back of the bus. Pulled back curtains showcase bunks that line the walls on both sides, two on each side, a top and a bottom. There's a shower to the right and a bathroom to the left. Another door in the rear leads to the only private bedroom in the bus. *Dylan's room*. The one he'll be sharing with Lucky.

My band has toured before. Admittedly, our bus looked nothing like this, but I know from experience that walls are thin and groupies have no qualms about who might hear. Hell, the sounds that came out of the back were often the topic of ball-busting the entire next day. I smile, thinking of Nolan's knack for mimicking a screamer he'd heard the night before. Yet the thought of hearing Lucky leaves a bitter taste in my mouth. The thought of anyone mimicking her downright makes me angry.

Eventually, the guys load onto the bus. Dylan and Lucky are the last to join, and the driver takes off for the arena as soon as everyone is situated. The only greeting I offer is a nod at the two of them. They disappear into the back of the bus.

"Welcome to our home." Mick opens his arms wide. "If you don't snore, you can take the bunk above me on the right-hand side."

"Thanks."

"Do you share?" Mick asks, plopping down on the recliner. He cracks a beer even though it's only eleven in the morning.

"Share? Like one woman and crossing swords?"

"There's no room for threesomes in this thing. Unless you use Dylan's room, and I'm guessing that he's on a sharing hiatus for a while." He shrugs. "I meant if your hookup is interested in touring the band. Works both ways, of course."

"I'm guessing you'll get all his hookups coming to you, seeing as he can't satisfy them anymore," Duff taunts.

"Fuck off. You don't share because you don't want them comparing." Mick grabs his crotch. "My kielbasa to your miniature hotdog."

Lucky walks to the front of the bus, eyes Mick still holding himself, shakes her head and sits down at the far end of the couch.

"So. You in or you out?" Undaunted by Lucky's appearance, Mick continues the conversation. I catch her eye before I respond.

"No, thanks. I'm not into sharing."

Tonight is Linc's last night of the tour. I'm looking forward to seeing the band and watching the interactions between the guys. It will give me some hint of what to expect when I join on stage two nights from now. So far, it's an easy fit. Mick and Duff are the most vocal of the group. They enjoy ball-busting, and since I can pretty much let shit roll off my shoulders after years of putting up with Nolan, I don't suppose we'll run into any issues. The three of us spent a little time jamming together on the bus this morning, and I get the feeling that I passed their unspoken test.

Dylan, on the other hand, I'm not quite sure what to make of him. He's standoffish toward me. There's a chip on his shoulder, but I honestly don't blame him—the guy has had a career most people in the music industry can only dream about. Even though he's never said or done anything specific to confirm it, I get the feeling he looks at me like a younger model. He's only thirty-five, but something tells me he sees aging as a threat, instead of seeing the benefit of experience. It doesn't help that the band had a dip in sales with the release of their last album. A dip to a volume most musicians would be ecstatic to achieve, but Easy Ryder's standards aren't those of most musicians.

Lucky and I haven't said much to each other either. We've exchanged a lot of quick glances and wordless smiles acknowledging some of Mick and Duff's comments, but when the backstage lounge finally empties and the rest of band is gone, we eye each other and both start laughing.

"This is weird," she says hesitantly.

"Only if we make it weird."

She smiles. "Then let's not make it weird. Come on. Let's go watch the show. It will probably be the last time you go unnoticed in a crowd." And just like that, whatever we had in New York City is back again.

Lucky talks me into watching the show from the floor, rather than the VIP area. It's a smaller venue—smaller by Easy Ryder standards, that is—and only the higher-priced tickets have seating. The roped-off section designated for VIPs is nearly filled with guys in grey suits, executives from the corporate sponsors. Lucky took one look, smiled a devilish smile, and tugged my hand toward the other direction.

So now we're in the middle of a crowd, among the real fans who are dancing and screaming. They're all riveted to the stage, the entire place alive as Easy Ryder sings one of their biggest hits, "Burn." A pyrotechnic show plays behind and between the members of the band, shooting flames up from the floor. Yet I find myself forgetting the show, distracted by the woman standing next to me. Lucky is dancing and enjoying the music, letting the vibe take her to her happy place. I watch as she closes her eyes and her body moves to the sound with a sensuality that has me mesmerized. Sensing me watching her, her eyes flutter open and she smiles sweetly when she catches me staring. I force my gaze back to the band I should be watching.

When Dylan hits the chorus, the whole arena sways in unison and sings along. Bodies push in, and the drunken woman behind Lucky stumbles, shoving her forward. I grab her before she falls and the woman apologizes with a slur. A few minutes later, the band changes things up and Linc strums the first chord of "Just Once More"—the song I'll be singing after tonight. Knowing I'll be up there in two days, Lucky grabs my arm and looks up at me excitedly. Unlike Dylan, who prowls the stage, working the crowd as he sings, Linc is much more subdued when he performs. It's an incredible song, with a kick-ass falsetto that people love to sing, but Linc's performance mellows the crowd from the near hysteria Dylan had built. It's not a bad thing, just different. And also very different than my style. I hope the crowd likes my delivery as much as Linc's.

Lucky can barely contain her excitement when the song finishes. "That's going to be you up there."

I smile. "I hope I can do it justice."

"'Do it justice'? I've heard you sing live. You're going to kick its ass!"

The drunken woman crashes into Lucky again. I stop her from stumbling too far a second time; this time the drunk woman spills a little beer on Lucky's shoes as she leans forward to slur another apology. Lucky is gracious and waves her off politely. Rather than waiting for a third time, I step behind Lucky and stand between her and drunk girl.

We stay that way for the next few songs, her dancing in front of me, both of us enjoying the show and the electricity of the crowd around us. The few times her ass brushes against me, I'm pretty sure it's innocent, but my thoughts are anything but.

When one of Easy Ryder's more mainstream pop-style songs comes on, Lucky turns to face me and we dance together. The entire crowd is moving and grooving and we both fully let go, allowing ourselves to become part of the audience, rather than part of the band. Even though we have limited room, I spin her around a few times and we both laugh. On the last twirl in, she folds into my arms and, with my arm around her waist, my hand resting at the top of her low riding jeans, I pull her against me and we begin to move. Really move. My front against her ass, my hands holding her pressed to me tightly, our hips moving in synch, grinding to the rhythm. It feels wrong, but yet oh-so-fucking-right.

When the song ends, moving to something heavier, more hardcore rock, our dancing comes to a natural stop, but she doesn't move away from me. And I don't loosen the grip my hands have on her waist.

An hour later, the show's almost over and we're backstage in the lounge. We laugh and talk and even share a beer—literally share—both of us drinking out of the same bottle. Then the band comes back. They're pumped from the show, the electricity flowing with them as they bring the lounge to life. Dylan grabs a beer and pulls Lucky to his side. We exchange glances a few times. But she and I are back to being strangers.

I move to the other side of the room and get some much-needed time with Linc. He's more subdued than the other guys in the band, less of a ball buster and full of passion about the music. I try to prevent my eyes from wandering in Lucky's direction, but when Dylan's mouth goes to her neck, our gazes lock. What the fuck am I doing?

chapter fourteen

Lucky

I wake to the same dull vibration I fell asleep to last night, only now the constant tremor of the bus is shaking me awake rather than lulling me to dreamland. The large picture window above the bed is masked by a blackout shade that keeps the room perpetually dark. I have no idea if it's six in the morning or two in the afternoon.

I slip from the bed, careful not to wake Dylan, and make a stop in the bathroom. The golden glow of early morning sunshine filtering through the opaque window tells me my internal alarm clock is still ticking. My reflection catches the effect of the cool morning air under my t-shirt as my perky nipples salute a new day. I wash up, pile my unruly hair on top of my head, and brush my teeth before going in search of a coffee pot.

The bathroom is next to the band's bunk area, and as I quietly pass through, I wonder which bed Flynn is sleeping in. And if he's in there alone. Yesterday afternoon we danced and acted like two teenagers. *Two teenagers who were very into each other.* I start to blush, thinking of the way his body felt behind mine. The way his fingers dug into my hips, guiding my body to move the way he wanted it to. It made me wonder...

Lost in thought, I startle when I pass through the door to the living area of the bus. Flynn's already there. He's standing in front of a coffee pot, arms spread wide, gripping the counter in front of him, head hanging down, seemingly in deep thought. And. He's shirtless. Stunningly shirtless.

I'm not sure if he hears my small gasp or senses my presence, but his head turns and our eyes meet. His blue eyes sparkle and the corner of his mouth tilts up. Lord he even looks like that in the morning.

"Good morning," I whisper.

His gaze drops to my chest, then flicks back to my eyes with a goofy half grin. "Certainly is."

He watches every step I take toward him. I can see why women would find him irresistible. Two words and a look and he makes me feel desired. Before I've even had morning coffee, no less. Add in a guitar and a voice like an angel, and the line will be wrapping around the bus after his first show.

He reaches into the cabinet above his head and pulls out two mugs. I guess I'm not the only one finding him irresistible this morning. My stomach turns a bit at the thought. "Sleep good?" I say, trying my best to sound light.

"Like a baby. You?"

"I did, actually. It's been a long time since I was on a tour bus."

"You always up this early?"

"Yep. Pretty much every day. Six a.m., whether I go to bed at eight p.m. or four in the morning. You?"

He grins before turning his attention to the coffee pot, which beeps as it finishes brewing. "Same."

He fills two mugs. "Cream and sugar?"

Oh. So he's not taking coffee for an overnight guest. I perk up at the thought of us having morning coffee together and take a seat at the table. "Yes, please."

He grins again.

"What?"

He shrugs. "I take it the same way." He brings a coffee mug to the table and waits for me to sip. "Good?"

It's exactly the way I like it. "Perfect."

He turns back to tidy up. Living on a tour bus teaches you to put things away faster than the tire hits the next bump. I'm treated to the sight of his naked back as he cleans up. It's strong, lean but muscular, and I'm delighted by the way the muscles ripple when he reaches to put the milk away. I totally shouldn't be getting so turned on watching the man open a damn refrigerator door and close it. I just walked out of the bedroom I'm sharing with my boyfriend, and he's sleeping less than thirty feet away.

Flynn turns around and catches my stare. Another boyish grin. Damn him. Does he have to be so adorable? With that body? I force my eyes to my coffee and sip again.

"What do you normally do at six a.m.?" he asks. "Do you exercise or something?"

"Exercise? Me? Have you seen the size of my ass?"

"I have. And that reminds me." He turns back, opening the cabinet above his head, and takes out a few Hershey's Special Dark bars. "Saw these at the store before we boarded the bus last night, figured I'd grab them in case you weren't well stocked." He winks. "Gotta keep that ass in its fine shape."

Lord help me. The man may be more sinfully sweet than my chocolate bars. "I actually didn't have any. Thank you." Flustered, because he's still watching me, I change the subject quickly. "I write."

He slides in on the opposite side of the table from me. "What do you write?"

I feel silly for having said anything. No one knows I write poetry. Not even Dylan. "Poetry mostly."

"Huh. Poetry."

"What?"

"I write music in the morning." He dips his chin toward the notebook sitting on the table. "It's the same thing. At least, if it's good it is. A good song is just poetry set to music."

"Are you writing a song now?"

He nods. "I'm still working on the lyrics. Right now it's just random thoughts and words that need to be sewn together. But I have the concept and, I think, the title. I need to hear the music in my head before I can write the actual lyrics. Once I have the rhythm set, the words come easier."

"What's the title?"

"'Blur.'"

"Hmmm..." I sip my coffee. "Intriguing. What's it about?"

"It's about how two very different things can be closely connected. Sometimes polar opposites, yet the line that separates them is very fine. And as you get closer to the line, things become a blur. The blur is almost a state of euphoria between the two sides, but you can't stay in the blur forever. Something pushes you from one side to the other, and then there's no coming back."

"Like love and hate?"

"Exactly like love and hate." Flynn reaches for his notebook and flips a few pages, then points to sets of words. The first set is *love* and *hate*. He smiles at me, then covers the rest of the page with his hand. "I was thinking of writing it like a bunch of sonnets. Fourteen lines for each pair of connected words...each verse a sonnet on its own. Okay, smarty pants, what else you got?"

"Hmmm...give me a minute, I don't have enough caffeine in me yet." We sit quietly for a while, then I say, "Pleasure and pain." The blush creeps up my cheeks before I even get the words out.

"Very good." He opens his notebook and points to the pair of words. "That pair is *definitely* all about the blur zone. The state of euphoria from pleasure as it dips in the range of pain, or pain as it dips into pleasure, is complete bliss. But push too far, leave the blur zone on the other side of the line, and there's no coming back. It's pain without any pleasure. Stay too far from the line on the pleasure side and you miss euphoria."

I wiggle in my seat, a bit of a swell going on between my legs as I listen to him. It makes me wonder what the blur zone would be like with him. I attempt to steer the conversation to a more clinical place. "It's the endorphins."

"It's about the feeling, not the chemistry. Plus, 'Blur' is a much better title than 'Endorphins.'"

I laugh. "Genius and crazy."

"I didn't have that one. But you're right. The blur between genius and crazy must be an awesome place to be. Imagine the incredible high your mind gets as the line between the two comes closer. Too bad people don't get to stay there forever and genius sometimes turns into crazy passing through the blur."

"Why can't we stay in the blur?"

"I don't know. But once you cross that line, there's no coming back."

We spend the next three hours spiraling through conversation. He hums some music that's flowing through his head for the song's rhythm. I tell him about my life on a tour bus with my dad. He shares stories about his niece, Laney. We're so engrossed in our own little world, I almost forget there are four other people on the bus. Until Dylan opens the door to the back. He looks back and forth between the two of us for a moment and then comes to plant a kiss on my mouth, his head leaning down so it's basically over the table, between Flynn and me.

"Morning," he says. Then looks at the two of us again. "How long you two been out here?"

Flynn responds, "Not long." He lifts his chin toward the other side of the room. "There's coffee in the pot."

Dylan turns around, opens the refrigerator and grumbles, "Don't drink coffee."

A minute or two later, Flynn excuses himself to take a shower. Dylan takes Flynn's seat and I find myself looking across the table at my handsome boyfriend, wishing he were someone else.

We arrive in Miami at two in the afternoon. Our home for the next four days. Dylan has a busy schedule of radio station stops and sponsor meet-and-greets, so we agree to connect at the venue later tonight. The band has never played the American Airlines Arena and wants to get an idea of the setup before checking into the hotel we'll be at for the next few days. Flynn and I are going to the arena early so we can work on his voice training.

The cavernous host to the Miami Heat is intimidating to say the least. With its modern white-and-glass façade and inviting views of Biscayne Bay, the arena reminds me how different Dylan's tours are than my dad's were. Dad's stops were more like the bars across the street, waiting to take in the after-crowd from the main show.

"Wow. It's beautiful," I say after the arena manager lets us in. Easy Ryder's tour manager called ahead and made arrangements for the two of us to spend some time here today. There are no performances tonight, so the tremendous complex is almost eerily quiet.

"It is," the manager says and overtly licks her glossy lips. She's looking at Flynn like he's a mouthwatering steak and she's a pit bull that hasn't been fed in days. Seriously? She doesn't even know my relationship with him, yet she completely disregards me. "What can I do for you?" She tilts her head, addressing Flynn, offering him much more than a tour of the arena.

"We're just going to take a look around and then head to the stage, if that's all right with you."

"Anything you want." She slips her card into the front pocket of his jeans. *Into the front pocket of his jeans. Really?* "My cell is on the back. Call me if you need anything."

Flynn nods.

I wait until she's out of earshot. Barely. "Could she be any more obvious?"

"What do you mean?"

"Don't play coy with me, Mr. Beckham. That woman practically threw herself at you."

"Oh. That."

"Yes. That. You make it sound so commonplace."

Flynn shrugs.

"Oh. My. God. Seriously?"

"What?"

"That's how women react around you?"

"Sometimes." He looks down, almost a little embarrassed about it.

"It's like having free room service at your fingertips."

Flynn's brows draw together.

"You know. You can whip out your phone when the mood strikes and pick whatever you want from the menu."

Holding out his hand to me, a charismatic smile adorning his ridiculously handsome face, he shrugs. "Problem is, I'm in the mood for something that's not on the menu."

I roll my eyes and shake my head, but it's really to cover the flutter in my belly. Then, hand in hand, together we tour the stadium.

An hour later Flynn is up on stage and I'm sitting in the first row. "Why do I need to be up here while you're down there?"

"So I can see you in action."

"You wanna see me in action?" He wiggles his eyebrows.

I smile. "It's like when you run on a treadmill, you don't run naturally...your feet have to fit the limited space that you have to run, so it changes your stride. When I watched you in the studio, it was different than watching you on stage. Performing in a real live setting will allow your natural habits to show through better."

"Do you have any requests?" he teases.

"Just sing something that comes easily. What's the most popular song you sang when you were on tour with In Like Flynn?"

"'Back on Top.'"

"Okay, sing that."

The song is one of his band's slower ones, but it's actually a perfect display of everything I need to see—range, reach, falsetto, reverb, movement. His voice is expressive, deep and rich at some points, with a flawless transition into the falsetto that makes women go crazy. He sings about being broken, climbing back to the top after falling hard. His delivery is so convincing, I find myself mesmerized by the story he's telling, really listening to the lyrics when I should be watching him with a clinician's eye.

As the song comes to a close, I softly sing along to the final chorus. "Wow. That was...incredible. You showed your feelings rather than singing about them. I felt everything you gave."

"Thank you," he says, with a modest smile this time. It's absolutely endearing that he still hasn't gotten used to praise.

"You're going to steal the show." The words leave my mouth before I think about them. Before I think who it is he'd be stealing the show from.

"Not sure that would go over well."

I'm positive it wouldn't. In fact, after watching his performance, it makes me a bit nervous. Linc is a good singer, his voice complements Dylan's well. But that's what it does, it complements. It doesn't compete with. Flynn's voice...it might just give Dylan a run for his money on stage.

"Come up here and sing one with me," Flynn says, surprising me.

I shake my head.

"Come on. It's just us. No one will see. We'll take off our shoes and everything."

I force a smile. "Thanks. But it will take a lot more than that to get my ass on that stage."

"I'm willing to take off more than my shoes if it helps."

"You're so dedicated to the cause."

"Hey. I'm all in for you, baby." He winks.

"Thanks. I appreciate it. I really do. But…"

Flynn walks to the end of the stage and sits on the edge, his long, lanky legs hang almost to the floor. "Come here."

I hold his stare for a moment before rising from my front-row seat and walking to him. He reaches out to offer me his hand. I take it without hesitation and he weaves our fingers together.

"This stage is just higher off the ground. It's no different than the one you sang on at Lucky's."

"It's step six. I'm only up to step five."

Flynn's face expresses I've lost him…understandably.

"My therapist and I made a twelve-step-ish program to try and get me back on stage. It's not actually twelve steps…but you get the idea. One foot in front of the other on the road to recovery. Step four was singing in front of three people at Lucky's."

"There were more than three people there."

"I know." I smile

"So you kicked step four's ass. Just take a flying leap over step five and land on step six."

"I'm moving along. I'm just doing it at my own pace."

"How long have you been working on the list?"

When I say it aloud, it sounds even more ridiculous. "Two years."

Flynn smiles. "Two years? Moving at your own pace? What are you, a turtle?"

I laugh. "It sounds worse than it is."

"I'm sure it does," he says, not believing a word of it. "Come on. Let's do it. I'll carry you up here. You won't even have to walk the steps."

"Tomorrow," I blurt out, nervous that he might hop down from the stage and actually carry me up there.

Flynn squints. "Tomorrow, huh?"

I nod my head.

"All right. But I'm holding you to it."

We work for two more hours at the arena. I notice that he isn't arching the soft palate as much as he should, which is limiting his throat space and causing him to strain a bit when he moves into his falsetto. A few other minor posture corrections could also help reduce the tension on his cords and minimize the chances of reinjuring his voice. He's only singing lead on two songs, but the two songs are challenging for any voice to perform without strain, no less one coming off an injury.

We make plans to return early tomorrow to practice the techniques I suggested so he'll have a few hours of rest before his debut show tomorrow night. As seems to have become a running theme with us, as soon as the band arrives at the arena, Flynn and I slip back into being distant friends. At this point, it's easier to ignore each other than it is to hide our obvious attraction. But it makes me wonder how long we can continue to ignore the obvious.

chapter fifteen

Lucky—
Eight years earlier,
age seventeen

"Are you nervous?" Avery is lying belly-down, diagonally across my bed, her legs kicking as she talks.

"Not really." I shrug.

"How many people will be in the audience?"

"I'm not sure. A lot. My mom doesn't play small places." I've never been to Town Hall, but I know it holds well over a thousand people. Mom thought it would be a good venue for my debut as her opening act. *Opening act.* Me. In three hours, I'm going to be on stage in front of a shitload of people living my dream. I still can't believe my dad is letting me go on tour with Mom. When I mentioned it to him more than a year ago, he was initially dead set against it. He wanted me to go to college, have something solid to fall back on, before trying my hand at a career that isn't an easy one. But somehow Mom and I changed his mind. Now, two weeks after my high school graduation, and one week from my eighteenth birthday, I'm getting ready for my first night as one of two opening acts for Iris Nicks.

Avery rolls onto her back and stretches the gum in her mouth out between her lips and extended fingers. "Wouldn't it be awesome if some hot guys had a picture of you in their room someday?" She motions to my wall of posters, at the center of which is none other than Dylan Ryder.

The sexiest rockstar in the world. I met him once—well, I was in the same room as him and he brushed by me on his way off the stage. But it counts.

"Imagine all the jerkin' they'd be doing to your half-naked body pinned to the wall."

Only my best friend would already have my poster visualized in her head. Not to mention guys fantasizing to it. "Let's get through the first night of the show before you start selling posters outside, okay?"

"Shit!" She jolts upright. "I didn't think of that. I could make posters and sell them! Fuck college. I'm totally getting rich off of your rockstar ass."

I laugh and take one last look in the mirror before turning. "What do you think?"

"You look like a cross between a saint and a sinner. Total wet dream. Guys are going to want to lift that little plaid skirt to see where the garters lead to, and girls are going to be running all over the city trying to find blood-red Mary Jane stilettos." I'd decided on sexing up a Catholic school uniform for my debut stage outfit. It went well with "Choices a Girl Makes," the first song I'd be singing. A song about a girl struggling between her beliefs and her desires. Mom loved my choice. Dad…not so much.

"You know, the majority of my mom's fans are older. So you talking about guys whacking off to me and lifting my skirt is sort of icky. They're old. Like my parents' age. Gross, Avery."

"I thought you liked older men?"

"I do. Like twenty-five. Not twice that. Guys our age are immature." I take one last look in the mirror and a deep cleansing breath. "You have your backstage pass?"

"Of course. You think I'd chance watching my best friend with the common people? I'm totally standing on the side of the stage and mouthing every word into my fake microphone. When they scream your name, I'm going to pretend they're screaming mine."

One of the things Dad insisted on was that I was not the only opening act. He didn't want me carrying the pressure of being singlehandedly responsible for delivering an enthusiastic crowd. He wanted me to be able to take a break if I needed one, and have someone to share the burden of opening a sold-out tour. It meant I didn't get to bring my band from high school; I'd be fronting the guys from After Sunday, the band that Lars Michaels plays with right before me.

At the time, I thought Dad didn't have enough confidence that I could make it as an opening act on my own. But standing on the side of the stage, waiting for my turn to go on, I finally get it. The opening act has a huge job. People are coming and going, everyone is here to see someone else, yet somehow, through all of the preshow distractions, we are responsible for getting people pumped up. It's not an easy task.

To lukewarm applause, Lars announces that a second act will be playing the preshow. He makes a big deal about telling the crowd it's my first tour show and they need to make me feel welcome. Then the stage lights go dark, so the crew can change up the layout and I can walk to the center of the stage. The spotlight won't come on until I've sung the first line of the song in the dark. It's a bit overly dramatic, but I've watched the practice video and it really seems to work.

Mom squeezes my shoulders as people work around us in the dark. "Ninety seconds." A guy wearing a headset yells in our direction as he lifts an instrument that was just knocked over near his feet. It's chaos on stage. Ten men run around reconfiguring things, and drills buzz while they call out to each other.

"You're going to be great," Mom says from behind me.

"Sixty seconds," Headset Guy yells again.

"Mom." I cover her hand on my shoulder with my own. I never call her Mom. When I talk about her to other people she's Mom, but I've always addressed her as Iris as long as I can remember. Until now. I didn't think about it. The word just came out.

"Right here, baby." She squeezes harder. "You can do this. By the end of the day, no one is going to remember my name. They'll all be too busy talking about the songbird who opened for whatshername."

I take a deep, relaxing breath.

A few of the workmen jog from the stage.

"Thirty seconds."

"You'd better go. I'll be right here. Dad is in center stage, row three. Go show your parents how it's done."

"Fifteen seconds."

My hands shake as I walk toward the center of the stage. We've rehearsed so many times, I can probably do this on autopilot. At least, I'm hoping I can do this on autopilot, because I'm pretty damn sure I might have forgotten the words now.

Shit. I don't know the words.

I put my feet on the pink X taped to the floor to indicate where I should stand.

"Five."

I think I'm going to vomit.

"Four."

Shit. I really don't remember the words. What's the first word?

"Three."

Panic sets in. The first line is supposed to be sung acoustic, then the spotlight comes on. The band joins in after that. My hands are trembling. And I can't feel my knees.

"Two."

Fuck. I have no idea what the first word is. *And* I'm going to vomit. Right in the center of stage. On the stage Iris Nicks is going to be on in a half hour.

"One. And go."

I don't.

I can't. Because I don't know the first word. Seconds tick by. I can hear the audience milling around, a loud chatter going on. They don't know I'm supposed to be starting. Yet.

The spotlight hits me, as timed. I should have already sung the first line.

Nothing.

The band is supposed to join in.

They don't. Conversations in the audience cease like someone just flicked the off button. I can't see any of them. But I'm sure they're all staring at me.

"Lucky," my mother whispers from the side of the stage, but I don't turn my head.

I wish I could see the audience. Where's Dad? Row three, center stage. I remember Mom saying it right before I walked out. But I still can't remember the damn words to the song I'm supposed to sing.

I hear Mom's yell again from stage left. "Flood the first five rows. Center only. Turn off the stage."

A few seconds later, lights come on in the first five rows, and the spotlight shinning on me flicks off. My eyes search the rows until I find him. Just like Mom promised. Third row, center stage. He smiles at me.

I take a deep breath and smile back, even though he can't see me.

Dad nods. The look on his face isn't full of panic, like mine. He's calm, and pride beams from his smile.

A few seconds pass and the words just come to me. So I sing them. In the dark, while looking at my Dad's soothing smile. The first line done, everything snaps into place.

Lights flick off in the audience.

The stage spotlight shines on me.

The band kicks in. And I go on to sing the entire song.

Flawlessly.

By the time I'm on the third song in the set, I'm walking the stage like a pro. As if it's rehearsal and not a live show with a couple thousand people watching.

The roar of applause isn't even necessary when I'm done. I'm high just from being up here. My arms and legs are filled with goose bumps from head to toe. I even hear a few people yelling, "Encore!" as I walk off the stage.

Mom congratulates me and pulls me in for a quick hug before she's whisked away for last-minute show prep. Avery, of course, is jumping up and down like she just won the lottery. Tons of people come by to tell me how good I was. No one even mentions my momentary meltdown.

I keep looking for my dad, but he doesn't come backstage. Knowing him, he probably wants to give me time to enjoy the post-show high. But all I really want to do is thank him. For being there for me. And not just for today. For every day of my life. I don't know what I'd do without him.

Avery and I stay on the side of the stage watching my mom's show. When the lights finally go dark, Mom comes off and grabs a water bottle. Security and the tour manager rush over to speak with her. The conversation looks serious, so I eavesdrop.

"There's a medical issue in the audience. The medics are working. They're going to need a clear path, so we don't want anyone to fill the aisles. Can you skip the break and go back and play the encore right away?"

"Sure. No problem. I'll go back out right now."

"Thanks, ma'am, we appreciate that," the security guard says.

Mom goes back out onto the stage and starts talking to the crowd about what her next song means to her. I follow the security guard.

"Sir."

He turns around.

"What happened? Did someone get injured?"

"No." He shakes his head. "Young guy. Heart attack. Just keeled over in his seat. Doesn't look good."

Somehow, in the pit of my stomach, I just know. My life forever changed tonight. And it wasn't just from my debut on stage.

chapter

sixteen

Flynn

I've never been a morning person. I might rise at the ass crack of dawn, but that doesn't mean I look forward to being awake. Most days after my eyes see the first rays of daylight, I pull the blanket over my head and try my damnedest to go back to sleep.

But not today. I'm looking forward to having coffee. At six in the morning. And the fucked-up thing is, I wish I were back on the bus. I've come to look forward to seeing those thin little shirts that Lucky wears to bed. Chances are, she's going to cover up before heading downstairs to the lobby for her coffee.

I throw on a pair of sweats, t-shirt, knit hat and some sunglasses to shield my identity as much as I can. Word got out that Easy Ryder was staying at this hotel, and last night the place was flooded with groupies when Mick and I came back from dinner. A few even recognized me. Mick, of course, happily indulged. Last I saw him before I called it a night, he had a blonde on each knee at the bar. And his bed hadn't been touched when I got up this morning. I suppose I should be grateful that he didn't bring the party back to our room.

Despite the fact that Lucky had just casually mentioned that the lobby lounge serves coffee beginning at six a.m., I'm pretty sure of myself that she'll be down there. But when I step off the elevator, the lobby is quiet. Empty. The coffee urns are just being set up in the lounge. I pour two mugs, make them just as we like it, and settle on one of the couches on the far side of the room where it's private, yet I can still keep an eye on the door.

I grab a newspaper and begin to flip through to kill time. Then my eyes catch a pair of pink-painted toes in flip-flops. I don't know why, but it's in this moment that I realize, *I'm fucked.*

The sight of her toes makes me smile.

I'm falling for another guy's girl. Something I promised myself I'd never do.

But then I reason with myself. I haven't done anything wrong. Thinking a woman is beautiful and spending time with her doesn't have to turn into anything, right? They're just toes after all. *But look how cute they are.* I've never been a foot guy, yet I wouldn't mind sucking... *Stop. Just stop.* We're just friends.

Because I've been friends with so many hot women in the past and *not* fucked them? Yep. I'm screwed. *I need to get the hell out of here.*

"Good morning," she whispers and smiles down at me. My eyes lazily travel up from her toes.

I'm totally not going anywhere.

I hold up her mug of coffee. And then I realize she still has the thin shirt she wears to sleep on and I'm eye-level with the sexiest taut nipples I've ever seen.

Screw sucking her toes... "Certainly is." I grin.

We spend nearly three hours in the lobby lounge, drinking coffee and turning the pairs of words for my song into sonnet verses. The only reason we decide it's time to leave is because we need to get ready to leave again. The tour manager got us access into the arena at noon so I could practice the new techniques Lucky showed me up on stage. And today Lucky is getting her ass up on that stage if I have anything to do about it.

My phone buzzes as I step from the shower. The face flashing on the screen makes me smile. I wrap a towel around my waist and answer it before it goes to voicemail.

"Hello."

"Hi, Uncle Sinn!" Laney screams. She's got it in her head that she needs to talk louder when people are farther away. My sister can't convince her otherwise. I actually hold the phone away from my ear when I answer, knowing she's already drilled Becca on how far away I am. Long car ride equals loud; plane equals screaming. I hear my sister yelling from somewhere in the background, "I told you, Laney, you don't have to yell. He hears you just like as if you are sitting next to him."

"Hi, beautiful. How are you?"

Laney spends the next five minutes telling me all the songs she learned on her new karaoke machine. Lady Gaga, One Direction, Taylor Swift. My sister's music taste is like mine—rock, blues, a little Johnny Cash—definitely not Top 100 pop charts. She must be ready to kick my ass.

By the time Laney decides to hand the phone to her mother, I'm pretty sure my niece must be tinted a lovely shade of blue. Not one pause for a breath in five minutes. My sister needs to introduce commas and periods to our little princess.

Bec and I catch up. The last time we talked, I didn't even have all the details about filling in for Linc yet. "So, when do I get to meet her?"

"Who?"

"The girl you're crazy about."

"What are you talking about?"

"You sound normal. The only time you sound normal is when there's a woman you're trying to impress."

"Normal? What the hell does that even mean?"

"Are there any women in your room right now?"

"No."

"Did you go to sleep before midnight?"

"Yeah. I was wiped out."

"Look around the room, are there empty beer cans all over?"

I scan the room. Not one. "No."

"Have you showered already today?"

"Yes."

"Normal. You're acting like a regular person instead of a rockstar."

"Whatever, Bec. I'm just trying to make a good impression with the new band, that's all."

"What are you doing now?" My sister is a bloodhound. If she thinks I'm hiding something, she doesn't stop sniffing until she finds it.

"I'm going to meet my voice coach and head over to the arena to work on some things."

"Is your voice coach a woman?"

"Yes."

"What's her name?"

"Lucky. Why?"

"The same Lucky you had Laney dedicate a song to?" she says with a tone that tells me she thinks she's figured out the puzzle she's been trying to solve.

"You need to get a life, Bec. You spend way too much time analyzing me." *And, shit, you know me so well.*

"That's actually why I was calling. I went through the tour schedule that you emailed, and I was thinking maybe we could fly out for the Austin show next week. I've been promising Alana that we'd come to visit, and since Professor Douchebag gave me a decent-size guilt check instead of coming to his own daughter's birthday party, I have some extra cash."

I love that I have even her calling her ex Professor Douchebag. "That would be great. We're there for three nights, and one of the days is a big festival. I'll book a suite at the hotel they put us up at."

"Laney is going to be so excited. You can get us tickets to the show, right?"

"Sure."

"Will Lucky still be there?"

"I think so. Why?"

"Because I'm looking forward to meeting her."

"Good-bye, Bec," I say in a warning tone.

"Good-bye, Flynn," she says in that singsongy way.

The blond manager is slightly less aggressive when we arrive at the arena today. Although, she does mention she'll be at the show tonight if I need anything. Her smile makes it clear that *anything* includes fucking. I already tossed her card in the garbage when I emptied my pants pockets yesterday.

"So, you wanna go first or should I?" I ask Lucky as we enter the massive seating area. It's transformed since only yesterday. The stage is set up for tonight's show. The floor level is filled with red cushioned folding chairs, and a VIP area with new seating has been installed and sectioned off with velvet ropes.

"I was thinking. I don't think I should skip step five. What if step five is critical to my overall success and I fail after going through all this work, just because of poor neglected step five?" She's teasing, but it's obvious there's real fear in her voice.

"You're going to be fine. I'll be right here with you." I put my hands on her shoulders and speak into her eyes, trying to reassure her.

"But…"

"We got this."

"But…"

"What's step five, Lucky?"

"I have to write a letter?"

"Step five is a writing assignment?"

"Yes."

"Well, let's sit down. We can knock it out quick. We wrote three sonnets before our second cup of coffee." I smile at her. "We're a good team."

"That gets you whatever you want normally, doesn't it?"

"What?"

"The dimples. The smile. The…" She waves her hand up and down my body, frustrated. "The whole hot-guy package."

"You think I'm hot?" I grin.

She rolls her eyes. "Can we get back to the point, please?"

"You mean a point other than *you think I'm hot*," I tease.

"Seriously. That smile probably gets you laid all the time. But it is not getting me up on that stage."

"Are you offering to have sex with me rather than go up on the stage?"

She blushes. "You're in a mood today, aren't you?"

"I'm always in the mood."

She smacks my abs playfully and I grab her hand. "Seriously, Lucky. I want to help. If you really don't want to get up there, I won't push. But I think you want to. For some reason, I think you need to. And I think you need me to push. I get the feeling no one has pushed you for eight years and, you know what, everyone needs that someone who will be that person for them."

Our gazes hold and I watch as her eyes soften. "Thank you," she says.

"Anytime." And, oddly, I really mean it. *Any damn time.*

She nods. "How about we work on your performance first. I want your voice to have as long of a rest as it can before you sing tonight."

"Whatever you say, teach."

She shakes her head and chuckles. "How about showing me what we talked about yesterday. Did you get a chance to practice?"

"I did."

She squints, not believing me. But the truth is, I stood in front of the mirror and practiced singing the damn song with my mouth and neck in the position she wants me in. If only I'd put in this much effort in school. Then again, my teachers never looked like Lucky.

Gently push. It's an odd saying. Can you really gently push someone? And does it even matter if you were gentle or not when the end result is the same? *I pushed him over a cliff, so what that he went careening to his untimely death…it was a* gentle *push.* I seriously doubt the last thing that goes through your mind before your brain is splattered all over the ground is, *I forgive him, it was a* gentle *push.* Yet here I am, pushing anyway.

"We can do this the easy way or the hard way. I'll carry you up there. Although I can't promise my hand won't connect with your ass when your body is slung over my shoulder."

Even though she smiles, I can see in her eyes that she's terrified. She has the kind of eyes that betray her, showing everything she's feeling even though her face attempts to tell a different story.

"I'm going, I'm going." She looks like any second tears might come. I'm just about to tell her to forget it—gentle or not, I don't want to be the cause of her splatter. But then she closes her eyes, takes a deep breath and walks toward the stairs on the left side of the stage. I take a seat front and center.

She climbs the stairs and stops on the side of the stage. At first, I think she's steadying herself, taking a deep breath before the plunge. But then a minute passes, then two. I want to give her time, let her do it when she's ready, but I know from personal experience that the longer you stand up there and think about what you're about to do, the more the panic starts to set in.

Another minute passes. She's just staring into space, but I get the feeling she can't see whatever is in her line of view. She's seeing something else. Remembering.

More time passes.

Nothing.

Whatever haunts her, I can't let her face it alone.

Without saying a word, I walk to the stairs and climb them. I stand next to her and wait until she looks over at me. I wait until her eyes focus, really focus on mine, and I know she's back in the moment. Then I offer her my hand. A sad smile attempts to hide her pain, but fails ruefully.

I take the first step and look back. Even though there is a pleading in her eyes, there's also a question. An unspoken one. I nod and wait for her to take the step on her own before continuing. Ever so slowly, we walk to the center of the stage. Hand in hand, we stand there until she eventually turns and faces the empty seats in the massive auditorium. Her eyes focus on an area in the center of the first few rows.

The sound comes before the tears. It's low, but gut-wrenchingly painful—an awful anguish-filled sob. It shreds a hole right through my heart. Whatever causes her pain, I want to slay it. I want to bear the pain for her.

And then everything she's been holding back releases. Her body begins to shudder, tears stream from her eyes, and she loses it. "He died while I was on stage. I never even got to say good-bye."

I catch her before she falls, wrapping my arms around her and hugging tight. Her body trembles against mine and my own tears burn in my throat as I hold them at bay. This cry has been kept contained for a long time. It isn't a cry from a bad memory. It's an avalanche of pent-up pain that has been building, waiting, needing to release. And it does. Shit, does it ever.

We stay that way for a long time. Until eventually every last sob has wracked its way through her body and I feel what amounts to a sigh of relief wash over her. Her tense limbs ease and she takes a deep breath before she pulls her head back and our silence is finally broken.

"Flynn," she whispers, and I lean my forehead against hers and watch her eyes close. When they open again, something is different. Her eyes are still filled with emotion, but the sadness is replaced by need. Our gazes lock and both our breaths change, becoming more labored, more heated. My heart pounds in my chest, and it takes every bit of willpower in my body to not take what I so desperately want.

Her lips part and I think she's about to say something, but then, suddenly, her mouth is on mine. *Jesus Christ.* My self-control goes out the window, chased out by desperation. Desperation to kiss her. Feel her. *Consume her.*

She may have started the kiss, but it takes less than a heartbeat for me to take over. One hand fists her hair, wrapping it snuggly around my fingers, while the other tightens around her back, pulling her even closer against me.

Our kiss deepens, tongues frantically find each other, but it's the little moan that escapes her body and travels through our sealed lips that does me in. Resolve shattered, fire pulses through my veins, any fleeting uncertainty is forgotten by both of us. She reaches up, her fingers tugging at my hair. Her soft curves contour to fit my body. We grope, pull, scratch, tug—to get closer—to get more. Just more.

When we finally break the kiss, we're both panting. My lips move over her neck, my ragged breath intensifies the rawness of my words when I speak. "I've wanted you since the minute I laid eyes on you," I whisper into her ear. "God, I fucking want you."

Between the sound of my heart ricocheting loudly against my chest, our heavy breathing and the lust pulsing through my veins, we don't even hear the sound of a person approaching, until the voice startles us.

chapter

seventeen

Lucky

"**S**orry to interrupt," the blond facilities manager says snidely. Startled, I jump. My instinct is to back away from Flynn. Unravel myself from his arms. But when I try to, he tightens his grip and holds me in place.

"What can we do for you?" Flynn says, impatience obvious.

"The electricians need to turn the power off to wire in some pyrotechnics for tonight's show. It will only take about fifteen minutes, but the lighting needs to be off." She plasters on a smile that is way too sugary to be sweet. "Doesn't look like you'll mind a little darkness though."

"By all means." Flynn shrugs. I'm not sure if he doesn't pick up her sarcasm or just doesn't care.

With a toss of her bleached hair, she turns and disappears. The clickity-clack of her heels sound in her wake until the door slams closed. I look at Flynn. "I don't think she was happy."

"I don't think I care." He grins.

Reality begins to come flooding back, hitting like a tidal wave. My head spins. *What did I just do?* "Flynn…I…we…"

He pulls his head back, taking in the confusion that's written all over my face. His grip around me loosens a bit, although he still doesn't let go. "You okay?"

I'm not. I'm elated, sad, happy, guilt-ridden, emotionally spent and entirely bewildered. *What the hell did I do?* I'm the one who initiated the kiss—it wasn't like it just happened. "Yes. No. Yes. I mean…"

Flynn grins. "You sound sure of yourself."

"I'm sorry. I…I shouldn't have."

The look of disappointment on his face makes my heart break into a thousand little pieces. He releases me from his hold, taking a step back. Blowing out a thick stream of air, he rakes his fingers through his hair. "No. I shouldn't have. I'm sorry."

"But I kissed you."

"Pretty sure we were both involved in *that* kiss."

"I know. But I…" I look away, guilt beginning to eclipse my other emotions, making me see things more clearly. Making me feel sick.

The sound of a door opening and workmen coming in interrupts our conversation. A man's voice calls out to us, "We're about to cut the electricity. You might want to step down from the stage. Gets pretty dark in here."

Awkwardness has descended between us—the first since the day we met. We leave the arena and ride back to the hotel in deafening silence. I'm lost in thought, my mind whirling between what I've done and why I did it, but mostly I find myself thinking about how right it felt, even though it was clearly wrong.

"Hey," Flynn says as we pull up to the hotel. I'm looking out the window and barely notice we've stopped. With his thumb and forefinger, he lifts my chin, forcing my eyes to his. "You kicked step six's ass."

I smile. "You're being kind. I didn't kick its ass. I tripped over it and fell. But you were there to save me."

"You don't give yourself enough credit. But whatever part I had, the pleasure was all mine." He opens the door to the SUV and hops out. Standing, he offers his hand to help me exit, then closes the door behind me and raps on the hood twice to let the driver know to take off.

We're almost at the entrance to the hotel when I slow down. "Flynn."

"Hmmm."

"I'm sorry I kissed you."

He winks at me. "I'm not."

Dylan was supposed to hit more radio stations this afternoon, so I'm surprised when I open the door and find him lounging on the bed, watching TV.

"I didn't think you'd be here," I say, almost accusingly. Not a very nice way to greet your boyfriend.

"You don't sound happy that I am." His brows knit together.

"I am. It's just…I thought you had to go to the radio stations, so I was surprised. And I'm sort of not feeling well."

"Mick went missing again." Dylan sits up on the edge of the bed and pats his lap.

"Missing?"

"Yeah. He does that every once in a while. Ties one on and no one knows where he is, so we wind up changing our schedule."

"Doesn't that bother you?"

Dylan shrugs. "The tour manager hates it. But we're all used to it by now. Used to happen every few days. He's slowed down in his old age. Why are you all the way over there still? Come here."

I walk to him, my steps heavy, laden down with guilt.

He pulls me onto his lap. "I'm actually glad the interview was canceled. They've had me so booked with crap, we haven't had a chance to enjoy being off the tour bus and properly take advantage of this big bed." He nuzzles against my neck. The exact same spot Flynn was nibbling on only an hour ago. A real wave of nausea hits me. I seriously think I'm going to be sick.

"I'm sorry. I think I'm going to..." I dart to the bathroom.

I splash my face with water and look in the mirror. Unable to stand the sight of myself, I slide down the wall behind me and sit on the floor with my head in my hands. How long can I hide out in here? Dylan will eventually check on me. I decide to take a shower, wash some of the guilt away, or at least the remnants of another man's mouth on me. It's the least I can do.

When I emerge in a towel, Dylan's on the phone. He smiles at me and his eyes drop to my bare legs.

"No. Just cancel it. I have other plans for this afternoon now."

Other plans? I really need to be alone right now, and something tells me his other plans are *me*.

He hangs up just as I've pulled out a change of clothes from the drawer. He comes up behind me and gently kisses my bare shoulder. "You feeling better?"

"Not really. Sorry. Must be a stomach flu."

He turns me and parts my towel at my stomach. Bending down, his lips brush against the skin of my belly. "Let me kiss it and make it feel better."

"I...I don't want to get you sick."

He drops to his knees and tugs harshly so my towel falls to the floor. "I won't catch anything. Not from the parts I'm going to kiss."

Part of me really wanted to skip the concert tonight. Feign sickness and stay in bed all night to avoid seeing Flynn. Seeing anyone, actually. But a bigger part of me wanted to see him up on stage. It's his first night filling in for Linc and playing with Easy Ryder. He's been there for me and my big moments lately, so I want to be there for his.

The backstage area at the American Airlines Arena is huge. Somehow, we manage not to run into each other before the show. After Dylan leaves to get ready to go on stage, I head down to watch the concert from the floor. Winding my way through the maze of halls backstage, I make my way to the floor exit. As soon as I turn the last corner, I catch a glimpse of Flynn at the other end of the hall. He's talking to a woman. She's super tall, almost as tall as him, and model-waif thin. Between her cropped top and low-waisted skirt, the bare expanse of her skin runs a mile long. Flawless, exposed skin. Long, wavy chestnut hair hangs loose, framing her abundant cleavage. She has one hand on Flynn's chest and her head is tipped in that provocative, flirty way that makes a man's eyes focus on her neck.

As I step closer, Flynn's head turns in my direction and Waif Girl follows his line of sight. I've never had an issue with confidence, but suddenly I feel short and regret eating that donut an hour ago.

"Hey. I was just coming to look for you," Flynn says with an easy smile.

My brain short circuits watching his lips move as he speaks. Lips I can almost still feel on me. I'm momentarily lost, remembering the way his hands threaded tightly through my hair. I blink myself out of the haze. "Well." My arms rise and fall at my sides. "You found me." Seriously? *Nice moves, Lucky.*

I watch as his eyes drop to my lips. Knowing his mind is in the same place as mine makes it that much more difficult to focus.

He cocks his head, a smile dangling at the corner of his mouth. "Can you give us a minute?" he says to the waif, without taking his eyes off me. She walks away, annoyed.

"You okay?" He takes my hand, his thumb rubbing along the top of mine.

I nod.

"I've been thinking about this morning all day…"

So have I. God, so have I. "Me too."

"I'm sorry if I pushed too hard."

"You didn't push. *I kissed you.*"

He grins. "I meant step six. I'm sorry if I pushed you too hard to go up on stage."

"Oh."

"But I'm glad to know you were thinking about our kiss all day."

"I wasn't…I meant…I…"

He leans in and whispers, "I was too. I can still feel your body against mine."

A voice comes over the backstage intercom. "Five minutes, Easy Ryder."

"Guess that's me now, too."

"Guess it is."

"You going to watch from the audience?"

I nod.

"I'll see you from the stage, then."

"You won't be able to see anyone in the audience with the lights."

"Don't need to." He taps his finger to his temple. "When I close my eyes, I see your face right here."

Even before Dylan and I started dating, I'd been to dozens of Easy Ryder concerts. They're legendary, even after only twelve years of playing together. The type of band that is so in tune, the show is never the same because someone makes a change on the fly and the band just goes with it seamlessly. Tonight is no different. The pull of the show has been intense and there's a crackle in the audience, a sort of slow burn that feels like it will turn into a wildfire when the spark hits the flint in just the right spot. That flint has been "Sins of Mine," the latest single that is climbing the chart. I know for a fact that the song was written with Dylan's voice in mind, and it's obvious the crowds have loved it so far.

Not having the play list, I assume we're about to get to that moment with "Sins of Mine," when the stage goes dark. I'm surprised when the first chord strums and it's "Just Once More," Linc's song. But tonight it's Flynn's to sing. I hold my breath until we're pulled from the darkness and a spotlight shines on only him.

Jesus. Holy mother of all sinners. I seriously need to remember to breathe.

He looks like a rock god on the stage. Perfectly magnificent in the spotlight as he sits on a stool with a guitar resting on his lap. It's impossible to tear your eyes away. The crowd stands in silent worship as he looks down and leisurely strums the intro. Then slowly, from the darkness behind him, the drums start to roll...at first low, then louder and louder. Until we can feel the vibration in our chest. Flynn stops playing for a moment, the spotlight dims, the arena goes dark again, and when the lights come back on, the full band starts playing. Right before he begins to sing, Flynn closes his eyes for a moment and then finally looks up and smiles to the audience. That lazy, slow-spreading, dimple-bearing, completely titillating smile. And the place goes mad.

Flint to spark.

Fire.

Even though the place is rocking, I seriously don't move for the entire performance. I'm captivated. By every note. Every lyric. Everything about the man. If I were fifteen, his poster would definitely be pinned on my wall...maybe even right over Dylan's.

After the show, I head backstage to the band's lounge. It takes me a solid fifteen minutes to get through because security is flanked by women. More than one has the name Flynn Beckham on her lips. I'm so excited for him, I'm still smiling even after being pushed and shoved as I attempt to show my badge to the guard.

Unfortunately, Dylan isn't feeling the post-show happiness that I am. "What's the matter? You guys were incredible," I say.

"Mick came in three bars late in 'Solace.' Duff played the recorded version of 'To the Wall' instead of the live version, and I couldn't hear out of one of my earpieces. It was a shit show," he says angrily.

I may be partial to the band, but I didn't pick up on Mick's or Duff's flubs. "I didn't catch it. I'm sure no one else noticed."

"You were probably too busy dancing around in the audience." I know how Dylan can get when he's not happy with his music. He's a perfectionist. It's a large part of why Easy Ryder has been successful for so long. But usually his attitude isn't directed toward me.

Security brings back a half dozen women—they're winners of a radio contest and the prize was tickets to the show and meeting the band. Dylan unenthusiastically shakes their hands. The other members of Easy Ryder at least act gracious. They stand around and chatter to the star-struck fans, making them feel at ease.

Eventually, Flynn walks in and I sit back and observe the reception he gets. Everyone is congratulating him, slapping him on the back and telling him how great he did. Everyone, that is, except Dylan. Security begins to usher the contest winners out when one brave woman yells, "Wait! We didn't get to meet the last member of the band. Flynn, I love you!"

Flynn turns and smiles. Dylan looks at Flynn on one side of the room, then back at security. "They're done. He's not part of the band."

The thing about lead singers is, they're the face of the band. So while that often leads to overinflated egos, it also leads to singers bearing the weight of the band on their shoulders. Sometimes it's difficult to tell which of the two is causing the front man to act a certain way.

"Remember when we were his age and hit our first tour?" Duff lifts his chin toward the bar area where Flynn has just walked into the after-party at a club on the strip in South Beach.

"Nope." Dylan knocks back the remainder of his glass. He's usually a beer drinker, but tonight he's drinking vodka on the rocks and the effect is noticeable. He's relaxed a little, his anger seemingly dissipating more with each refill. He holds his glass above his head, rattling around the ice as the waitress passes.

"Another one, Mr. Ryder?"

"Keep 'em coming."

"Well, I remember," Duff continues without being asked. "That first year. It was better than the highest high. Probably why I ended up in rehab a couple of times after that first tour. Chasing that high was like a dog chasing his tail. The kid's good. He's gonna do well."

"It's not his first tour."

"You can't count road trips in a van with truck-stop showers as a tour. Or the little gigs he played before this. *This* is a fucking tour. Sold-out arenas, a coach bus with gold fixtures in the bathroom. Groupies who want to do shit to you beyond your wildest dreams."

"I didn't mean it wasn't his big show. I meant it's *our* fucking tour, not his. He's filling in for Linc and then he's in the opening act in a few months."

"Why do you got a hard-on for this kid? You jealous because he's prettier than you?"

"Fuck off." Dylan stands. "This waitress is taking forever. I'm going to go get my own drink."

Seeing him stand, Dylan's security walks over. "Just going to get a drink."

"The bar is pretty crowded. That's not advisable, sir. Would you like one of us to get it for you?"

"No. I'm going to get it myself," Dylan snaps before storming off to the bar.

Duff watches his friend walk away and turns back amused. "Never thought I'd see the day."

"See what?" I ask.

"The day Dylan Ryder starts to question his greatness. I'd say he's a little bit jealous of the fresh meat."

Duff motions toward the bar. As security had warned, the crammed bar has turned into mayhem. Fans mob Dylan before he even orders a drink. "That should make him feel a little better."

"What? Getting mobbed?"

"Yep. Love him like a brother, but the arrogant fuck just needed some attention. He's not used to anyone else in the spotlight. Never been good at sharing."

Two hours later, Dylan is happily shitfaced and I'm ready to call it a night. Flynn and I have been playing cat and mouse with our eyes all evening, but I haven't had a chance to speak to him. Until now. Dylan's in the men's room and I'm standing with security, waiting to leave. He walks over, nods at the hulking security guard to my left, and turns his back so we can talk in something approaching privacy.

"Congratulations," I say. "You were absolutely incredible on stage."

"Are you referring to this afternoon or this evening?"

My eyes nearly bulge from my head and I look around to see if anyone heard. "I meant the concert. You were...amazing."

"So I wasn't this afternoon?" He arches an eyebrow.

"Behave," I warn.

"Nope." He shakes his head slowly.

"No? You're not going to behave."

"Nope. I've decided what happened today was too good. It needs to happen again. Frequently, in fact."

"How much have you had to drink?"

He holds up his glass. "Water. All night."

My eyes widen. "But…" I stagger to find the right words. "I'm not a cheater. Really. I wasn't anyway…until today," I say softly.

Flynn looks me in the eyes. "Neither am I. Not talking about cheating."

"What…then, what are you talking—"

"Here comes your soon-to-be ex." He tips his glass in Dylan's direction as he approaches.

My heart almost stops when Dylan arrives next to us. He scowls at Flynn, then says to me, "Let's get out of here."

"Good night, Flynn."

I look back over my shoulder twice on my way to the door. Flynn is watching with a devilish smile and gleam in his eye. My mind is jumbled as I climb into the back of the SUV, but one thing is clear…*I'm totally screwed.*

chapter eighteen

Flynn

The bus was rocking last night, but it had nothing to do with the hundreds of miles we traveled in the darkness after the final show in Miami. The roads were smooth, although not nearly as smooth as Mick Stonewood. I have no idea how he even made the logistics work, bringing two women back to his little cubbyhole of a bunk. Yet somehow he kept the wall on our side of the bus banging half the night. I finally put my Bose noise-canceling headphones on and lulled myself into pretending the steady rocking I was feeling was the road beneath the tires, rather than the drummer beneath my bunk. I suppose I should be grateful the bastard fucks like he drums...with the rhythm of a master.

I stretch out my body as I wait for the coffee to finish brewing, then pour two mugs and jot down some notes for "Blur." One more set of connections and I'll have a decent first draft. Turns out, I've saved the best for last. I'm looking forward to Lucky's poetic tongue helping me with this one today.

It's not long before she rises. I hear the click of the bathroom door, and a few minutes later she's quietly closing the door to the living area behind her.

"Morning," she whispers.

"Good morning." I nod. The day just got a whole lot better.

She eyes two mugs on the table. "One of them for me?"

"Just as we like it."

She smiles and slides into the seat across from me, wrapping her hands around the mug and bringing it to her lips. "I could get used to this service."

"There're plenty of other services I'd be happy to provide." I cock one eyebrow.

"I walked right into that one, didn't I?"

"You did." I sip my coffee, watching her over the brim of my mug.

"How did you sleep?" she asks.

"Not so good. A lot of banging kept me up." It's the truth, wrapped up in politeness.

"You felt that too?"

How could I not, my bunk was literally rocking. "Yep."

"I thought we might be getting a flat tire at one point."

I was hoping that damn thing would deflate. "Seems like the ride is smooth this morning. You ready to finish off 'Blur'?"

"I was hoping you'd want to do that this morning."

"I think it needs one more verse. Another sonnet for the last set of connections."

"I'm ready. What line are we writing about crossing today?"

"Friends and lovers." Our eyes lock and my mouth spreads a slow grin.

Fourteen lines, ten syllables each. It may not look like much on paper, but there's nothing quick about writing a sonnet that's a song. Especially with Lucky. Even though I clearly had less-than-virtuous reasons for suggesting friends and lovers as the topic of the last verse, she still gives no less to our writing. We're sitting here for three hours discussing and debating words and feelings that shift from friends to lovers, yet I still have to bait her to take the conversation out of the realm of professional.

"No, if we use the word *certain* when crossing the line, that would mean crossing the line is inevitable," she says.

I shrug. "Sometimes it is."

"Nothing is inevitable except death."

"That's where you're wrong. Some things are just fate. And you can't fight fate."

"But—"

I interrupt her. "You keep telling yourself you can fight fate. But I promise you, you're wrong. Some things are just meant to happen."

She stares at me, I can see the wheels in motion—she's inwardly fighting the truth. At the sound of the door behind me, my head turns. Mick stumbles in with one of his two half-dressed brunettes in tow. I collect my stuff from the table and decide it's time for a shower. But not before I lean down and quietly leave Lucky with one last thought. "I can't wait till the day I get to wake up next to you and kiss the hell out of you in public."

Both the shower and the bathroom are occupied, so I try to get in a little exercise. I haven't been to the gym in almost a week, and I'm going to have to figure out a routine that works on a bus or I'll look like an aging forty-year-old father of triplets before we make it to LA.

In the hallway between the front lounge area and back bedroom, there's a storage area with a pull-up bar installed. Duff gave me the quick tour the other day—there are free weights in the bottom of the lower cabinet and even a collapsible bench for pressing. I hit the floor for fifty pushups, do some lunges to stretch out and let my muscles relax, then grab the pull-up bar. My muscles burn, but it's a feeling I relish. I'm on number eighteen when the door to the front lounge area opens and Lucky walks in.

Muscles tensed and straining, my eyes are glued to her as she stands there while I slowly finish the last two pull-ups. Even though my muscles were starting to falter only a minute ago, I suddenly have perfect form and control over my body while I fluidly rise up and down. Thank you, testosterone.

I watch as she swallows, taking in my shirtless torso flexing while I lift and slowly come back down. The look in her eyes conveys what she hasn't accepted yet. I jump to my feet after I finish the set of twenty I'd set out to do. It's a narrow hallway and she can't get by without my moving, so I step aside to give her room to pass. Well, to give her *some* room to pass. I could definitely back up so there's enough room for two without touching. But what fun would that be?

"I thought you were going to shower," she says to my naked chest, with a huskiness in her voice that makes me harden instantly.

"Occupied," I say as I catch my breath.

She nods. Then moves to pass me, turning her back to sidle through the little room I've left. But in the tight confinement of the hallway, her ass brushes up against me and my self-control slips. I put my hand out to stop her from passing, fingers gripping her hip tightly. My shirtless, sweaty front to her back, Lucky's breath hitches and I exhale a jagged breath. I want to run my lips across that neck and push her up against the wall she's standing in front of. Show her what being near her does to me as I press myself up against her ass. She doesn't try to move.

I exhale again, my warm breath landing on her neck.

She inhales sharply.

I hear the shower water turn off in the distance, but I'm stuck in this bubble, interpreting what she feels by only the sound of her breathing and the reaction of her body. Normally, I like music when I have a woman beneath me. A rhythm we can both let flow through our bodies and move to. But I want the first time I'm inside of her to be quiet. So I can listen to her breathing and let her breaths tell me what she needs from me.

Jesus, this woman tests every bit of restraint I have. My body aches for her. Without a doubt I want her. But not like this. Not with her boyfriend twenty feet away. Not with her still sleeping in his bed at night. I drop my hand and release her, backing away. I'm going to walk away because I want her. And not this way.

I manage to accomplish the impossible, keeping distance from Lucky when she's with Dylan, on a bus where there are few places to hide. The sun is setting by the time we pull into Little Rock. The tour manager hops on the bus at the airport and hands Mick two plane tickets. Mick has a fistful of ass from the woman on his left, and his tongue in the other one's mouth.

Duff and I are sitting on the couch watching the end of a movie. He takes a draw on his beer, lifts his chin toward Mick and his two fuck buddies and says, "It's like having live porn. Watch the next move. He's gonna turn his head to the other side and stick his tongue in her mouth. The left hand will slide up to that one's back while the right hand grabs a handful of the other one's ass. Then he's gonna whip two signed postcards out of his back pocket with his autograph next to the city he met them in."

Amused, I sit and watch the end of the Mick show rather than the movie. The last scene plays out exactly as Duff described it. The two women giggle when he hands them the postcards and escorts them off the bus. I chuckle. "Guess he's been using those moves for a while, huh?"

"Yep. Two-on-one gets a signed postcard. Mick's an ass man. Taking it Greek gets you tickets to the next night's show *and* an encore performance before you're handed the one-way first-class plane ride and a kiss-off at the airport."

"Shit. He kept me up half the night with those two. Guess I should be glad they weren't Greek or I wouldn't sleep again tonight at the hotel."

Duff finishes off his beer. "Nah. They would have been postcarded anyway. We're in Little Rock, it's wife night."

"Mick's married?"

"Yep. Going on fifteen years. Married his high-school-fucking-sweetheart. Lydia. She's a bitch. But who could blame her, married to that jackass? Two kids, a dog and a white picket fence around his house in the suburbs too."

"No shit. You married?"

"Divorced." He shakes his head and laughs cynically. "It's ironic. I'm the only asshole that stopped dipping my pen in the tour ink when I found a good woman. Surprised her one night by coming home early from a gig. Had flowers in my hand and all when I found her blowing our CPA. A fucking *accountant* for Christ's sake."

"Wow. Sorry."

"The worst part? She stopped giving me head after the wedding, and here she is on her knees for some pencil dick."

"What did you do?"

"Broke the asshole's nose, divorced the bitch and vowed never to get married again." He shrugs. "I like getting head too much to try it again anyway." Duff reaches into the small fridge on the side of the couch that's only stocked with beer and pulls us each out one. "You got a girl?"

"I'm working on it."

He nods. "Well. Wife night usually means the band goes out to dinner. Tour manager has a steady woman who will come and won't say two words. Lydia will pick a fight with Mick during appetizers. And Lucky will obviously be there."

Not wanting to call attention to my interest in Lucky, I haven't poked around any. But a little poking here won't seem out of the ordinary. We've already chatted about all the other guys' women. "Those two serious?" I ask casually and crack open my beer.

"As serious as Ryder gets."

And that means? "Not the settling-down type?"

"He wants to spawn. Lucky seems like a good woman. I'd bet he makes it official sooner rather than later." He sips his beer and I think he's done, but then he adds, "But doubt it will stop him from banging groupies. He's got a twenty-nine-year-old retired porn star he hooks up with every time we pass through Vegas the last ten years. Be interesting to see if he disappears for a few hours while Lucky's on the tour with us."

With no sign of Mick since we pulled into Little Rock, I'd suggested Lucky and I work on my voice rehab in my room. She'd hesitated to agree at first, taking that plump bottom lip in between her teeth while she mulled it over. When she'd said yes, I'd smiled in victory, doing a little internal fist pump.

But as I wait for the knock to come at my door, I realize it probably wasn't the smartest of ideas. Privacy, a big bed, and a woman I want beneath me so badly, I'm fucking dreaming about her at night. Yeah...not too bright.

The full-of-myself part of me thinks if I pushed, there's a good chance we'd wind up clawing each other's clothes off. But I don't want to be the other guy. She's inside me, I want to be inside her. And, for a change, not just my cock.

A few minutes later, the knock comes and I open the door to find her standing there. She's wearing white shorts and a tight white tank top that has the Rolling Stones' iconic mouth made from crystals of some sort. I step aside for her to enter, and light from the tall windows streams in and hits her at just the right angle so her glossed lips sparkle as much as her shirt. Fuck. *Definitely a bad idea.*

chapter

nineteen

Lucky

I told myself I was being silly for being nervous about coming to his room. It's my job, I reasoned, and Flynn is a friend. We both just got caught up in the moment that day on the stage. I was emotional. It was a moment of weakness. That's all.

The door clicks closed behind me. The room is...all bed. I turn around, and Flynn hasn't moved. He looks at me, his gaze dipping to my breasts, then down over my bare legs, before his eyes return to meet mine.

He stares.

Really stares.

Like he wants to eat me.

Shit. We may be having another moment.

My heart thumps.

His eyes once more sweep over my body and devour me.

I watch his throat work as he swallows.

I'm trying to keep my cool, but I have some serious flips going on in my stomach.

Then he groans. The sound is a haunting mix of pain and frustration, but goddamn if it's not sexy as all hell. Suddenly, I'm aware of how many nerve endings must be inside the human body. Because I feel every one of them abruptly zap to life. I seriously wouldn't be surprised if I was lit up like a Christmas tree.

He paces back and forth a few times. "This isn't a good idea."

"Why?" The reason is obvious, but I ask anyway.

He stops pacing and looks at me. "You want me to say it?"

Swallowing hard, without saying a word, I hold his gaze and nod. My body trembles as he stalks in my direction. Invading my personal space, our bodies just shy of touching, he looks down at me, the height difference between us making me tilt my head back to maintain eye contact.

"I'll tell you why. Because if we're alone in this room for another minute, I won't be responsible for my actions." He pauses and I watch as his pupils dilate and his chest rises and falls. "Because I want to pin you against that wall behind you and hold your hands over your head while I suck on those nipples that I've been staring at every morning while I was forced to drink coffee instead of you. Because I want to keep you pressed up against that wall while my face is buried between your thighs and your legs are dangling down my back. Because I want to make you soaking wet so when I bury myself into you hard and deep, I won't have to go easy. Because it won't be easy. Because I won't be able to take my time with you like you deserve the first time. Because I won't be able to control myself when I'm buried so far inside of you that I'll literally explode when you explode around me. Because I want to feel you tremble from the inside out while my mouth is crushed to yours until you can barely breathe."

I'm shocked I'm still even standing. I'm breathless and dizzy and never in my life have felt as desired as I do in this moment. I hate to do it, but I have to break our gaze just to catch my breath and slow my spinning mind.

His warm fingers lift my chin to meet his eyes. "You should go," he whispers in warning, his voice strained.

"But what if I want to stay?"

We stare at each other for a long time. His eyes challenging me, mine daring him. His gaze burns into mine. Fire. Passion. And maybe even a little anger pulses through his veins.

"I told you to go," he growls. Narrowing the distance between us, he moves in so our bodies aren't quite touching, but I can feel the heat emanating from his. I take one step back, bumping into the wall behind me. He takes a step again, arms caging me in on both sides of my head. His eyes blaze so hot, I think I might melt. The muscle in his jaw flexes and I know he's hanging by a thread. "Is this what you want?" He searches my eyes as one hand moves to gather both my hands and he lifts them over my head. "Tell me. Is this what you want?"

I nod. "I—"

The words are lost as his mouth crushes down over mine. I completely forget everything else except this kiss.

This kiss.

It's the most consuming thing I've ever felt in my life. I feel it everywhere. My mouth, my nipples, the wetness responding between my legs, from the top of my head to the tips of my toes. It's as if my entire body has been asleep for the last few years and suddenly...*this kiss*...has awakened it.

One hand glides down the side of my body, caressing slowly as it comes to slide along the back of my thigh and lifts. I whimper when I feel the hard length of him through his jeans for the first time.

Instinctively, I reach for him, wanting to urge him closer, dig my fingers into his hair, but I forget he has my hands bound together. I attempt to pull away, but it only makes him tighten his grip.

Oh, lord. I've never been subdued before, but the feeling could only be described as decadent. My body hums and I kiss him harder, wild with need. His free hand wraps into my hair and he tugs, giving him better access to my neck. He sucks and bites his way from one ear to the opposite collar bone, then back up to the other ear. "You're so beautiful," he groans.

He makes me feel that way. *Beautiful.* Like it's an honor for him to have me, instead of the other way around.

My nipples harden as his thumb brushes over my breast through the soft cotton of my shirt.

"These things," he confesses, pinching one and then the other. "These things have been taunting me every goddamn morning."

I gasp when he pinches again, much harder this time, shooting a jolt of fire directly from their stiffened peaks down to between my legs.

Desire races through me as he lowers his head, lifts my shirt, and his thumb slips down the cup of my bra so he can blow on my already pebbled nipples. He alternates between licking and blowing, teasing me into a frenzy. By the time he catches the swell of my nipple between his teeth, I'm thinking I might finish before we even start. A soft moan billows from my lips.

I need more. Just more. So I lift my other leg and wrap it around his waist, locking my ankles together. Arching my back from the wall, legs spread wide around him, I get the friction I desperately need. His jeans, hard with his straining bulge, rubs against my sensitive skin—the thin fabric of my shorts doing little to impede me from feeling every inch of him. Every. Many. Inches.

Flynn keeps me pinned against the wall, ravaging my mouth, inflicting sweet torture on my breasts, until I'm a panting mess. Then he lets go of my hands, my legs drop, and he takes a step back. For a second I think he's going to put an end to this recklessness, but then he smiles. It's a slow, devilish smile, with so much intensity in his eyes it almost sweeps my breath away.

"Flynn…"

"Take off your shorts."

Mr. Nice Guy has a bit of a bossy edge to him. I like it. A lot. Turns out I'm finding out a lot about myself today, things I wasn't aware could be so ridiculously hot.

Slowly, I hook my thumbs into the sides of my shorts and shimmy them down my legs. I'm generally not self-conscious about my body. I like my curves, and I've been blessed genetically to be able to eat whatever I want and remain thin, but if I had any body issues, they'd disappear with the way Flynn is looking at me.

He doesn't leer. He appreciates. As if he's looking at fine art that should be treasured. I'm not sure if it's another one of his intangible talents or if he truly adores what he sees, but in the moment I could care less. Because I feel how he makes me feel. Beautiful.

After taking his time drinking me in, he drops to his knees. He's making good on all the things he told me he wanted to do when I asked him why I should leave. Still keeping me pressed with my back against the wall, he looks up at me, locking eyes as he lifts one leg over his shoulder.

The cool air on my wet, sensitive skin, coupled with the way he's watching me, makes me gasp. The sound makes his eyes blaze even darker.

"Watch me," he says, and then his mouth is on me. Licking and sucking, his face buried between my legs as he devours every inch of me. His tongue lashes against my clit, twirling and flicking until I can barely form a coherent word.

"Oh god." My fingers dive into his hair as I climb higher and higher, my body greedily rocking against him as he strokes and strokes with his tongue lapping hungrily until my orgasm rips through me. I shake almost violently as he continues to draw more and more from my body with an unrelenting vigor. Just when I think my body is over the edge, that I'll begin the slide down on the other side of the orgasm rainbow, he pushes two fingers inside me. Gently but firmly, he twists while he pumps, literally stroking one orgasm to roll directly into another one.

Still trembling, it barely registers that he's lifted me up until he's setting me down on the bed. With dexterity that I don't want to think about how it was earned, he unclasps my bra and sheds the rest of my clothes before starting on his own.

He guides my back down and follows. With a rough timbre and a wicked grin, "You've been inside me since the day we met. It's time I return the favor. Only I'm going to be much more literal."

I reach down to grab him, wrapping my fingers around his thick shaft, but he quickly peels my fingers back. I look at him questioningly.

"I won't last. I'm already teetering on the edge just from the taste of you on my tongue. When I come, I want it to be inside you." Those damn dimples dip into cavernous wonderlands. "Plus, it's been a while."

Out of everything he's said since I walked in the door, something about that last sentence does me in. "Well, then we shouldn't wait any longer," I whisper hoarsely.

He quickly rolls on a condom and is poised at my entrance. Our gazes meet and hold. With one hand around his neck, I pull him down for a kiss and, just as our lips connect, he slides inside me.

We kiss for a minute as he inches his way in and then, once he's completely seated, once I'm completely filled, he pulls his head back and our eyes hold again.

He thrusts in deep, but slow as he studies me. It feels like he's memorizing my body's reactions to everything he does. Sliding his hand under my ass, he tilts my hips just slightly, but it allows him to penetrate even deeper. The feeling is heavenly. My eyes flutter closed, succumbing to the incredibly full feeling, as he whispers in my ear, "Beautiful."

Finding our rhythm quickly, we move in perfect unison, as if we've been doing it for years, rather than it being our first time. It feels so…right. My body climbs yet again, a faster build, but no less powerful when it crests. I shudder and hold his gaze as I begin to come again and then he starts pumping harder. "You feel so. Damn. Good."

He groans my name as he releases into me before my own orgasm has even fully ebbed. Afterward, we hold on to each other tight, slowly rocking back and forth as we catch our breaths.

But I catch my breath too soon. Because I only lose it again when the pounding knock comes on the door.

chapter twenty

Flynn

"What if it's—" she asks, a look of panic on her face.

"I'll deal with it." I'm pulling on one leg of my pants when the knocking comes again. This time louder, more insistent.

Lucky searches the bed frantically for her clothes. "But if he's...I can't find my clothes. I should hide."

"You're not hiding."

"What? Why?"

"Because we're not sixteen and I said I'll deal with it."

She looks at me wide-eyed, like I've lost my mind. "Look." Pulling my jeans over my hips, I don't bother buttoning the top button before lifting my knee onto the bed and leaning over. "Stay naked. I don't give a shit who's at the door, I'm getting rid of them." I pull the sheet she has gripped to her chest back and peek down between the sheet and her skin. "Fast. I'm getting rid of them fast." I wink.

The knock is more of a banging as I swing the door open to catch whoever is on the other side off-guard. It works. The two girls jump back so fast, they nearly fall over.

"Shit. You ladies okay?" I reach out and grab the one on the right's elbow, just as she's about to fall. As soon as she's recovered, she throws her arms around my neck, swamping me in a big hug.

"Oh my god! It's really you!"

I pull my head back and attempt to disentangle myself from her grip. "Yep. I'm me. And who might you be?"

"Oh my god!" she squeals to her friend in a glass-shattering pitch...right into my ear. "He wants to know my name."

I can smell the alcohol on her breath, and it looks like these two may still be dressed from last night. "It's very nice to meet you, ladies, but I'm sort of in the middle of something important. Will I see you at a show soon, I hope?"

"Yes! We're going to follow the bus to the next show. We went last night. We went to see Easy Ryder but...oh my god...you were incredible."

"Thank you." I smile. "Well, I'm hard at work. So I'll see you ladies in a few nights then, yeah?" I turn around to the door I've been holding open just a crack. "What're your names, sweethearts?"

I hear Lindsay and Jenna yelling and jumping around even once the door is closed. I walk back into the bedroom, shaking my head.

"*Hard* at work, huh?" Lucky arches an eyebrow.

"Just telling the truth." I unzip my pants. Her eyes follow the sound. The glazed look in her eyes has me hardening again as I slip off my jeans.

She swallows. "Sounds like Lindsay and Jenna were excited to meet you."

"Yeah." I hold her eyes while I stroke myself up and down leisurely. "Looks like I'm excited too." I pull away the sheet and climb on top of her, hovering.

Her voice is soft, but etched with concern that matches her eyes when she looks up at me, our noses an inch apart. "What are we going to do?"

"Right now? I'm going to make you forget there's anyone else. The rest we'll figure out later."

We've both been quiet for a while. Her head is lying in the crook of my arm while one finger traces a path over the tattoos woven above one bicep. I know there's something she wants to talk about, but I give her time to let her thoughts form the right words.

"I'm not a cheater," she whispers.

I kiss the top of her head, and the arm I have wrapped around her squeezes reassurance. "I didn't think you were."

"But I am now. I mean. This is the first time I've ever cheated on anyone."

"Me too."

"Really?"

"You sound surprised." Her comment stings a bit, and my voice bites right back.

"I didn't mean it that way. I mean…you just…you're sort of a flirt and, you know, the whole rockstar thing."

"And that makes me a cheater?"

"No. I really didn't mean it that way. Can we please start over?"

"How about we've established we're both not usually cheaters and move on from there?"

"Okay." She's quiet for a long time before she speaks again. "I've been with Dylan for almost a year."

It's not like that's news to me, but the reminder slaps me in the face. I don't respond. Because what do you say to that?

"I thought I was in love with him."

Apparently, the slap was just a warm-up for the punch in the gut. "Thought?"

She nods. "But I'm confused now. I was lying in bed the other night trying to figure out if I fell out of love or never was in love, or if I do love him but just not the way I should."

I shift, lifting her from my chest and easing her back to the bed so I can see her. I hate this conversation, but I need to see her eyes. "Did you figure out the answer?"

She shakes her head.

"Do you feel like today was a mistake?"

"That's the thing. Today felt…right. It didn't feel like a mistake at all."

"Every minute since the day I met you has felt that way." I'm pretty sure I sound like a pussy, but fuck, I don't even care.

She looks up into my eyes. "What are we going to do?"

"The question isn't what are *we* going to do. It's what are *you* going to do. Because I'm right here waiting for you to figure it out."

She swallows. "Can you give me a few days?"

I nod. Hating that she needs it, but the reality is, it feels like I've been waiting a lifetime for her. A few days more shouldn't kill me. Or will it?

chapter twenty-one

Lucky

It's been two days since I slept with Flynn. Two days since my head started spinning and I haven't been able to think straight. I look over at Dylan lying next to me as the bus hums peacefully along the open road in the middle of nowhere. A man I've wanted since I was fifteen. I'm living every girl's fantasy. Only, I'm not a girl anymore. I'm a woman. Yet I'm still unsure if I know the difference between lust and love, infatuation and dedication.

I do have feelings for Dylan, I'm sure of that, and I thought those feelings were love. But if I loved him, would I have done what I've done? He's good to me. A relationship with a musician on the road isn't easy. Yet he's worked at it, finding time for me and even arranging it so we can be together on this tour. And look how I've shown him appreciation.

The last two nights I've pretended to be asleep before he came into the bedroom. I feel guilty even lying here. The funny thing is, my guilt is less toward Dylan and more toward Flynn. I've been with Dylan for almost a year, yet I feel guilty for sleeping next to him. Deep down, I know why that is—because guilt is an offense of the heart, and by lying here, I'm committing a crime against a man who has captured a piece of mine. But can two men have a piece of my heart at the same time?

I was pretty good at geometry, but the logistics of this triangle makes my head spin. Even if I end things with Dylan, where would that leave Flynn with the tour? He still has another few weeks of filling in for

Linc, and then his band is joining the second half of the Easy Ryder tour. It's not like I could break things off with Dylan and Flynn and I would walk off on our merry way.

Once Dylan found out we were together, he'd know things started behind his back. And *that* would definitely not sit well. I wouldn't put it past him to fire In Like Flynn and make it out to be their fault in an attempt to blacklist them.

And I know from experience that keeping any relationship private when you're in the public eye is nearly impossible. Any way I look at it, Flynn seems to lose. So I just keep looking at it. Over and over again.

I toss and turn for a half hour more, thinking about tomorrow night. We arrive in Austin and I can't wait to see Avery. She's never been a fan of Dylan, so I'm sure when I fill her in, she'll be all team Flynn. I might be shopping for a forum to validate what my heart is telling me to do.

Even though it's early, even for me, I slip out of bed, tiptoe into the bathroom to wash up and head out to the lounge area.

"Hey," Flynn's voice surprises me. He's in his usual morning position, arms spread wide on the counter, waiting for the coffee pot to finish brewing.

"You're up early."

"Couldn't sleep." He looks down at my t-shirt, where he's undoubtedly greeted with a stiff salute, then back up to me with a flirty grin. "Come here," he says in a low, incredibly seductive voice. The simple two words make my belly flutter in that delicious way. Then he slowly crooks his finger at me.

I deliberate for a second, turning around to look at the door closed behind me, and then back to Flynn. He simply waits with that sexy smile for me to come to him. Totally sinful.

I want him.

No, I don't.

God. Yes, I absolutely do.

I walk the half dozen steps to stand before him, my feet barely finishing their last step when his hand wraps around my neck and his mouth crashes down on mine. One hand keeps a tight grip on the nape of my neck, his thumb snugly holding my throat; his other goes to my ass and he pulls me firmly against him. Oh god. *Firm.* Firm is definitely what I feel.

The man truly steals my breath away. I'm a puddle on the floor by the time he releases me. "Morning." The sound vibrates against my lips, but I feel it much lower.

My good sense finally returns, and I take a step back. I'm on a bus with my boyfriend and the rest of his band and any one of them could walk in at any moment. I clear my throat, still shaken from his kiss, and go to sit down. "Yes. Umm. I couldn't sleep either."

Flynn fixes our coffees and brings the two steaming mugs to the table. Unlike every other morning, he slides in the booth next to me, rather than across from me.

It's a tight fit, our shoulders and thighs pressed up against each other. "What are you doing?"

"What do you mean?" He lifts his mug to his mouth—the mouth with the wicked grin—and sips with a devilish gleam in his eyes.

"Why are you sitting on this side?" I squint.

"Ah. Because it's harder to reach from the other side."

I'm afraid to ask. "Reach what?"

Instead of answering me, he trails his fingers along my thigh and then, with eyes blazing, he pulls my thighs wider apart under the table.

My breath audibly hitches. I should stop him.

Should.

Yes, I'm going to.

Stop! Wait…I screamed that in my head, nothing actually came out.

His fingers travel up the inside of my thigh.

I should stop him.

No, don't.

Higher. Yes. God, yes. Do.

No, don't. I'm really going to stop him.

The words get stuck in my throat. And the next thing I know, his fingers are stroking me. Up and down, over the thin material of my night pants, but it feels incredible nonetheless. The way he watches me so intently, with so much desire in his eyes, shoots through me and I can feel my wetness grow.

Oh, God.

His fingers find my clit and he rubs small circles, the lace of my panties causing just enough friction that I think I might actually be able to come with only his fingers on me through my pants.

"Oh god."

"Feel good?" His voice is hoarse.

I nod and let my eyes flutter closed. Pressure inside me starts to build.

And build.

I'm so consumed, I can hear the sound of my own heartbeat pulsing loudly in my ears. Which is probably why I don't hear the door open.

Luckily, Flynn does and his hand is gone.

"Why are you up so damn early? Come back to bed." Dylan's sleepy voice jolts me from my pre-orgasmic haze, like I'd just stuck my finger on a live wire.

I almost choke trying to speak—my mouth is suddenly so dry. "Umm...I couldn't sleep."

Dylan looks from Flynn to me, eyes narrowing suspiciously. "Come on, I'll wear you out until you're tired enough to sleep for a few more hours."

Not knowing what the hell to say or do, definitely feeling guilty as hell, I nod.

"Excuse me," I say with a shaky voice to Flynn. For a second I panic that he's not going to move, that everything is going to blow up in my face. Flynn turns and catches my eyes, searching for something. His jaw clenches and then he stands to let me out. I feel his cold stare following me the entire way back to my room.

I try to get a minute alone with Flynn the rest of the day, but he's either very sleepy or intentionally avoiding me, because he spends the remainder of the bus trip in his sleeper. I'm pretty certain it's the latter, only I have no idea how to fix things. Well, that's not exactly true. I know how *Flynn* would have me fix things. Me, on the other hand, I'm not sure what it is I want to fix. My stomach churns with a mix of guilt and grief. I don't trust my own judgment anymore. From the moment I laid eyes on Dylan so many years ago, I fell deeply. But my feelings have never grown. Whereas, every day I fall a little deeper for Flynn. Do I really not know the difference between infatuation and love at twenty-five?

The sun is quickly disappearing behind the city skyline as we arrive in Austin, and everyone is anxious to get off the bus, especially Flynn. We pull into a spot and Flynn hops off the bus and walks toward a car parked a few spots over. A guy gets out and the two bear hug, slap each other on the back a few times, and then promptly disappear.

"You ready?" Dylan's been curt with me since this morning. I went back to the room, but I just couldn't bring myself to fool around with him. Not after Flynn's hands were on me. It's not the first time I've rejected Dylan's attempts over the last few days and he's beginning to grow impatient.

"Sure."

"Do you have everything? The bus can't park here tonight, so you won't be able to come back and search for a pair of heels, or whatever it is you forget this time, after we get out."

"I have everything. Wait. Do I need heels?"

Dylan rolls his eyes. "I don't know, Lucky. What do you normally wear to a club?"

"A club?"

"Yeah. A club. I told you earlier, but you weren't paying attention. *Again*. A friend of Flynn's owns a club in Austin and is going to rope off an area for us. So bring shoes, or whatever other shit you're going to need."

Great. Just great. I can't wait. A night out on the town with not one, but *two* men who are angry with me.

The Capitol may be the largest nightclub I've ever seen. And that's saying something, having grown up in New York and traveled half my life with my dad's band. During the day I would bet people pass right by the unremarkable building and assume it's just an old warehouse. But the line that stretches all the way across the front of the club and disappears around the side tonight is a testament to its popularity. If *this* place is at capacity, the rest of the bars and clubs in the city of Austin must be empty.

Easy Ryder's security breezes us from the dark SUV directly into the club, skipping the line that people are waiting on and causing a murmur of interest as we pass. Inside, the first floor has a live rock-and-roll band, a tremendous dance floor, and bars outlining almost the entire expansive perimeter. Looking up, I see two more floors, a balcony wrapping around each, protected by a wall of glass. People mill around, watching the crowd dance beneath them. Men who resemble tree trunks guard the entrance to the upper levels.

All the guys from Easy Ryder and their dates, except Linc and Flynn, pile into an elevator, and we're escorted to a glass room on the second floor above the dance floor. It's truly glass—the floor, the walls, everything. I look down and watch a mob of people swaying on the dance floor. Distracted, I don't notice the guy I saw pick up Flynn outside of the bus today walk in. He takes one look at my face and smiles, knowing exactly what I'm thinking. "It's one way…they can't see up your skirt."

I look around the room—there's a bar in the corner, a couple of guys who look vaguely familiar, but no sign of Flynn. Lydia, Mick's wife, walks over and hooks arms with me. "You look like someone ran over your dog." I've met Lydia a few times. She's smart, sarcastic and has zero filter—if it pops into her head, it comes out her mouth. She'd get along great with Avery. I'm actually looking forward to introducing them tomorrow night at the show.

"I'm just tired. Haven't slept so good."

"Life on the road is tough." She looks over at Mick and Dylan. "Even tougher with moody assholes like them." We both laugh. "C'mon, Lucky. Let's go live a little. These old bastards are going to stand around and drink beer. I see a cute bartender with shot glasses and a dance floor calling our name."

I do one shot for every two that Lydia does; the two I drink have my head spinning and yet she seems perfectly fine after her four. I've got to be the biggest lightweight to ever own a bar.

An hour later I'm on my second fruity drink. The music is pumping and I feel it in my veins. Or perhaps it's the alcohol. Either way, it flows through me, taking away all my worries. The crowd downstairs has thickened, the music has changed from rock to more of an R&B. Bodies sway with a sensual vibe.

"Come on. Let's go dance." Lydia grabs my hand. We stop by the booth that Dylan and Mick are sitting at. Mick waves off his wife, not caring where she's going. Dylan, on the other hand, gives me a look of annoyance.

"Why don't you come with me, then?" I yell over music that seems to have gotten louder since we started talking.

"Go. But save some of your energy for me later," he says. I've feigned everything from tired to a headache the last few days every time he's tried to get intimate.

Down on the dance floor, the music is so loud that I can't even hear myself think. Which is exactly what I need. A new song with an incredible beat fills the air and I start moving my body, letting the music take control of my mind.

"There you go, beautiful girl. Let whatever is bothering you go," Lydia says, but I more or less have to read her lips. She closes her eyes and joins me in getting lost in the music. A few guys try to dance with us, but we shoo them away and keep to ourselves. I lift my arms over my head, letting my hips sway from side to side, and my eyes drift closed.

I'm at the fringe of awareness, lost somewhere in my own semiconsciousness, when I feel it. Goose bumps break out all over my skin before I even understand what it is that's happening. I open my eyes and, like metal to a magnet, I see him. Flynn. He's two floors up, standing against the glass wall, and his blue eyes are burning into mine. Even with all the space between us, the anger is clear in his eyes. I watch as he tosses his drink back and hands the scantily clad waitress his empty glass without so much as a glance in her direction.

"You okay?" Lydia asks, noticing I'm frozen on the dance floor.

"Yeah. I. Uh. I was just looking at the VIP rooms upstairs, trying to figure out which one we're in."

"Oh. We're right up there." She points to the second floor. To the room directly below where Flynn is standing. Still zeroing in on us, Flynn follows our gaze, and I watch as he looks down and sees all the guys from Easy Ryder beneath him. He can see down, they can't see up. It makes me wonder how long he's been standing there. Was he watching me the last hour in the room directly below him?

Not knowing what to do under the scrutiny of his stare, eventually I attempt to dance again. But I've lost the vibe—the atmosphere changed from being lost in the moment to being lost in the man. Another drink is definitely in order. Lydia pouts but leaves with me, again hooking her arm into mine as we make our way into the elevator to return to the second-floor VIP room.

Security pushes a button and the doors slide open. Inside, the guard presses number two…but then I realize there is no button for the floor above us. "There're only two floors on the panel. How do people get up to the third floor?" I ask.

"You need a security card." He motions to the top of the panel. "Slips into the slot and takes you upstairs. Boss man, his friends and employees only."

I know I've had way too much to drink when I start singing in public. It's only a whisper of the words, but the beat thumps along in unison with my heart and I feel the words as I sing the song "Someone New" along with Hozier. The last few lines of the chorus croons about falling in love a little bit more every day with someone new. I sing the words looking up, wondering if Flynn's singing them looking down at me too.

Eventually, the song comes to an end. Still staring up at the opaque glass ceiling, I blow out a shaky breath. Feeling bereft, I decide I need a few minutes of privacy to clear my head. Dylan's busy arguing with the tour manager when I excuse myself telling, him I need to find a ladies' room, but really I head to the elevator to search for some desperately needed fresh air.

The security guard is on the phone, but he opens the door to the elevator when I arrive. A few seconds later, the doors slide open—I hadn't even noticed we weren't going down. "Boss man wants to see you." The hulk of a man extends his arm, gesturing for me to exit the elevator.

I don't have to ask which way to go. I walk toward the same room I was just in, only one floor up. My insides churn at the sight of a woman vying for Flynn's attention as he stands in the corner, arms folded tightly over his chest. I may notice the tall, svelte blonde, but Flynn...his eyes are trained on me.

We stand at opposite ends of the room, our gazes locked, until he pushes off the wall and, with a few long strides, stalks to me. I can see the flex of his jaw and the darkness in his normally light-blue eyes.

His friend from today approaches us, his face going through a mental Rolodex before recognition dawns. "You're Dylan Ryder's girlfriend, right?"

Flynn looks at his friend, then back to me. His response is spoken into my eyes, even though his words aren't for me. "Can you clear this room, Blake?"

Through my peripheral vision, I see his friend's brows draw down, then understanding hits him. "Shit. You're asking for trouble." Blake shakes his head, but a minute later the room is cleared of everyone except Flynn and me.

Flynn looks down, then closes his eyes and takes a breath before speaking.

"My mother raised me and my sister, Bec, alone. She struggled every day to make ends meet and never had time for herself. Our dad left when I was eight. Had his secretary actually waiting in the car the day he moved out."

He drags a hand through his hair. I reach out to touch him, but he puts his hand up. "Don't." The disdain in his voice makes me want to vomit.

"Bec married Professor Douchebag. My niece, Laney, has a half-sister three weeks younger than her. Compliments of her father's TA."

"I'm sorry," I whisper. And I truly am. Although I'm not sure my words bring any comfort, since I'm the cause of his turmoil.

"I'm not the other guy."

The irony is, he was never the other guy. From the first time we crossed that line, *Dylan* became the other guy. But I nod anyway, respecting what he's saying a hell of a lot more than I respect myself at this moment.

Flynn looks down, my eyes following his to peer through the glass floor. We're standing almost exactly over where Dylan is sitting.

"Friends?" he asks. "Can we go back to being friends?"

It feels like a heavy weight is sitting on my chest as I walk to the elevator alone. He's right to put a stop to what shouldn't have started to begin with. But now, I wonder, can we really go back to being friends after we've been through the blur and crossed the line?

chapter twenty-two

Flynn

Alana Evans doesn't shut the fuck up. And I mean that in the nicest possible way. She's been my sister's best friend since third grade, and basically it's been twenty years of one long run-on sentence. I kid Becca that Laney is really Alana's daughter, with the lack of breaths when she gets on an excited rant, but the truth is, Laney is a lot like Alana because Alana and Becca basically grew up as sisters and they're a lot alike. Nurture trumps nature with those three.

We park in the short-term lot at Bergstrom and make our way to the terminal. I'm used to people staring now. For the past year, a lot of people have recognized me, although they weren't sure where from right away. These days, the recognition dawns faster, sometimes instantaneously. More heads than usual turn as we pass, but it takes my conceited ass a minute to catch on why. Alana is drop-dead gorgeous. It's not new—she didn't grow from an ugly duckling to a beautiful swan or anything, she's pretty much been insanely hot since third grade. Around the age of seventeen, I thought about it for a few minutes one night when we were swimming in the neighbor's pool and she was wearing that white bikini that became translucent when she went in the water.

It was a hot July night, the stars were twinkling, my sister had fallen asleep, and the air was thick and humid around us. I'd had a few beers and my judgment was impaired, leading me to think with my teenage

179

dick. Luckily, one thing *didn't* lead to the other, and the next morning I woke to the sound of Alana's voice rambling on from the kitchen table. I love the woman. But there's not enough duct tape in the world.

My ears are nearly numb by the time I catch sight of Becca and Laney at baggage claim. The little pity party I'd been throwing myself for the last twenty-four or so hours abruptly comes to an end when I see Laney's face. Her eyes grow wide and she smiles so big, I could probably count all of her little baby teeth. She charges at me, her arms open, and nearly causes an old man to fall when she whizzes past him. "Uncle Sinn! Uncle Sinn!"

My sister rolls her eyes, but smiles and greets her best friend as I haul Laney up into my arms and spin her around in the air. "Squirt! You made it."

She squeals when I toss her around. I seriously hope she's never too cool for this shit. Because it's better than any medicine or high I've ever sought to relieve my pain.

I throw Laney's backpack over one shoulder and carry her in one arm to greet my sister. "How was your flight?" I lean down and peck her on the cheek.

"Good. Except I think the airline might ban us. Laney talked the entire flight. To the flight attendants, the guy next to her, the people in the row behind us, in front of us."

"Nah. I think you're good. If they banned people for excessive talking, Alana would have been grounded years ago."

Alana smacks my abs.

"By the way, she told everyone on the plane that her uncle was a rockstar and she was on her way to see him. I'm not sure if half the people believed her, but the teenagers a few rows up knew your name and asked if you would be at the airport."

As if on cue, two teenage girls hesitantly walk up to us and ask for my autograph. By the time Becca and Laney's bags pop out of the carousel, we've got a pretty good crowd around us. We'll have to teach Laney about discretion some day.

Normally when I travel for gigs, I take the cheapest room. Most times, I'm out partying until the sunrise anyway, so I never saw the point of wasting money on a room I was just going to crash in for a few hours. But this time, I booked a two-bedroom suite for the few nights we'd be in Austin, so me and Laney could hang and my sister and Alana could have enough space to throw their clothes all over the floor and still walk.

Becca puts Laney down for a nap, which I'm thinking is a kick-ass idea as I eye the spot next to her little body on the king-size bed. But Alana begs me to go to the pool with her. After my over-indulgence last night, I'm not in the mood for the scorching Texas sun beating down on my head, but she's never going to shut up if I don't go along. So I give in sooner rather than later despite my headache, hoping to catch some Zs on a lounger at least.

I open the gate to the pool area for Alana to walk through first and follow behind her, slipping on my sunglasses and already feeling the blaze of the afternoon sun on my back.

"How's this?" Alana asks, pointing to two open cushioned lounge chairs.

"Fine. Whatever you want," I say, looking down. My phone just pinged with a text from Nolan. I respond and look back up just as Alana lifts her cover-up over her head. *Damn.* I shake my head. *What a shame.*

I tug the shirt off my back and set myself up on the lounger next to her. It's only when I'm settled in that I look across the pool and see her. And *him.* Dylan is out cold and Lucky has sunglasses on that hide her eyes. Yet I can tell from her face that she sees me. Sees *us.* I offer a slight nod, which she returns, and then I set my seat all the way back so I'm lying flat. There's no doubt where my eyes would be if I were sitting up.

"Flynn. Can you get my back with the sunscreen?" Alana waited until I settled in, of course.

"Lie on your back and you won't need it."

"If I lie on my back I won't fall asleep. Which means I'll need to keep talking to you."

I groan. And get up. The sunscreen soaks into her skin almost as soon as I rub it on, so it doesn't take me very long to cover her back.

"Can you do my butt?"

"If you didn't wear half a freaking bathing suit, you wouldn't need to put sunscreen on your ass. Seriously, half your ass cheeks are hanging out."

"Shut up and get your hands on my butt. You know you've wanted to touch it for fifteen years anyway," she teases, jiggling her butt cheeks.

Normally, I'd savor the opportunity to lather up a woman's ass sticking out of a tiny bikini bottom. But this is Alana. It's a great ass, but after so many years, it amounts to rubbing lotion on my sister's.

"Done," I announce. "Anything else before I lie down?"

She turns over. "Actually. Could we go in the pool? I'm hot."

"You just made me rub lotion on your ass. *Now* you want to go for a swim?"

She unfolds from her chair and grabs my hands, pulling me to stand. "You are one pain in the ass," I say.

"But you love me anyway. Come on. I'll tell you all about my new job."

Duct tape. There is not enough duct tape.

We spend the next half hour in the pool. My dark sunglasses conveniently conceal my eyes as they drift back to Lucky every few minutes. Fuck, she's beautiful. She has to know I'm watching her, even if she can't see my eyes. Although Alana doesn't even seem to notice…she's too busy babbling on about some guy at her new job.

I grit my teeth when Dylan rolls onto his side, then leans over and kisses Lucky's belly. It's one thing to know they're together, a completely different thing to have to watch any intimacy between the two of them. Pool time is definitely over. I need to get the hell out of here. "This sun is kicking my ass. What do you say we get a drink at the bar and head back upstairs?"

"Can I get a lemonadey drink?"

"You can have whatever you want."

Unfortunately, I'm not the only one opting to leave the oven for cooler pastures. Dylan and Lucky pass by as we're packing up. "Catching some rays, Beckham?" Dylan says to me, but his eyes are all over Alana. Forget that he has no idea who Alana is to me, he's standing right next to his girlfriend. The asshole has no respect.

"Yep. Packing it in. Just about to head back up to our room." The statement doesn't seem odd until I see Lucky's face. It looks like mine did when I saw Ryder put his fucking lips on her stomach.

"Aren't you going to introduce me?" Alana says. I completely forgot that meeting Dylan Ryder would impress anyone.

"Alana. This is Dylan and *his girlfriend,* Lucky." The words taste bitter.

"Nice to meet you," Alana says with stars in her eyes.

"You too." Dylan grins, enjoying the adulation.

"I can't wait to see the show tonight. I love Easy Ryder."

"Well, make sure Flynn gives you an all-access pass."

Alana smiles. "Okay. He pretty much gives me whatever I want or I use my secret weapon on him." She takes my arm, then leans in like she's telling them a secret and winks. "My mouth."

I almost choke. Totally Alana. She meant it innocently enough—I'll do anything just so she'll shut up. But Dylan's eyebrow-jump and dirty grin tell me how it was received was definitely not as she intended. As does the scowl on Lucky's face.

Perhaps a little of her own medicine doesn't taste so good.

chapter

twenty-three

Lucky

This afternoon Dylan and I had yet another fight. The poolside playtime with Flynn and his new friend left me in a mood I couldn't seem to shake. I was relieved when Dylan didn't try to come with me to the airport. Traveling with him makes everything into a production, and I really just want some alone time with Avery.

After two hours of delays, I finally have my best friend. We walk to the waiting car with her two bags in tow. *Two bags...*for a two-night trip.

"What the hell did you bring?"

"Clothes."

"We're in Texas in summer, it's not like it's sweater season. You really couldn't fit everything in one bag?"

"I brought some extra outfits for you."

"For me? Why?"

"To cheer you up."

"But I'm not depressed." Well. Maybe a little. But that's a story I can't get into now as we sit in the back of a car being driven by security. *Dylan's* security.

"What did you have for breakfast?"

"Breakfast?"

"Yes, breakfast."

"A chocolate chip muffin and coffee. Oh. And maybe a few pieces of bacon."

"Did you sleep until after seven?"

"Yes. I slept in for a change. What's that got to do with anything?"

"This morning's sonnet. What was it titled?"

"'Ruin.'"

"That's what I thought."

"What are you talking about?"

"You're depressed. When you're down, you eat, get up late and write depressing poetry." She shrugs like it's a known fact.

"I do not." Then I think about it. "Do I?"

Avery's look says *duh*, even though she doesn't.

"But even if that's all true, how did you know that all the way from New York?"

"The sighing."

"What are you talking about?"

"You have this little sigh at the end of your sentences when you're depressed. It's like talking is an effort. You sighed on the phone when you called to confirm my flight info last night."

"You're absolutely insane, you know that?" A barely there sigh comes out after my last word. *Oh my god.*

Avery arches an eyebrow and grins. "A glass of wine while I get to pick out what you wear tonight. Then you can spill your guts when we get home. If you spill them before, you won't want to go out."

"Thanks, Dr. Phil."

"No problem." She ends her response with an over-pronounced, intentional sigh.

The Easy Ryder show is sold out again and the VIP section is filled with corporate sponsors in suits. Avery and I forgo our five-hundred-dollar reserved accommodations in favor of the cheap seats on the floor. Even though Avery isn't a fan of Dylan Ryder, there's no denying she loves their music. Together we dance around and sing along with the crowd.

I try to focus on the music and enjoy my time with Avery, ignoring the man standing on the right side of the stage, but it's virtually impossible when it's time for him to take the microphone.

Flynn has the women swooning before he even sings the first note. A woman screams something obscene and rushes past security to throw underwear on the stage. They land at Flynn's feet and he looks down with almost an embarrassed grin and shakes his head with a flirty half smile. Absolutely charming.

"Lord, that man is delectable," Avery says. "How the hell have you been traveling on a bus with him and not jumped his bones?"

I stare up at the stage. Flynn is absorbed in the song, eyes shut; the sound that flows from him seems to come from somewhere even deeper tonight. The words more soulful, more achingly beautiful as he sings Linc's song about losing the girl he loves. Tears fill my eyes. He's absolutely hypnotizing.

As the song ends, I notice they've changed the transition back to Dylan. Rather than a hard finish, which gives the crowd a chance to applaud, the set seamlessly moves from Flynn's solo performance right into Dylan's next song. When the spotlight leaves Flynn, there's an ache in my chest at the loss.

"Oh my god. You fucked him!" Avery screams. I turn and find my friend's eyes flashing shock, her face filled with excitement.

"What are you talking about?"

"Don't play coy with me, Luciana Valentine."

Oh geez. She's channeling my father.

"It's…complicated."

She claps her hands and jumps up and down. "Why didn't you tell me?"

The truth is, I wanted to tell Avery. But I'm embarrassed at how I've acted. She's my best friend. I'm pretty sure if I committed murder, she'd grab a shovel instead of judging me. Yet I kept putting off this conversation because I knew what would happen after she buried the body. We'd talk about it. And she'd push me to figure out why I did what I did and make sense of it. Keeping my head in the sand wouldn't be possible anymore. "I'm sorry. I just wasn't ready to talk about it while it was happening."

"Was? As in it's not anymore?"

I shake my head and a tear rolls down my cheek.

"Oh, honey." Avery wraps her hand around my shoulder. "Come on. Let's go backstage and have a drink."

The concert is less than half over, which makes getting through security a breeze compared to the line of women who will be vying for backstage access at the end of the show. Behind the scenes is quiet—most people are stage-side, watching the show, or in the VIP area. I'm surprised to find anyone in the lounge. Two women are seated at the bar. My stomach drops when I catch a glimpse of one of them. Flynn's poolside plaything from today.

"Hey. From the pool today, right?" she asks with a friendly smile. She's stunning, and it makes me feel insecure—something I pride myself on not being.

I nod.

"Dylan Ryder's girlfriend," the woman explains to her friend. "Flynn and I saw them down at the pool today."

"Nice to meet you. I'm Flynn's sister, Rebecca."

"Really? You're Laney's mom?"

The woman cocks her head. "Yes. How did you know?"

"Flynn talks about her all the time."

She smiles. "Yep. That would be my brother. Had his heart stolen the day she was born. This is my friend, Alana. She lives here in Austin. Laney and I flew in last night to visit and watch the show."

"Nice to meet you. I'm Lucky, and this is Avery."

"Lucky? The voice coach?"

"That's me." I pause. "But how did you know I was a voice coach?"

She smiles. "I hope you don't find this inappropriate, but I'm pretty sure my brother has it bad for you."

Avery pipes in from next to me, "I'm pretty sure the feeling is reciprocal."

My eyes flare. I look at Alana. "He doesn't. I'm sorry."

She shrugs. "Why are you sorry?"

"Aren't you two...?"

"Me and Flynn?" She crinkles her nose. "Gross. No. Why would you think that?"

"I saw you at the pool together today. And you said..."

She looks at me funny. "What did I say?"

"You said you could get him to do anything. With your...mouth."

"By talking his ear off. He'll do anything to shut me up. What did you think I meant?"

The heat rises in my face. Becca, who is mid-sip, actually spits her drink out all over the place. "Oh my god!" She laughs. "We need a drink and a do-over, ladies."

Something about the ridiculousness of our conversation and the warmth that Becca radiates makes the stress ease, and all four of us have a good laugh. Along with a shot or two. A little while later, it feels like the four of us have been friends for years. Watching Becca and Alana is like looking in a mirror at Avery and me.

The roar of the audience suddenly grows louder and the endless music quiets. "Sounds like the show is ending. What do you say the four of us go have a girls' night out?" Alana asks.

"We're in." Avery jumps up, leaving me no choice. Not that I would have declined. It's actually exactly what I need.

The four of us are toasting to our newfound friendship, and one for the road, when Flynn walks in. He takes one look at our new little posse and actually looks a little scared.

chapter twenty-four

Flynn

You don't need to have ever been in a hurricane to know to run the other way when you see one coming. I walk into the lounge area backstage after the show and four women are smiling, holding up shot glasses in a toast. My sister, Avery, Alana and Lucky.

From the looks of things, it's not the first toast of the evening. They slam back the clear liquid in their shot glasses, make faces like they just smelled a rotten case of morning breath and turn around to see me.

"Well, well, if it isn't my favorite brother," Becca says. Of course, I'm her *only* brother. But my mother didn't raise a fool. Now is *not* the time to point that out.

"Ladies," I say apprehensively.

Avery stands. "Hi there, Flynn. We're going to go out dancing." She motions to the four ladies. "With our new friends. Want to join us?" There's a gleam in her eye.

"Ummm. Think I'll pass."

Alana kisses my cheek. "Good choice."

Becca takes her purse off the bar. "We were going to find a karaoke bar. But seeing how I've had my fill of karaoke lately, we thought we'd try something different." My sister walks to me, kisses my cheek and then grins. "Did you know my new friends Lucky and Avery own a karaoke bar?"

I shake my head. One by one, they walk out the door. The last to leave is Lucky. "Love your sister. Have a good night."

It's almost four in the morning when I hear the hotel room door open and the sound of female giggling. Laney spent the night at Alana's mom's house, so there was no reason for Bec to make it an early night. I'm actually glad she had a night out for a change. Although curiosity has kept me awake for the last few hours, seeing as with whom my sister was spending the evening getting acquainted.

The door to my bedroom creaks open slowly. It's dark, but a shadow comes toward the bed. I push up on my elbows. "Everything okay?"

The voice that answers is not my sister's. "Can I sleep in here with you tonight?"

"Lucky," I warn.

"I know you're mad at me. Yesterday morning, I didn't…when I went into the bedroom with Dylan, we…"

"I really don't want to hear about it."

"We didn't. I couldn't. Nothing happened."

"Why not? You were certainly in the mood when you were with me."

"I couldn't…because I felt like I was cheating. *On you.*"

The bed dips and she crawls into bed with me, slipping under the covers. "We'll stay dressed. I just want to sleep with you."

"How much did you drink?"

"Not enough to make me stop thinking about you."

She rests her head on my chest and releases a loud sigh of contentment. Having her here feels too right to turn her away. I wrap my arm around her shoulder and pull her tight. "Get some sleep."

The next morning, our bodies are tangled when we wake. I swear it's like seeing the sunrise for the first time when I watch her eyes flutter open. Fucking beautiful. She smiles and snuggles closer. Yep. I could get used to this...every damn day. Maybe the two of us wouldn't wake up so early if this was the way we woke up.

"Morning," she says.

"Sleep good?"

"I did. What time is it?" She arches her back and stretches.

I reach over and swipe my phone from the nightstand. "Eleven."

"Wow. I haven't slept this late in years."

"Me either."

"Maybe we both get up early because there's no reason to stay in bed."

"If I woke up with you next to me every morning, I'd give you a reason to stay in bed."

She giggles, and the sound makes me feel all warm and fuzzy. It also makes my morning erection harden a little more.

"You know what I was thinking about last night?"

"Me," I say confidently. The fact that she wound up in my bed might have been the first clue.

She chuckles. "I was thinking it was strange that we kept on pretending we barely knew each other, even after it made sense that we would be friends. I mean, we worked together a few hours a day, yet we never let on that we were even really friends."

I knew exactly why I did it, but I'm curious to hear her explanation. Unfortunately, a loud knock at my bedroom door interrupts us. "Uncle Sinn."

Mini–motor mouth is back. "Give me a minute, squirt."

"Oh, God. I don't want her to see me in here with you."

"What? Why?"

"She's a little girl."

"So?"

"Do you want her thinking it's okay to sleep around?"

"Considering she's never seen me with another woman, my guess is she'd think you were special."

"That's sweet. But still. No. Go. I'll wash up quick. Do you think you can occupy her in the other room so I can sneak out?" She jumps up and runs to the en suite bathroom.

Not exactly the morning I was hoping for after waking up with Lucky wrapped around my body.

chapter twenty-five

Lucky

I slip my key into the door of the penthouse suite, hoping by some miracle I'll find it empty. No such luck. Duff and the tour manager, Brett, are sitting on the couch in the living room. Dylan is across from them, his feet propped up on the ottoman. He extends his hand for me to come to him and pulls me down for a kiss.

"Have fun last night with Avery?"

"I did. Thank you for flying her in."

He nods. "We just ordered lunch up, should be here in a little while. Need to finish going through some tour stuff, then I'll kick these guys out and we can spend the afternoon together."

"That sounds nice." I force a smile. "I'm going to take a quick shower."

I head to the bathroom to attempt to wash the guilt from my body. Only today, it's not really my body that's guilty. Flynn and I slept next to each other last night—I'm sure Dylan would not be happy about that if he knew. But nothing happened. Although, the guilt from physical cheating might actually be easier to wash away this morning than the affair I'm having with my heart.

Lunch is delivered when I return to the living area feeling clean on the outside. The inside is a whole different story.

"Ticket sales are up," Brett says. The three men are now sitting around the dining room table, a platter of sandwiches in the center. "We sold out the rest of the next four shows. Beckham is giving us the recharge we needed. He's bringing in the younger crowd...the eighteen-to-twenty-two demographic that does the bulk of the spending on music."

"He's a showboat. Linc runs circles around his cocky ass. Teenage girls don't know music from shit," Dylan spits back.

"They buy tickets."

"Until the next cookie cutter comes along. We've seen a hundred of these guys over the last ten years."

"I don't know. Beckham's got talent. He's more than just a pretty face," Duff adds, stuffing a sandwich into his mouth. "What do you think, Lucky? You know his chops better than anyone. Is pretty boy a phase or does he have staying power?"

The right answer would be to say no. Dylan's insecurity about becoming an aging rockstar at the ripe old age of thirty-five does not need to be fueled by my gushing about a younger singer. But the need to defend Flynn wins out. "He's vocally gifted. He can run from E2 to E6 and his falsetto has major endurance."

Dylan's brooding stare is piercing into me when I glance in his direction. Ignoring him, I quickly turn my attention to fixing my plate.

"Told ya," Duff gloats. "And he's a pussy magnet. He's good for the tour. Enjoy it. He's bringing us new fans, not taking them away."

"The change from his head voice to his falsetto is choppy. Linc's is smooth." Dylan's tone is definitely less than agreeable; he's challenging my assessment of Flynn's vocal ability. I don't take the bait—no use in arguing over the better vocalist. We're both influenced by the artist—for entirely different reasons.

"Whatever, man." Brett shrugs. "I can't sing for shit. That's why I manage pains in the asses like you. But I can count pretty damn good and there's more to count with Beckham on the tour, so I'm happy."

The afternoon is peaceful, although Dylan is on the quiet side. We watch a movie, then sit around talking about the upcoming venues for the rest of his tour. He frowns when our conversation falls to an awkward silence, and not for the first time today.

"Is everything okay, Lucky?"

"Ummm. Yes. Why?"

"I don't know. You just seem…off, lately. Like there's somewhere else you'd rather be."

"I'm sorry. I didn't mean to make you feel like that."

He pushes a lock of hair behind my ear and searches my face. "Is there?"

I furrow my brow.

"You said you didn't *mean* to make me feel like you'd rather be somewhere else. You didn't say there *wasn't* somewhere else you would rather be."

I'm a crap liar. Luckily, there is a truth I can grab onto. "It's just a big change. I haven't been on a tour bus in a long time. I feel sort of…unsettled."

"You'll get used to it." He gives me a sly smile. "You know, I had an ulterior motive for bringing you out on this tour."

"Oh yeah, what is that?"

"Trial run."

"For what?"

"A full-time position."

"As a traveling voice coach?"

"As my permanent traveling companion." His face is serious as he watches me.

I blink in surprise. We've been together almost a year and never talked about changing our relationship. My immediate reaction is acute. My palms sweat and a cloak of claustrophobia hits me. I look down to hide my apprehension. "Oh."

"Don't sound so excited."

"I'm sorry. It's just…my life is in New York."

"Is it? You finally let go of Lucky's, and your boyfriend is on the road."

My heart feels heavy. The truth is, down deep, my hesitation has little to do with my life back home and more to do with the commitment I'd be making. The only carrot I see dangling in front of me from his offer is that Flynn's band would eventually be joining the tour as the opening act. But agreeing to essentially move in with my boyfriend just so I could be closer to another man is definitely not the right thing to do. "I don't think I'm ready for this yet, Dylan."

"It's been almost a year, and I'm thirty-five years old. I'm ready." He sighs and sits down next to me. "Don't answer me yet. We have another week and a half before you're done traveling with us, for work anyway. Let me convince you."

Not knowing what else to say or do, I nod.

A strain fell upon the peacefulness of the afternoon after Dylan asked me to go on the road with him full-time. It wasn't anything he said—the unspoken blared much louder. Or maybe it was that I knew I didn't need to consider my answer.

Avery and I skipped the Easy Ryder show, choosing instead to stay in and drink wine in our PJs. I was pretty sure she didn't fly halfway across the country to sit in a hotel room, but she insisted and, to be perfectly honest, it was exactly what I wanted to do.

Dylan asked me to sleep with him tonight, rather than spend the night with Avery again. So I called it an early night, knowing he wouldn't be back from the post-show party yet, but that the wine would lull me to sleep quickly.

The next morning, I wake to a feeling of melancholy. The man I thought I was in love with is sprawled next to me, his bare ass peeking out from beneath the sheet. I always loved how he slept naked; it made the mornings more interesting. But in this moment, I'm questioning everything. What I've felt in the past, what I feel today. The only thing I don't question is heading downstairs for coffee and hoping I won't be drinking it alone.

chapter twenty-six

Flynn

Being on tour with a legendary rock band certainly has its perks. I've never really struggled to capture the attention of women. My sister lovingly says it's because I'm a "full-of-myself dimpled whore," although I like to think it's my glowing personality. But last night no personality was required backstage, that's for damn sure.

What I thought was the post-show laidback style of Easy Ryder, with only a few women permitted through security into the inner sanctum, turned out to have a qualifier—the laidback style of Easy Ryder *when girlfriends and wives are around.*

The backstage lounge was filled with women who didn't require small talk. One of whom made that abundantly clear when she greeted me by sticking her tongue down my throat and grabbing my crotch.

When I left, alone, I reasoned that my sister was visiting. That it's normal for a single guy to turn down a hot redhead who whispers in his ear that she has no gag reflex, in favor of going back to his hotel to wait for his sister and her five-year-old daughter. The fucked-up part? I didn't even have a hard-on when she pushed her breasts against me and suggested we step into the bathroom.

Yet here I sit, six-o-fucking-clock in the morning, and my dick starts to turn to steel when I see a woman in a tank top and baggy sweats.

But look at how those sweats hang just at the curve of her hip. Sweats can be hot.

I'm totally fucked. Choosing sweats over a woman with her uvula pierced. I need to get my head out of my ass and stop hanging around Lucky like a puppy.

"Good morning," she whispers and smiles down at me. I'm sitting in the breakfast lounge, having already made her coffee. My eyes languidly feast on her hip before moving up to her perky nipples.

Maybe she likes puppies.

I hold up her mug of coffee. "Morning. How do you feel about dogs?"

I'm thrilled as shit to learn she begged her father for a dog for years, but never got one. Maybe it's time.

Three hours later, we finish our morning coffee. "You up for a road trip for my coaching session today?" I ask as we head toward the elevator bank.

"Road trip?"

"Yep. Becca has a rental car. I'll drive."

"Where are we going?"

"It's a surprise."

She smiles. "I'm going to take the ride with Avery to the airport at one. How about after that?"

"Works for me. Text me when you're ready."

"You ready, squirt?"

"What's her name again?"

"Lucky."

"That's right. It's a funny name."

"It's a beautiful name for a beautiful woman."

Lucky's smile when she sees me strolling to the lobby, hand-in-hand with my favorite girl, lights up her entire face. It might just be the best greeting ever bestowed upon a man.

"Well, this beautiful young lady must be Laney," she says.

"Uncle Sinn thinks you're beautiful, too!" Laney shouts. And there goes the talk we had five minutes before we walked out the door about not repeating things.

Lucky arches one eyebrow at me. "Oh he does, does he?"

Laney nods her head fast. "He likes your name, too. He said—"

I cut her off. "Okay, motor mouth, let's go or we'll be late."

Shockingly, Laney doesn't spill where we're going on the way to the theater, although there are plenty of hints. She's wearing an Elsa crown and halfway there asks, "Uncle Sinn. Sing my favorite song!"

"I sang it once last night and twice in the hotel room before we left."

"Sing it, Uncle Sinn!"

I look at Lucky and laugh. "My sister is raising a tyrant."

"I can see who's in charge," she teases me.

"Oh yeah." I glance at Lucky and back at the road. "Laney, you know Lucky sings too. She's actually better than me. I think she probably sounds more like Elsa than I do.

"Really?" Her voice screeches with excitement.

"You bet." Lucky has no idea what she's in for yet. It's hard to keep a straight face.

"Lucky. Will you pwease sing *Frozen* for me?"

"I would love to, Laney. But I don't know the words."

"You don't know the words?" Through the rearview mirror, I catch Laney's little nose crinkling in confusion. She's baffled that someone doesn't know every word to the entire *Frozen* soundtrack.

"Actually, Laney, I think she'll know them soon." I turn and pull into the parking lot at the theater.

"We're going to the movies?" Lucky asks.

"Sort of."

She squints at my cryptic answer, but goes with it anyway. I unbuckle Laney from her car seat and pull the baseball cap I tossed in the back down over my head, adding a pair of aviators for good measure.

"Rockstar disguise?" Lucky teases.

"I prefer 'rock god'."

She rolls her eyes.

Inside, I skip the long line and head to the woman collecting tickets at the door. She directs me to Carolyn, the woman I arranged today with on the phone.

"What are you up to?" Lucky asks suspiciously as we head into the theater.

"Just multitasking."

"Multitasking?"

"Yep."

The eyes of the woman with the clipboard indicate she recognizes me immediately. Guess my disguise sort of sucks.

"Mr. Beckham. I'm so excited you made it."

"It's Flynn. And we're excited to be here. Right, squirt?" I look down at the girl squeezing my hand tight, and she nods her head vigorously with a smile from ear to ear.

Carolyn laughs. I pull the tickets from my pocket and hand them to her. "Thanks for adding us."

"I'm a huge fan of Easy Ryder. My older daughter is thirteen. She didn't know who Easy Ryder was, but when I mentioned your name, she started to hyperventilate. Getting these tickets made me the coolest mom in the world." She hands me a numbered sign with pins at the top. "At least for today. Tomorrow is another story."

A girl about five or six runs up to Carolyn and tugs at her arm. "Mommy, that's the crown I want." She points to the tiara that has been almost permanently affixed to Laney's head for the last year.

"How about 'excuse me,' Deidre," she scolds.

"Excuse me. Mommy, that's the crown I want."

I chuckle. Guess all little girls are the same.

"Okay, Deidre. Why don't you go back and sit? The movie is going to start soon."

Laney looks at me, then back at the other girl. She doesn't have to say what she's thinking; I see the question in her face. I nod, telling her it's okay.

"You wanna borrow it for the movie?" Laney asks her.

"Really?"

"Sure." She shrugs. "I wear it all the time."

"Okay! You wanna come sit with me? We're in the front row and my sister is in the contest."

Laney turns to me, her eyes asking permission. "Sure. Just no leaving the theater." I look around. Most of the rows are filled, but there are a few vacant seats in the back. "We'll just be in the..."

"The gallery is empty if you'd like to sit up there so no one bothers you," Carolyn points up toward the small balcony. I'm twenty-five going on fifteen. *Shit, yeah, I'll take the balcony in the dark with the hot girl.*

"That would be great." I look at Lucky and wiggle my eyebrows.

"I'm almost afraid to ask," she says as we settle into the front row of the otherwise empty balcony. "What are the numbers for?"

"The contest." I shrug.

"Care to elaborate?"

"The local theater club for kids is putting on a *Frozen* musical. After the movie, the finalists for the lead role are singing."

"And you're trying out?"

"I got lucky, the organizer's daughter wanted to come to tonight's Easy Ryder concert, but it was sold out. Traded tickets for this movie and auditions for the Easy Ryder show tonight. Figured Laney would love it. She's obsessed with the soundtrack. Thought she'd get a kick out of me singing, too."

"That is so sweet."

"I'm glad you think so. Because you're singing later, too."

Her eyes flare. "What?"

The lights dim for the movie to start. She's still staring at me, expecting an answer. I lift my pointer finger to my lips, *shh*ing her, and whisper, "The movie is starting, no talking."

Ignoring her glare, I take her hand and mesh our fingers together. They stay intertwined for the entire movie.

When the lights come up, the theater applauds and Carolyn walks to the front of the stage. "Okay, everyone. We're going to take a five-minute bathroom break and then we'll get started."

Looking down, I see Laney jumping around. "Laney's doing the pee-pee dance. I better grab her."

"I'll take her. You can get me some popcorn for your Elsa audition. I have a feeling it's going to be amusing." She bumps my shoulder as we stand, but doesn't let go of my hand until we get to the restroom with Laney.

With a popcorn bucket bigger than my damn head, I wait outside the ladies' room. When the two of them walk out hand in hand, I realize for the first time what I've been missing, what I want more than anything. I thought it was having the world at my feet, singing up on a stage, being a rockstar. But the reality is...I want Sunday afternoon movies with these two.

chapter twenty-seven

Lucky

The little girls giggle at the man on stage singing his own version of "Let It Go." He's turned the epic ballad into more of a rock anthem—singing it without a single beat of music. I've watched him up on stage before; his talent is undeniable and his sexiness is utterly swoon-worthy. But watching him today, as he sings a song for a five-year-old he adores, puts the whole man into perspective. His beauty shines through from the inside out.

I'm leaning against the wall on the other side of the theater, taking it all in. A gaggle of moms stand nearby, as riveted as their daughters, only the look on most of their faces tells me their interest is far less innocent.

"You think he likes older women? I mean, we're more experienced."

"Look at him. Do you really think we have more experience? Giving Harold a BJ on his birthday and your anniversary doesn't equate to the type of experience *that* man must have. I bet he fucks like the devil."

"Victoria! You're so bad!" They both giggle.

"I'd like to be bad with him."

The women sigh loudly. "Do you think having all that rhythm makes him better in bed?"

Flynn's song ends, and the place erupts in applause that by far overshadows the clapping the end of the movie garnered. He winks at Laney in the front row and heads toward me. Through my periphery, I see the horny moms follow his steps as he strides closer to where I'm standing.

"Back to the balcony?" He offers me his hand.

I take it, walk two steps, and then stop, turning back to whisper to the moms, "The rhythm definitely makes him better." I wink and walk away, leaving their mouths hanging open and their eyes green with envy.

"What was that all about?" Flynn asks as we make our way back up to the balcony.

"Nothing." I smirk deviously. We settle back into our seats and he guzzles a full bottle of water. "Thirsty?" I tease.

"How did I do, coach? I did everything you taught me. Tilted my head so my throat was open, leaned back instead of forward. I think I earned an A."

Shit. I was supposed to be watching him for professional purposes. "You did great. You're a model student."

He smiles. "I had a good teacher."

"I don't even think you really ever needed me."

He stares at me for a long moment with his beautiful blue eyes. "Funny. I was just thinking you're all I really need."

My heart sighs and the entire world fades away as he slowly leans in and, ever so gently, brushes his lips with mine. We've been intimate, but this moment is at an entirely different level. He rests his forehead against mine, and I hold my breath while he speaks. "Lucky," he groans. "I want you. I keep trying to distance myself, but it's impossible. I wake up with your name on my lips every morning. I want you next to me during the day and beneath me at night." He closes his eyes, and when he reopens them, the pain I see crushes me. "Tell me to walk away and I will. But if you don't right now…" He shakes his head. "I'm not sure I'll be able to."

The thought of losing him sickens me. It's not a difficult decision. "Don't walk away. I just need more time to figure things out."

He closes his eyes, and I watch his face visibly relax. We sit hand-in-hand in the balcony until the last person sings. Then we go down to a very excited Laney. Carolyn is by her side, a hesitant look on her face. "Ummm...Laney told the girls you would sign some autographs."

Flynn's dimples appear along with his adorable crooked smile. "No problem." I'm pretty sure Carolyn blushes.

A half hour later, he signs the last autograph and thanks Carolyn. A few workers from the theater come to carry the portable stereo that acted as backup for the singers today. "Would you mind if we borrowed that for five minutes and I'll carry it out to your car?" His smile is less innocent this time—he absolutely knows it will get him what he wants. I have to stop myself from rolling my eyes when Carolyn gushes that she'd be delighted.

When the theater door closes behind her, Flynn turns to me. "You ready?"

"Ready for what?" I ask nervously.

"Our duet."

"Ummm...I don't think so."

He leans in so that Laney can't hear him. "'Let It Go' was the number-one karaoke song last year. You're not going to try to bullshit me that you don't know it like you did in the car, are you?"

Shit.

There may be no stage, but the big room is nerve-wracking nonetheless. I look around and swallow.

"We got this." He squeezes my hand and stares into my eyes. The way he looks at me, assuring me, I believe his words.

We do have this.

He smiles, knowing I'm giving in before I even do. Then, together, with an audience of one little princess smiling from ear to ear, we stand at the front of the theater and sing the shit out of the *Frozen* song.

Laney babbles almost the entire way back to the hotel. It's clear she adores her uncle, and he is most definitely wrapped around her tiny little finger. After we park, she insists on holding *both* our hands. She squeals with delight when we swing her into the air between us, and demands, "Again."

Busy entertaining the little tyrant, none of us even notice we walk smack into a row of three men as we enter the hotel lobby. The middle one being my very unhappy-looking boyfriend.

His eyes hard, he takes in the full scene before him. We must look like a happy couple playing with their child. The smile drains from my face along with the color. His jaw flexes. "You haven't answered your phone."

I fumble in my purse and fish out my cell, turning it on. There are five missed calls. "Sorry. I turned it off in the movie."

"The movie?" he snaps.

Shit.

My stomach roils. When I see the angry glare he directs at Flynn, I worry what might happen next. "We. I…"

Luckily, Flynn steps in. "I asked Lucky to come with us to a kid's event I sang at for my niece. Take her coaching on the road. This is Laney." Flynn locks eyes with Dylan and then points his down to the little princess we're both still holding hands with. It serves as a gentle reminder of her presence. After a long hard glare, Dylan's eyes drop down to Laney and it takes the tension down a notch.

"We're going to look at a new bus. I was trying to reach you so you could come look at it."

"A new bus?"

His jaw clenches and he searches my face. "I'm thinking about upgrading. So you have more space to put your things. You're going to want more than just a few outfits when we're gone for two months at a time."

He's assuming I'll agree to what he asked of me last night. But now is definitely not the time to point that out. I feel Flynn's eyes on me, too.

"You ready?"

"Umm. Sure." I look down at Laney, who is unusually quiet. "It was very nice meeting you."

She tugs at my arm, telling me to crouch to her level. When I do, she wraps her arms around my neck and squeezes a big hug good-bye.

I walk out of the hotel with a different man than I just walked in with, and an enormous ache in my chest. Turning back, my eyes meet with Flynn's. How much longer can I do this to him?

Neither Dylan nor I say another word about the encounter in the lobby. Oddly, it felt like we had just moved the discussion to the back burner, where it would simmer for a while, rather than letting things come to a boil in the moment. I also didn't mention, as we looked around at luxury buses that cost more than an apartment in Manhattan, that I hadn't agreed to go on tour with him. The conversation was coming, I just needed to figure a few things out first.

The next morning I wake even earlier than usual. I didn't have a chance to speak to Flynn after the tense exchange in the lobby and, taking the cowardly course of action, I went to bed before any of the guys returned to the bus after last night's show. Mick spent the night in Austin and is flying to meet us at the next stop in Vegas, and Duff had a woman with him, so that left just me, Dylan and Flynn. Not a trio I wanted to sit around with in the tight confines on the bus.

After failing miserably at trying to get back to sleep, I decide to head out to the lounge area and do some writing. A quick stop in the bathroom and then I tip-toe through the dark sleeping-berth area. Halfway, an arm reaches out and grabs me. Luckily, the other arm wraps around my mouth and stops the bloody-murder scream that was beginning to wail from my lips.

"Shhh," Flynn whispers into my ear and then hauls me up into his sleeping berth, drawing the curtain closed behind us.

My heart is pounding in my chest.

"You might want to keep quiet," he growls in my ear.

"But—" His hand comes back to my mouth, pressing gently.

"I thought I would help you figure things out." He glides his other hand down over my body and beneath my sweatpants, fingers coming to stop over the lace of my panties. "Can you keep quiet?" he asks, his voice strained and low.

I nod, but he doesn't immediately move the hand covering my mouth.

"When I slip my fingers inside you, can you keep quiet then?"

A muffled whimper escapes when he presses his fingers against my clit and begins to slowly rub tiny circles.

"When I fuck you with my fingers. When you're soaked and I'm pumping in and out of you. Can you keep quiet then?" His gritty voice at my ear sends a shiver through my body.

It's pitch dark in the small, curtain-concealed bunk, but I see the flash of need in the glow of his eyes. Longing ripples in my belly. One finger slips inside of me while his thumb continues to massage my clit—everything tingles, straight down to my toes.

"When I bury my face in your sweet pussy. Licking and sucking until I feel your body convulse around my tongue. Can you keep quiet then?"

His hand at my mouth clamps down harder, barely able to stifle my groan. My hips buck when he slips another finger inside me. He shifts to lie beside me.

"I'm going to take away my hand for a minute," he warns and waits for me to nod before moving.

His hand inside me slows while the other manages to undress me from the waist down. He pushes up my shirt and growls when he finds my erect nipples.

"Bend your knees. Pull your legs up and spread them wide for me." His head dips, his mouth sucking harshly on my nipple as he resumes the speed of his pumps between my legs. Wisely, the other hand moves back to cover my mouth.

My fingers dig into his hair, grasping handfuls, desperate to let out the burn flaring inside of me. Everything begins to spin, my mind forgetting anything exists except this moment.

Forgetting where I am.

Forgetting we could get caught.

Forgetting what's right and wrong.

My entire focus on one thing. This man.

The way he touches me.

His fingers inside me.

His heavenly, greedy mouth.

Biting.

Sucking.

His fingers pump harder. Furiously in and out.

The hand at my mouth clamps firmer.

I think I might burst.

And then abruptly his fingers slip out of me and his mouth leaves my breast. Only to drop lower, settling between my legs. There is no teasing first lick or promising suck. No. He just devours me. His tongue lashing out at my clit, sucking, licking, nuzzling.

"Oh god," Flynn's hand clamps down harder and catches the rest of my incoherent words. My body screams for release, stifled moans build. It's as if keeping it all silently inside me only increases the intensity at which I'm about to explode.

He spreads my knees wider, opening me completely to him as his fingers join his tongue and he licks in rhythm with his pumps. "You taste so fucking good." He pushes deeper and deeper.

My breaths grow short and shallow. Eyes roll toward the back of my head as I feel the wave crashing down upon me. My body trembles as I unfurl. Unravel.

The most powerful orgasm of my life takes over, everything else ceasing to exist. I cry out, sound muffled under his hand.

It takes a full five minutes before the last tremor runs through me and Flynn senses it's safe to free my mouth.

"Morning." He grins wickedly at me. "I just wanted to show you what I plan to have with my morning coffee every day."

Now *that* I could get used to.

Unfortunately, the twelve hours we spend on the bus after I slip unnoticed from Flynn's bunk are not nearly as incredible as the breakfast Flynn decided to have in bed. Dylan is in a bad mood, and the guilt I feel turns into a blaring headache. I throw together a quick dinner in the small galley of the bus, even though I don't really have an appetite.

Watching me push food around my plate with my fork, Dylan huffs loudly. "Not hungry again?"

"Not really."

"Did you take something for the headache?"

Do they sell anti-guilt pills? "No."

"The medicine cabinet in the bathroom is stocked. Take something. We should get in around nine. I have to do an appearance at Club Sixty-Six. Would be nice to go out and actually spend time together for a change."

I nod and force a smile.

Flynn walks in from the back—it's not a very big bus, but he seems to have successfully avoided us most of the day. Until now.

"There's ravioli in the pot on the stove top if you're hungry," Dylan grunts.

"Thanks. But I had a big breakfast."

I catch the glint in his eye, but Dylan seems oblivious. Flynn grabs a beer from the fridge and sits on the couch across from us. The closeness of the two men makes me nervous; the smirk at the corner of Flynn's mouth as he takes a long draw from the bottle makes me downright panicky. "Do you ever have breakfast for dinner?" he asks while I'm drinking from my water bottle. I almost choke. "I like my morning meal so much, sometimes I eat it twice a day."

A frown pulls at Dylan's lips. He wasn't in a good mood to begin with, and Flynn's presence doesn't do much to enhance it. "I skip breakfast most days," he mumbles, as if it's an annoyance to even have to respond.

Flynn's lips twitch as he brings the bottle to his mouth again.

Ten minutes later, Dylan declines a *Rockband* video game challenge in favor of taking a nap.

The minute the door to the back closes, Flynn grabs another beer and plops down next to me at the table. "Skips meals. Naps." He shakes his head ruefully. "Must suck to get old."

I crinkle up my napkin and throw it at his face. "You're in a devil mood tonight, aren't you?"

"Maybe." He shrugs. "Must have been the way my morning started."

"I think you should sit on the other side of the room."

"Can't keep your hands off me this close?" He takes my fork and pops a ravioli into his mouth.

"I thought you weren't hungry?"

"I wasn't. Guess I just get hungry for a good meal when I come closer to you."

A loud female moan comes from the back of the bus. Duff and his date were at it half the afternoon; guess he caught his second wind. The female voice gets louder. "Oh. Oh. Ohhhhh."

"Sounds like Duff might be having a late breakfast."

I feel my cheeks blush.

Flynn surprises me by getting up and pulling the door closed. Then he turns on *Rockband*, letting the sounds drown the rest of the moans out. He hands me one of the plastic guitars and waits for the game to start, not looking at me when he speaks. "New tour bus, huh?"

Of course, we didn't really have any discussion this morning, and the last time I walked away from him was after Dylan suggested I'd agreed to go on tour with him. "Dylan asked me to go on tour with Easy Ryder long-term. I didn't agree," I clarify.

The music starts up and Flynn begins to press the buttons on the guitar handle. He doesn't even have to focus much to hit all the notes. "He asked and you said no?"

Not exactly. "I suppose I didn't give him a definitive answer."

"What will your answer be? Is this how you see us a few months from now? When In Like Flynn joins Easy Ryder on the tour? Sneaking away when we can?"

I shake my head. I wish I had a better answer to give him. But honestly, I still have no idea how any of this will wind up playing out. I'm afraid to trust my heart blindly again.

He nods and says nothing more. We play together for hours, laughing and falling back into that comfortableness we've had since the first day we met. Only, we'd never let anyone see our true relationship. Eventually Duff and his date come out and join us, and the two guys battle it out on the guitars, cursing and drinking beer. It's not until Dylan walks back out into the lounge and eyes us strangely that I realize the relationship that Flynn and I have is starting to bleed through. We're no longer able to hide the bond that has grown between us, even when we try.

chapter
twenty-eight

Flynn

The last of my anonymity fades into oblivion as we walk into Club Sixty-Six in Vegas. In Like Flynn has toured before—I'd even been on TV—but after only a few weeks with Easy Ryder the vague recognition I was used to seeing on people's faces changed into instant identification.

Mick looks over at me as a group of women swarm us the minute we walk inside. Together we sign autographs on the way to the VIP area. More than one woman slips me her number. Instead of tempting me, it makes me wonder if Dylan really does indulge when Lucky isn't around. It's not really a question one can ask directly without raising suspicion.

"I can understand why no one brings their wives and girlfriends on for the whole tour," I say to Mick as we reach the bar and order two shots. We're the first two from the band here.

The bartender pours two tequila shots and Mick lifts one into the air with a toast. "Over the gums and down the hatch, keep the wives at home and collect the snatch."

I drink to his anthem with a chuckle, but then step out on a limb. "How is all that gonna work when Lucky's shacked up in the bus permanently?"

"It'll slow Dylan down, that's for damn sure. But I'd bet the bus it doesn't stop him from his visits with Jamie."

"Jamie?" I don't let on that Duff has already filled me in.

"Retired porn star. Been seeing her for a decade. Mark my words, Ryder will go missing one night while we're here in Sin City." He motions to the bartender for another round. "No ring is going to change that shit."

Ring? A figure of speech, I hope. "Him and Lucky aren't engaged."

"Not yet. Think he's planning on popping the question when we get out to LA."

I only realize how much I drank when I stand to go in search of a men's room and stumble up the step from the sunken bar. Turning back, I curse the step. "Who put that fucking thing there?"

Shit just goes downhill from there. Returning to the bar, I find Dylan, his arm wrapped around Lucky's tiny waist. Even the simple touch bothers me tonight. Maybe it's the familiarity his hands have on her body, I'm not really sure, but I find myself staring at his fingers. I've known what I was getting myself into from the get-go, yet anger bubbles from within tonight.

A petite young woman with dark hair, tan skin and pale blue eyes works at capturing my attention from a few feet away. Her eyes are so pale, with lashes so thick and dark, they hold me captive for a beat too long. She smiles, her tongue swiping over her glossed lips, then she leans in and whispers something to her friend.

My attention is diverted from the pretty little lady when Dylan says something to Lucky I can't hear and then kisses her on the lips. The alcohol has slowed my response time and, when he releases her mouth, he turns and finds me staring. His eyes meet mine, and in some sort of unspoken challenge, he turns back to Lucky and kisses her again. *Really* kisses her.

I clutch the beer bottle in my hand so tightly I'm surprised it doesn't break. Pale Eyes calls my attention away from the car accident in front of me. "Are you...Flynn Beckham?"

"That's me." I smile, turning on the charm. "And you are...let me guess...the woman with the most beautiful eyes I've ever seen."

Pale Eyes giggles innocently, but the way she's looking at me is in stark contrast to the sound. "I have tickets to the show tomorrow night." She takes a step closer and runs the nail of her pointer finger down my chest.

It's been a while, but it's just like riding a horse...so to speak. "And what are your plans for tonight?"

Her eyes light up and she cocks her head coyly. "Whatever you want."

Duff chuckles next to me. "Don't forget your old pal Duff." He turns to Pale Eyes' friend and says, "You and me should probably stay with them. Looks like they could use a chaperone."

If I wasn't feeling like such a selfish bastard at the moment, Lucky's face would shred me alive. Instead, I focus on the hand still wrapped possessively around her waist. I raise my eyes to meet hers before speaking to Pale Eyes, although my gaze doesn't leave Lucky's. "I'm starving. Haven't had anything to eat since this morning. What do you say we get out of here and take care of my appetite?"

Who knew blowing off a woman would be more difficult than picking her up? After a quick bite to eat, Duff is steering the ladies back to the hotel room we're sharing tonight, only I have no desire to join in on the festivities.

The elevator dings and the doors slide open at our floor. "Think you can host the party without me for a little while?" I ask, my arm holding the door in its pocket, allowing the trio to step out of the car, but I don't join them.

"You're not coming?" Pale Eyes giggles. "I was hoping we'd both be coming."

"I need to take care of something. Duff will entertain you while I'm gone. Right, Duff?"

Slinging an arm around each woman's neck, he grins from ear to ear. "You won't even know he's gone. I'm *that* good at entertaining."

I remove my arm, letting the elevator glide closed. After an hour with those two, I'm positive neither will be upset I have no plan on returning. A night with any member of the band and a signed-postcard departing gift would be enough. The face that came with the evening wasn't important to them.

Inside the lobby bathroom, I splash water on my face and stare at myself in the mirror. What the fuck am I doing? Everything I've ever wanted is right in front of me. Playing to sold-out stadiums, women with expectations of nothing more than a good time, traveling with a band of guys who are as passionate about music as I am. And I'm doing what? Leaving a very ready and beautiful woman and instead fucking up the chance of a lifetime by going down on the lead singer's girl while he sleeps five feet away.

Inhaling a deep breath, I gather my thoughts, tuck them away in the back of my mind and do the only thing I know I won't regret doing in the morning. Getting shitfaced in the bar.

The next morning I wake sprawled between two chairs in the dark lounge. Vaguely, I remember Brett trying to get me to vacate the bar at closing time, but by then I wasn't even capable of putting one foot in front of the other. A wad of bills stuffed in the bartender's hand later, I was in the quiet, dark bar—just me and my good old friend Jack. Daniels, to be specific.

A jolt of pain grips my skull as I straighten to upright. The new position arouses the slumbered headache that's been lurking in the back of my head. "Fuck," I grumble. My mouth taste like shit, my body aches from sleeping on a goddamn chair, and if the empty bottle wasn't next to me reminding me of just how much I drank last night, there's a good chance I'd think I had a brain aneurysm detonating in my head right now. Not to mention, my bladder might explode if I don't get my shit together and go in search of a bathroom.

Elbows on my knees, I drop my head into my hands and let a string of curses fly before finally standing my ass up. What the hell time is it anyway?

The artificial light in the hallway causes a throb behind my eyeballs. *That's new.* I squint to shield my retinas from the fluorescent glow and find the nearest bathroom. After relieving myself of a gallon of alcohol, I realize it's still early in the morning and I haven't slept for very long. Unfortunately, my natural alarm clock doesn't seem to have an off button, and has gotten me up somewhere between drunk and hung over. You're supposed to sleep through this shit.

Not surprisingly in the city that never sleeps, the lobby is alive. People come and go, some still sporting the dressed-up attire of the night before, others looking ready to start a new day. "Coffee?" I ask the woman at the front desk. She directs me to a nearby Starbucks inside the hotel.

I stop at the glass front door, peering in for a long moment before Lucky even sees me. Her eyes jump at the sound of the bells rattling to announce a new customer. Her beautiful face looks conflicted, a mix of relief and uneasiness. Exactly the way my insides feel. She offers a hesitant smile and drops her eyes to the table in front of her. Two coffee cups.

"Good morning," she offers uncertainly when I make my way over.

"That for me or your boyfriend?" My voice is flat, battling against the unevenness I feel inside of me.

She flinches. "It's for you."

I nod and take the seat across from her. We stare at each other, me trying desperately to hold on to my dignity and her reflecting back the pain I'd been clinging to as an excuse to wallow away my own sins since last night. The weight of the silence becomes too heavy. "Sleep good?"

"Not really. You?"

"Barely at all. I might have went at it a little too hard last night."

The facade she was putting up crumbles as she stares at me, speechless. Her lips screw in disgust. She abruptly stands. "I realize I'm not one to talk, but I don't need to hear the sordid details." She's striding away before I can replay exactly what I said that she misinterpreted.

Fuck.

I grab her arm. "I meant I went at *drinking* a little too hard last night."

Her face changes, but the anger only softens to hurt. The pain in her voice causes my chest to ache. "I'm sorry. I don't have any right...I...I should go," she whispers.

"I slept in the bar last night. By myself."

Her eyes are weary. "You don't have to explain..."

"I know I don't. But I want to." I lean in and lower my voice. "I watched him kiss you and I wanted to hurt you back." I search her eyes. "Did it hurt to think of me being with another woman?"

Her eyes are so expressive, she doesn't even need to respond verbally. "Yes."

"Then stay. Have coffee with me. Let me show you that starting our day off together is the way it's supposed to be for us."

She holds my gaze. I watch as a million thoughts fly through her mind until she lands on the one that matters. A small, but genuine smile tempts her lips and she sits back down. I breathe again.

We spend the next few hours sipping coffee and falling back into our daily routine. The hurt and fear behind us, I hate to leave our little bubble. I chance getting caught and weave her fingers with mine on top of the table before I speak softly. "I need you to choose. No more hiding. I want to kiss the hell out of you in public, whenever I want."

Her eyes jump to me. I'm determined to stand strong, keeping my gaze fixed and resolute. "We're leaving Vegas tomorrow night and then there's a break for a few days once we hit California. I want you all to myself. Go away with me. Tell him it's over before then. We'll figure it out after that. But I need you to choose, Lucky."

She considers my words, or more likely, the words I'm not saying. Choose me, or choose him. One or the other, because there's no going back anymore. We've crossed the blur line.

Uncertainly, she nods. I walk away with a knot in my stomach, knowing what she's likely walking into in L.A., if she doesn't choose me. Ryder is planning on making things permanent.

chapter twenty-nine

Lucky

Dylan has never been a neglectful boyfriend, but the flip side is, he's also not a very doting boyfriend either. Until today. It's almost as if he senses I'm on the threshold of making a decision about us and has decided to pull out all the stops. Or maybe he just feels guilty about having to leave tonight after the show for a business meeting up north with sponsors.

"I made us reservations for noon today. We have to be downstairs a half hour before that."

"Okay. I'll jump in the shower. What are we doing?"

"Helicopter ride over Grand Canyon."

"Really?" I've never been in a helicopter and it's been years since I visited the Grand Canyon.

"Yep." He smiles. "Figured between the bus and the hotels, you could use a little outdoors today."

"I love the Grand Canyon. My dad and I went camping there when I was fifteen. We'd always talked about going back someday, but never got around to it."

"I know." Dylan walks to me and wraps his arms around my waist. "I remember you telling me about it. Your whole face lit up, so I figured it would be a good choice for today. I haven't been making you smile enough lately. I'm going to work on that over the next week." He leans down and kisses me softly. "Go get ready, I know how long you can take."

I let the shower rain down on me, the heavy massaging pulses of water working to loosen my tense shoulder muscles. Hanging my head, I stare blankly at the water swirling around the drain. Dylan's right, he hasn't made me smile lately, but the truth is, I haven't given him the chance since the day Flynn Beckham walked into my life. Maybe today is just what we need. Just what I need to finally know I'm making the right decision as the bus rolls on to California tomorrow.

"We camped right down there!" I point to a clearing along the river's edge, yelling over the whirl of the chopper. There's a microphone built into the headset I'm wearing so that the pilot, Dylan and I can all hear each other.

Dylan reaches for my hand. "Maybe we'll go back one day."

The pilot dips to the left, taking my stomach with him and making me smile. Dylan catches my eye. "There it is. It's been hiding on me lately." He cups my face with his hand and runs his thumb back and forth on my cheek. The contact feels...nice.

The pilot's voice comes over our headset as he points out spectacular views—the Hoover Dam, Bypass Bride, Black Canyon. He brings us over an extinct volcano and then flies deep within the canyon for otherworldly views of the Colorado River running between multihued rock formations that are millions of years old.

I look down in awe of the natural beauty, a gift thoughtfully given by the man I've called my boyfriend for almost a year, and think to myself, *the shade of blue in the shallow part of the river is almost the exact same as Flynn's eyes.* It's at this moment I realize that although my brain may not have caught up yet, my heart has already made its decision.

The ride back to the hotel in the town car is quiet. Dylan's gaze is troubled when he calls my attention back from where I'm lost staring out the window. "Is everything okay, Lucky?" His forehead puckers to a frown that matches his lips.

"Yes," I lie. "I'm just tired. I've been having trouble sleeping. Guess I'm not used to being on the road anymore."

"It takes a while. But you'll get the hang of it. You need to stop getting up so early. You get out of bed like you're anxious to start the day."

I force a smile. "I'm just a morning person."

"Guess it's a good thing one of us is. Will come in handy when we have kids someday."

The frightened look on my face makes him frown. "What's wrong? You do want kids, don't you?"

"Sure. Someday. But that day is a long time away."

"I don't want to be forty-five when I start to have kids."

The ten-year age difference between us has never mattered. "I'm nowhere near ready to have a baby, Dylan."

"We'll have to negotiate that one."

"Negotiate?"

"Yeah." He raises my hand and pulls it to his lips, kissing the top as we pull up in front of the hotel. "Would it really be the worst thing in the world if you were pregnant now?"

Yes. It most certainly would.

I watch the show from my usual place on the floor, taking note of the jam-packed venue. Only a month ago, Easy Ryder wasn't selling out places as big as the MGM Grand Garden. Now ticket scalpers are getting twice the face value because the demand has spiked so high. Women in the audience are sporting T-shirts I've never seen before—the face of Flynn Beckham, not the usual Easy Ryder concert tee.

There's a noticeable shift in the air when Flynn sings the songs he leads. An energy that seemed to have been missing prior to his arrival. There's no playful banter between songs, like Linc and Dylan have, it's more of a necessary evil that Dylan tolerates. I watch Dylan's face as the crowd shrieks in delight when the limelight passes to Flynn for a song— he definitely doesn't appreciate all the newfound attention going to someone else.

After the show, I take my time going backstage, knowing that Dylan is being whisked off for his late-night dinner with the sponsor. He didn't ask me to join him tonight and I purposefully avoid running into him before he leaves so he doesn't have time to extend an invitation at the last minute.

I check in with Brett and tell him I'm going to hop in the first limousine that shuttles back to the hotel. Cars run back and forth after the show, taking roadies and guys from the band with their guests wherever they want to go. It all gets coordinated through the tour manager.

Avoiding the lounge area backstage, already filled with excited groupies, I slip out the black door and into the black stretch limousine that pulls up outside. The driver tells me it will just be a minute or two while he waits for a few more passengers that Brett radioed him to expect momentarily.

I'm texting back and forth with Avery when the door flies open and a man hops in. It startles me, but I quickly see why he's running. A gaggle of women are chasing after Flynn. He turns, not expecting to find anyone inside the sizeable back seat, and when he sees me sitting across from him, his trademark slow, lazy, smile washes across his face and he arches one eyebrow expressively.

"To the hotel, please. Too many fans out here."

The limousine pulls away just as Duff is walking out with one of the roadies and a few women.

"Waiting for me?"

I roll my eyes. "No. Running to me?"

He grins. "Always."

We stare at each other, and I watch the change in him occur right before my eyes. His mischievous smile turns heated, bordering on predatory. He calls to the driver, without breaking our gaze, "Can you drop us at the Wynn, please?

We're staying at the Bellagio a mile away. "In the mood to gamble?"

He shakes his head.

"See a show?"

Another slow shake.

"Dance?"

That's not it either.

"Dinner?"

"Only if we're having breakfast for dinner."

Oh my.

Neither of us says a word as Flynn whisks me from the reception desk to a suite, flipping the key around between his fingers impatiently as we board the elevator. When the elevator fills and half the panel illuminates with floors to stop at, he blows out an audible breath of frustration.

He pulls me against him to make room for an older couple, and his hard-on pokes against my ass. This time it's my turn for the audible breath. Flynn chuckles faintly and his fingers press into my hip as he nudges me against him even tighter.

Oblivious to everything around us except our growing need, neither of us realizes for a moment that the voice speaking is directed at us.

"Aren't you Flynn Beckham?" the woman says.

"No. But I get that a lot."

I laugh at his response and lean toward the woman and whisper, "He's not as cute as Flynn Beckham."

The fingers at my hip dig in a little harder.

A few more stops and we arrive on the seventeenth floor. With a swipe of the key, we're inside and don't bother to turn on the lights. The curtains on the floor-to-ceiling windows are wide open, the lights of the Vegas strip providing an oddly sensual backdrop as they flash and illuminate the dark sky.

Cupping my face tenderly in his hands, Flynn leans in and kisses me sweetly. He takes his time, his tongue exploring and hands sliding up my sides in a way that makes me feel worshiped.

He pulls back and looks at me. "I'm crazy about you." Eyes filled with sincerity, and something that takes my breath away, he reaches down and surprises me by hooking one arm beneath my knees and lifting.

His lips come back to mine again as he carries me to the bedroom and gently sets me down on my feet. "I want to take my time with you. No talking tonight. I'm going to *show* you how I feel about you."

We explore each other's bodies slowly. Listening to one another's breath as we trace the curves and feel the soft contours and hard ridges. His gaze caresses my skin so that I feel him warming my body, even when he's no longer touching me.

I kiss underneath his ear, the spot I've learned makes his body shiver. His tongue traces a path along my collarbone before his head dips lower and he takes my protruding nipple between his teeth and tugs.

I moan when he runs his finger from the top of my ass, his finger threatening at my rear, before sliding down and then up between my legs. A sinfully erotic groan echoes through the room when I lick the V on his lower abdomen, trailing my tongue from his hipbone down to his groin. With my head already low, I surprise him, taking him into my mouth.

"Lucky," he groans in warning, as if to say he won't be able to handle being inside of my mouth. I drop to my knees before him, his restraint only fueling my desire to see him lose control. Pulling back, but not all the way, I gently swirl my tongue around his tip and then loosen the suction around him as if I'm going to release him. But I don't. Instead, I wrap my fingers around the base of him and take him in as deep as I can, until my lips meet my fingers.

"Fuck. Lucky." His eyes darken as he watches me. Even though I can see the primal urge lurking just beneath the surface, he still holds back. So I suck harder. Deeper. Faster. Bobbing my head up and down until the room fills with a roar and the last bit of control he was trying to maintain shatters. His hands fist into my hair tightly and he begins to thrust into my mouth.

My own excitement grows as I hear him gasp for breath and he mutters all the things he's going to do to me when he has me beneath him. He tries to pull back before he releases, but I'm so turned on, the feel of his salty, warm finish might be enough to detonate my own spectacular orgasm.

Throwing back his head, his body trembling as he becomes undone, he releases into my mouth long and hard. I struggle to take it all, breathing jaggedly through my nose until his thrusts begin to slow and finally stop.

Then he lifts me from my knees, cradling my body in his arms, and holds me tight for a long time. Eventually, when our breathing returns to normal, he lays me on the bed and slips in behind me, his front to my back.

A few minutes later, his voice still hoarse from strain, he brushes my hair to the side and kisses my neck. "I thought I was showing you what I felt."

"Guess I had a lot to say first."

He chuckles. "Give me about five minutes, you won't be able to get a word in edgewise."

"Five minutes?" Half joking that he can retool and be ready again so quickly. He responds by pushing his already semi-hard erection up against my ass.

"Oh."

"The five minutes were for you, not for me."

The next time there is no race to lose control. Instead, it's beautiful and slow and everything he promised it would be. His eyes don't break from mine as he slides inside of me, not even as he brushes his lips tenderly against mine. And then we begin to move, a sensual and slow-burning rhythm that is so much more than just two bodies heading toward a magnificent finish. We're two souls colliding, rocking as one person, doing something I never realized I hadn't done before. Making love.

The rest of the night we speak only with our bodies, listening to each other's heartbeats, and truly feel each other in a way I've never experienced.

What I don't feel for once is guilt. Giving in to my emotions, allowing ourselves to truly let go and just be with each other leaves no room for anything else. There will be plenty of time for guilt tomorrow.

chapter thirty

Lucky

Not since I was fifteen and Avery and I snuck out to meet up with the Raven brothers at eleven on a school night have I felt so nervous creaking open a door to a place I'm supposed to already be inside of. I swallow a deep breath, attempting to calm my nerves. It almost works, but then I remember what happened when I returned from that decade-ago dalliance. Avery got her first real kiss with Kyle that night. I, on the other hand, walked straight into the angry glare of my father the minute the door opened. It was a solid two weeks before I saw the outside of our apartment again, aside from school.

Dylan isn't supposed to return until early this afternoon, but plans can change. Finally mustering enough courage to slip the key into the door, I brace myself for the consequences of my actions.

The room is dark.

I heave a sigh of relief when I flick on the lights and find the bed hasn't been slept in. Thankfully, I have a few hours to clear my head.

I'm in the middle of drying my hair in the bathroom when I hear Dylan call out my name. He's back early.

"Hey. I didn't think you'd be back for a few more hours." I force a smile as I step from the master bath to greet him, but my knees are actually trembling.

"Neither did I," Dylan bites out. *Uh oh.*

"Did the meeting not go well?"

He turns and stares at me, a very unhappy look on his face. "The meeting was fine. I felt guilty leaving you alone all night, so I came back early."

"Oh." I get the feeling he's angry with me, but I'm almost afraid to ask. "You didn't have to do that. I'm fine."

His jaw flexes and he turns away, emptying his pockets on top of the tall dresser. "So I've heard."

What's that supposed to mean? I don't respond, but I'm sure more is coming.

"What did you do last night, Lucky?" His tone tells me he's not making small talk. It's an interrogation, and I have the sickening feeling he already knows all the answers.

It would be the perfect time to come clean. I've dragged this out way too long already. Yet I can't seem to get the words out. Lies seem to flow from my lips with ease these days. "I gambled for a bit at one of the casinos."

His unrelenting stare makes me squirm, so I pretend to focus my attention on packing the blow dryer in my hand into my suitcase.

"At the Wynn?"

I freeze. I hate myself. What I've done is loathsome and vile. It was never meant to happen. I didn't mean to fall for another man. I wasn't looking, we just sort of found each other. And after last night, I finally realize that nothing can stop what is going on between Flynn and me. What we have is real, not a fantasy I'd spent years imagining.

"Yes, I'm sorry." I bow my head repentantly.

Dylan forks his fingers through his hair and edges over to me. He sighs loudly when I don't look up. "I'm the one who should be sorry. I fucked up."

Not what I was expecting.

My eyes jump to his, finding a pain that is familiar. Guilt? He places his hands on my shoulders and I wait for him to continue.

"I've been so preoccupied with the tour, how things are changing for Easy Ryder, I haven't given you the attention you deserve." He closes his eyes, and when he reopens them, remorse looms in the forefront. "I shouldn't have gone last night. It was a mistake." As if I didn't already feel like a horrible human being, he's apologizing for having to go to a business dinner, when I was with another man.

"You had a business dinner. I understand that. You didn't do anything wrong."

"I won't be going to any more business dinners. I promise." The declaration is so heartfelt, it feels like he's promising something much bigger. "You're what's important and I won't let you slip through my fingers. I'm going to fix things between us."

"Dylan. I...I need to tell you something." I steel myself with a deep breath and wipe my sweaty palms against my jeans discreetly.

A knock at the door interrupts what is about to be my confession.

He ignores it. "It can wait. Go on."

Like a coward, I cling to the interruption for a minute of reprieve. "It's fine, why don't you get it?"

Dylan lumbers to the door as the second knock comes. Just as I'm beginning to steady again, I hear the voice from the hall.

"Brett said you wanted to see me?" *Flynn.*

"I'm making some changes to the show," Dylan replies curtly and then looks back at me. Not a single muscle in my body has moved, I'm so tense. "But I'm busy right now. Lucky and I are"—the sneer on his lips grows to a full-blown self-satisfied smile as he adds—"going to enjoy our last few hours in a hotel room before we have to get back on the bus. I'll meet you in the lobby at three to talk."

If Flynn responds, it isn't audible, but the slam of the door makes me jump.

I convinced myself it was a bad idea to break things off with Dylan before he was going to have a sit-down with Flynn. Although the truth of the matter is, I'm just buying more time. I'm afraid that when I end things, Dylan will see right through whatever I say and know I've fallen for Flynn. And *that* won't be good. Dylan is already clearly bothered by the attention that Flynn's receiving. If he finds out we're together, it's Flynn who will pay the price.

The last show in Vegas is uneventful, and I'm anxious to speak to Flynn when they finish playing, but backstage is crammed with people and Dylan keeps me tight against his side. "Change of plans. Lydia flew in to tell Mick she got the all-clear from her doctor to try to get pregnant again." A few months ago she miscarried; I remember Dylan telling me she was really upset. "They want to go out to dinner to celebrate before the bus rolls tonight."

"Wow. That would be three, right?"

"Yep. We have a lot of catching up to do." Dylan nuzzles into my neck and I blanch, finding Flynn's eyes trained on me, watching us together from the other side of the room.

I down three glasses of wine at dinner, well aware that two is my max. Lydia and I spend most of the night talking about her two boys and plans to try to have a girl. But my mind keeps wandering back to Flynn. Before we leave, while Mick and Dylan are busy signing a few autographs, I take the opportunity to throw out a random question to Lydia.

"How did you know Mick was the one?"

"Wow, you get deep when you're inebriated." She smiles. "We dated casually for a while, both seeing other people. The band was taking off and we were young. When I was with Mick, I never thought about another man. But when I was with someone else and something funny happened, the first thought was always to call Mick and tell him. A nice guy could take me on a great date, yet I'd want to call Mick and tell him about something I saw." She sips her water. "My advice. Go to a comedy show or a place you've never been. If you don't have the urge to call him and tell him all the funny jokes you remember or something you saw, he's not the one."

The helicopter trip to the Grand Canyon immediately comes to mind. I was sitting next to Dylan, but couldn't wait to tell Flynn all about the things I saw when I got back.

It's almost two in the morning when we board the bus. The driver starts the engine as soon as the door closes behind us. "You want a few minutes to get settled before we get on the road, Mr. Ryder?"

Dylan looks at me. My stumbling will have nothing to do with the sway of the bus tonight. I shrug and head to the bathroom. The curtain on Flynn's sleeping berth is drawn, but I imagine snuggling up to him as I pass by. It physically hurts to know he's only feet away while I'm sleeping beside another man.

The next morning, I wake to an ache in my chest and throb in my head. It's as if someone ripped out my beating heart and reinserted it under my eyes so I can feel every painful heartbeat. Water. I need water. The alcohol left me severely dehydrated.

I make my way through the bus in the dark to the galley, hoping to find Flynn in his normal position, anxiously awaiting the coffee pot. Discovering the living area empty, I slump with disappointment. The clock on the microwave reads almost six—perhaps I'm a little earlier than usual.

Ignoring the nausea of a wicked hangover, I force down two bottles of water with a couple Tylenol. After an hour of staring at the door that leads to the sleeping area, I grab a blanket, curl up on the couch, and eventually the vibration of the bus lulls me back to sleep.

A soft kiss on my cheek wakes me. Groggy, I smile with my eyes still shut. "It's about time."

"Come back to bed."

My eyes spring open. *Not the voice I was expecting.* "What time is it?"

"Almost ten."

Pushing up with one elbow, my other hand rubs my eye. "I fell back asleep for almost four hours?"

"I guess so. I don't get why you jump out of bed so early anyway."

I look past Dylan toward the rear of the bus. It's quiet. "Is everyone still sleeping?"

He shrugs. "Come back to bed."

"Actually. I have something I wanted to work on before the bus gets loud." I hold up the notebook that must have fallen from my hands when I nodded off. "Do you mind?"

The muscles in Dylan's face tighten. "Whatever." Letting out a frustrated sigh, he retreats to the bedroom and slams the door.

My second cup of coffee does the trick, and with the aide of the Tylenol and water earlier, I feel human again sitting at the dining table in the galley. I'd hoped Flynn and I could have a few hours to talk this morning. Think about how we're going to handle things once I break up with Dylan. I reach up to the cabinet where Flynn seems to have a never-ending stock of Hershey's Special Dark for me, and find he's replenished my bars with bags full of Hershey's Special Dark chocolate kisses. My heart melts faster than the chocolate in my mouth.

Around noon, Duff stumbles from the back. "You still writing in that notebook?"

"I am."

"Why don't you write us some songs instead?" He pours himself a cup of coffee and collapses in the seat across from me, one hand fighting back his unruly morning hair.

"I'm not good with finding the music in my head."

"Me either. You need a partner, then. Someone who can put your lyrics to music."

"That's how my dad and mom actually met. He was a drummer but played a little of all instruments. They wrote my mom's bestselling song during an all-nighter the week that they met." I smile, thinking of how many times I heard Dad proudly tell that story.

"Maybe you and Dylan will become the next Simon and Garfunkel."

The truth is, music is the biggest thing we have in common, yet after all this time, we've never even thought of working together in any way. Unlike Flynn and I, who naturally gravitated to music to bring us closer. Maybe it's because Dylan's older and more experienced, but he and I have our roles—roles *he* defined for us. He's the rockstar, I'm his girlfriend. The picture he paints for our future becomes clearer and clearer the more time we spend together. The thing is…I want to paint too.

"I think Dylan's more of a soloist."

Duff snickers. "That's one way of describing the fame-hog bastard."

"He doesn't really share the limelight well, does he?"

"We've been friends since we're six years old. Fucker didn't even share his toys. Linc is the only one he never seemed to mind stepping aside from the stoplight for. Probably because the poor bastard is homely looking and there's no real competition there." Duff downs half his mug of coffee and makes a loud *ahhh* sound.

"How is Linc? Probably be tough to leave the babies in a few weeks and rejoin the tour."

"In a few weeks? You mean in a few nights."

"It's only the thirteenth. Flynn's filling in through the thirty-first."

"Guess boss man forgot to give you the memo."

"What memo?"

"Beckham's gone. Bus left him behind last night when we pulled out of Vegas."

Nausea threatens as I stand in front of Flynn's sleeping berth, curtain still tightly drawn. With a hollow feeling in my stomach that tells me Duff isn't just screwing with me, I slowly pull back the thick, dark fabric.

chapter thirty-one

Flynn— Yesterday

ylan Ryder strides from the elevator to the lobby with purpose, ignoring the heads that turn as he passes. The guy's had an issue with me before anything even started with Lucky, but today the scowl on his face is more hateful than most.

Coming directly to where I'm sitting, he tosses an envelope down on the table in front of me, eyes narrowing to crinkled slits. "Here's the change to the show."

I wait for an explanation, but he isn't offering one. Nor does he look like he plans to sit down. Unsealing the envelope, I shake the contents into my hand.

A plane ticket.

One way, back to New York.

Swallowing, I look back up and our eyes meet. His voice is stony, words spoken through gritted teeth. "I'm not fucking blind. The way you look at her."

I say nothing. Whether I like the guy or not, the least I can do is not play games and pretend I don't know what he's talking about. Plus, I have no idea how much he actually knows, and there's no reason to make it any more difficult for Lucky than it needs to be. She works at the record label he's been with for the last decade.

"Did you think I would put up with you sniffing around, trying to get into her fucking pants? Keeping her company while I'm taking care of business?"

I stand to meet him eye to eye. "Taking care of business? Is that what you call Jamie these days? You paying for her services, so it's considered a business transaction?"

"What I do is none of your damn business." An evil smile twists his lips. "But if want the best blow job you'll ever get in your life, stop by 3225 Honeycomb on your way to the airport to catch your flight tonight."

"You don't deserve a woman like Lucky."

"And you do?"

We glare at each other.

"Go back to New York. Now that Easy Ryder has made your pretty-boy face famous, there will be a line of women to suck your cock." He turns to walk away. "If you try to contact Lucky, your little band won't be opening for Easy Ryder, and the only gig you'll be able to book will be in a garage. And if she's stupid enough to be interested in you, you won't be the only one on the unemployment line."

"Fuck you."

He takes a few steps and turns back, a sadistic smile on his face. "Flight leaves at midnight after the show tonight. Be on it."

chapter thirty-two

Lucky

"Where's Flynn?" Reaching over where Dylan's soundly sleeping, I tug the bottom of the blackout shade so it rolls up with a loud snap, revealing the large rectangular back window of the bus.

"Good morning to you too." He squints from the flood of light.

"Did you kick Flynn off the tour?"

He pulls the cover over his head and tries to ignore me.

"Answer me."

Nothing.

I tug at the cover. "Answer me."

"What the fuck, Lucky?" he shouts, springing upright.

"Did you or did you not kick Flynn off the tour?"

The muscles in his face tighten. "Linc is coming back."

"So sending him home had nothing to do with me?"

He glares through angry eyes. "You tell me, Lucky. Does it?"

My irritation flickers while I hold his indignant stare. A silent standoff ensues until Dylan finally rips the covers back in a huff and rises, ramming his bare feet into his jeans before storming out of the bedroom.

An hour later, I'm still sitting in the bedroom when he comes back in. He rakes his fingers through his hair and I wait through another lengthy silence. My mind is a whirl of questions, most of which I probably shouldn't ask.

Finally, he sits. His voice is low. "We're going to be at the next stop in an hour."

I nod.

He blows out a loud stream of air. "I asked Linc to come back early."

"Why?"

"Because." I'm still not looking at him, so he moves from beside me to kneeling in front of me, leaving me no choice but to face him. When I look up, he continues. "I want to be with you, Lucky. I want to settle down, have a couple of kids and plant roots somewhere."

"I'm...I'm not ready for that."

"You're just nervous. That's all."

I shake my head. "No. It's more than that."

He searches my eyes. "Then what is it?"

"I'm not sure about us, Dylan."

"You were sure last month."

"Things change."

"What changed?"

Dawning realization hits and his eyes narrow to accusing slits. "You have feelings for Beckham?"

I lower my head and nod.

"He's a snake. Slithering in and giving you attention when I'm too busy running a fucking tour."

"It's not his fault."

"Don't give me that shit. I saw the way he followed you around. He wanted in your pants. That's why I sent him packing."

"I'm sorry."

"Let's just move past this. He's gone. We both have baggage. It's time for a fresh start. To build our future on a clean slate."

I don't respond. With two fingers under my chin, Dylan gently lifts until our eyes meet again. "I love you, Lucky."

"I'm sorry," I whisper.

"You're sorry? What the fuck does that mean?"

I remain silent, but words aren't necessary.

"You have got to be fucking shitting me." He stands. "Think long and hard about what you're doing, Lucky. You can walk away from me if you want. But just try to walk to Flynn fucking Beckham, and not only will his band not be opening for Easy Ryder, but I'll be damn sure he doesn't play anywhere for a long, long time."

Seething, he slams the door behind him so hard, the walls of the bus shake from the force.

I stay in the back after the bus pulls into California. It's so quiet without the hum of the engine and radio blaring, it makes me wonder if I'm the only one left on board.

Wheeling my bag out into the lounge, I discover I'm not the last one on the bus. Dylan lifts his eyes to meet mine. "Give me tonight?" There's a vulnerable tone to his voice that I've never heard before. "I have to do an interview this afternoon, but let's have dinner afterward. Let's talk."

As much as I'd rather get on a plane this afternoon, run away from my guilt, the right thing to do is to end things like adults. I nod.

The car ride is uncomfortably quiet on the way to the restaurant. Dylan stares out the window, tugging at the collar of his shirt, seemingly as lost in thought as I am. It surprised me when he told me to dress for dinner, surprised me even more when he slipped on a jacket and tie.

The driver pulls up outside Chateau La Roque and Dylan tells him not to get out. Instead, he opens the door at the curb and offers me his hand.

"Thank you."

"You look beautiful." Lacing our fingers together, he walks us into the trendy French restaurant. I'm shocked he picked such a public place for us to talk, knowing the topic we will be ultimately discussing.

"Mr. Ryder," a man with a thick French accent says. "Right this way."

After we're seated, the first ten minutes are filled with awkward small talk. It reminds me of a bad blind date.

"Dylan," I say at the same moment he says, "Lucky."

"You go first," he offers with an appeasing smile.

"I just wanted to say I'm sorry. I'm not sure what happened along the way, but I'm sorry. You've never been anything but kind to me." I truly mean it. I hate myself for what I've done.

He takes my hand into his. "Me too. I'm sorry for a lot of things. First and foremost, for not giving you the attention you deserve. But that's going to change. This afternoon, the thought of losing you made me realize how stupid I've been—"

"You didn't—"

"Let me finish, I need to get this out. I waited too long already." He stands. And I must be the most clueless person on the planet...because I'm watching the entire thing unfold right before me, and yet I still don't see it coming.

He takes something from his pocket.

The next thing I know...he's bending down on one knee.

Oh my god. No. This cannot be happening.

I hear gasps around the crowded restaurant, and then his words through a fog. "Lucky." He clears his throat. "I've written hundreds of songs, yet I don't know the right words to tell you how much you mean to me. I was planning on doing this once we got down to LA, but today I realized I've already waited too long. I know you aren't ready for marriage and kids tomorrow, but I'm willing to wait. Until then, I want you to have my ring on your finger to remind you every day how much I love you."

I don't even notice tears are falling from my cheek until his thumb wipes them away. "Don't cry." He smiles at me, mistaking my angst for tears of joy. "I know what I want. Be my wife, Lucky. Not today or tomorrow. But promise me, someday?"

"Dylan." My wary voice cracks as I pull him up from his knee to stand. I can't do this to him publicly. Two minutes later, the entire restaurant is clapping and snapping pictures.

chapter thirty-three

Flynn

"**A**rghh," I groan. Cracking one eye open, I scan the room, grateful when I realize I'm at Becca's and not in an alley somewhere. How the hell did I get here? I try to recall the last twelve hours: Nolan's apartment for a few beers, Molly's Irish Pub for a few more, then over to the Royal in Union Square when people started to recognize me. That's where things start to get fuzzy. I remember the long bar, a cute bartender named Alexa...and wall-to-wall TVs.

Shit. The TVs. There must have been forty of the damn things. Every single one of them flashing the same news story. A picture of douchebag Dylan Ryder down on one knee, then of Lucky hugging him.

I moved to hard liquor after that. Tequila. Plenty of it, too.

It takes a few minutes before I piece together the bits and pieces that followed. Nolan. And the redhead. She had a deep voice. I vaguely remember teasing Nolan to check for an Adam's apple before taking her home with him. What came next?

The redhead's friend.

Shit.

Bella? Belinda? Beth? Something with a B. I think.

I remember the four of us stumbling out the door at closing time. What the hell did we do after that? Betsy? Bianca? Bailee?

Dragging my ass out of bed, I answer Mother Nature's call and splash some cold water on my face. My head feels like I ran into a Mack truck last night. It's a distinct possibility, for all I know. Headed back to my sister's guest room, I abruptly halt when I hear her voice.

Barbara? Brooke? Bridget?

Skittishly, I head to the kitchen in search of the women's voices.

"Good morning, sunshine." My sister arches a brow. "How you feeling?"

"Like I look."

The woman from the bar last night smiles like it's normal for her to be sitting at my sister's kitchen table.

"Hey," I tentatively offer.

"I'm glad you woke up, sleepyhead." She gets up from the table, pushes up on her toes and kisses me on the cheek. "I have to get to work, but I didn't want to leave without saying good-bye."

"Umm...I'll walk you out." In the hallway, I try to fill in some more blanks. "Where did we go after the Royal?"

"You don't remember?" She looks surprised. I must have faked sobriety pretty damn good.

I shake my head.

"Some karaoke bar, across town."

Shit. "Lucky's?"

"Yeah. That was the name of it."

"I'm sorry." I drag my fingers through my hair. "I don't remember a thing after leaving the Royal."

She smiles. "You were pretty lit. But nothing much happened. Except you sang."

"I sang at Lucky's?"

She nods.

"Do you remember what I sang?"

A few things. "An old Tom Petty song, a Springsteen song and a Dave Matthews one I never heard of."

I don't have to ask the songs. "You Got Lucky," "My Lucky Day" and "So Damn Lucky."

"Did we...?" I motion between us.

"Nope. Not for my lack of trying either." Her cheeks pink up. "You weren't interested."

"I'm sorry...it's not you...I..."

She holds up a hand, motioning for me to stop. "It's okay. You told me all about her."

"I did?"

She nods.

"She's a lucky woman. You were a perfect gentleman, even in your state. I slept on your sister's couch because I was worried about you getting home, but then you didn't want me traveling by myself at night."

"Well, thank you."

She takes the phone I'm holding in my hand, punches a bunch of buttons and offers it back to me with a sweet smile before turning to leave. "In case you ever want help getting over her."

Walking back into my sister's apartment, I look down at the name she's typed into contacts. "Zoe." I was close.

A long shower, even longer nap and a half gallon of water later, I feel halfway normal. Becca's getting dinner ready. "Sorry about bringing Zoe here last night." My sister's never laid down any house rules, I just don't want Laney to get the wrong impression.

"I'm pretty sure she brought you home, not the other way around."

"Yeah. Guess I got carried away with myself."

"I thought you were going to be gone a few weeks more."

I rub a hand over the three days of stubble on my chin. "So did I."

"I saw Lucky on the news last night. That have anything to do with it?" she asks cautiously.

"I did something I'm not proud of."

"You fell in love. I saw that when I was there."

"Yeah. That still doesn't make it right."

"Neither of you were married. Don't compare yourself to him. I know what you're doing."

"Thanks. But looks like that's about to change."

"I saw the picture in this morning's paper. I don't care what the news prints, that woman's as in love with you as you are with her. Did you speak to her yet?"

"Douchebag Dylan threatened to get her fired from her new job if I spoke to her."

"Douchebag Dylan? Is he related to Professor Douchebag?" Becca bumps her shoulder into mine.

"They're like long-lost brothers."

"You need to talk to her. Something isn't right."

chapter thirty-four

Lucky

Music has always been the medicine to cure all of my ills. But these days, it's also the source of much of my anxiety. The cab line stretches almost a full city block in length outside of JFK; Pandora blasts through my headphones as I attempt to occupy my spinning mind with a soothing melody. But of course, the song that comes on would have to be an Easy Ryder song.

Things didn't go exactly as planned. After Dylan's proposal in the restaurant, and my not-exactly-yes-or-no hug, half the restaurant, it seemed, came over to congratulate us. I didn't want to embarrass Dylan in public and say no while phone cameras were clicking and rolling, but it made clarifying that I hadn't said yes that much more difficult. Especially when he pulled me in for a deep kiss and ordered a bottle of Cristal *for every table in the restaurant*, to celebrate.

It wasn't until we went back to the hotel and were in the privacy of our room that I had the chance to set things straight. Needless to say, Dylan did *not* take it very well. Barely two hours after his loving proposal, the man who was prepared to spend the rest of his life with me was threatening my job. And worst of all, Flynn's music career.

I hopped the first available flight the next day and spent six hours deliberating what to do about Flynn. If there is one thing I'm certain about as I walk away from Dylan Ryder, it's that his threat to destroy

Flynn was not idle. For some reason, he's had it out for the man before he even learned that I had feelings for Flynn Beckham. I'm thankful he doesn't know the half of it.

"Well, look what the cat dragged in." Avery wipes down the top of the bar. It's early; only a few college students from down the street are in Lucky's.

I glance around the bar with intentional exaggeration. "What did you do with all my patrons?"

She throws the wet towel she's using to clean the counter at my face. "Nice response to my texts."

"Sorry, it's been a crazy few days. Just got in last night."

"And you were too busy to send a one-line text?"

"I didn't know what to say. Where to start."

She leans over the bar. "How about starting with *Hey, I'm marrying one rockstar and fucking another.*"

Well, that certainly caught the attention of the few people sitting within earshot. I shake my head and walk behind the bar, wrapping my arms around my best friend for a much-needed hug. "God, I didn't realize how much I needed this," I sigh.

"Two men *and* a hot babe like me? You're a nymph. You might need therapy," she teases.

"I definitely do. The Avery Logan kind. Can Jase cover the bar for a while?"

"I always knew Ryder was a sleazeball." Avery and I are in the alley behind Lucky's, camped out on milk crates as she smokes her daily *I don't smoke anymore* cigarette.

"Umm. I think in this case, you have it reversed. I'm the sleazeball."

"Well, yeah. That too." She grins. "But he's going to try to ruin your career and Flynn's to get even. Besides, I'd bet your half of the bar he cheated on you."

"How is that a bet...you're betting my half of the bar?"

"If I learned something since you were gone, it's that I *do not* want to own this thing without you."

"You missed my sleazeball self, didn't you?"

"It does kinda suck without you here to boss me around."

We laugh. God, I missed her. Missed this place. Even the back alley that smells like month-old stale beer mixed with cigarette butts. It may not have a white picket fence around it, but this place is my home.

"You need to tell Flynn what's going on."

"How can I? Dylan will definitely kick In Like Flynn off the tour if we're together now."

"Shots of Dylan down on one knee and you hugging him have been all over the news. Flynn thinks you're engaged, Lucky. You need to tell him the truth."

"I don't know. What if his decision is to be with me anyway and Dylan makes good on his threat? He'll lose the tour...and who knows what else."

"It's his decision to make."

"Honestly, I can't imagine he believes I would say yes to Dylan's proposal anyway, after the last month."

"I wouldn't be too sure of that."

I squint. "What are you not telling me?"

"He was here last night."

"At Lucky's?"

She nods.

"Was he looking for me?"

"Not exactly."

"Stop being cryptic. He came in and didn't ask for me?"

"He wasn't exactly in a sober state."

"Oh."

"Although he was definitely thinking about you."

"How do you know?"

"Jase cut him off after the third song about Lucky was slurred pretty bad."

"Oh."

"There's more." Avery digs her cigarette pack out of her bag and jiggles it so one falls halfway out, extending the offering to me.

I shake my head. I hate smoking.

"He came in with a woman."

"A woman?" It's crystal clear what she's telling me, but I make her spell it out anyway.

"She was all over him. They left together, too."

I light that cigarette she's still offering.

chapter thirty-five

Flynn

"**W**ant a beer?" Nolan yells from the fridge to where I'm still crashed on the couch from last night.

I pick up my cell to check the time. "Dude, it's ten in the morning."

I hear the bottle crack open and then footsteps shuffling toward the couch. Sensing a body near, I open one groggy eye, and instantly regret it. His junk is swinging in the wind. "Put some fucking pants on."

He shrugs and takes a long draw from the dark-green Heineken bottle. "You know, I've pretty much had my bare ass on every surface in this place."

I pull up the blanket and attempt to ignore him, but of course, that's pretty much impossible.

"Yep. Yesterday I was sitting right about where your head is now. Scratched my balls for a while watching the Kardashians. Then let 'em dangle to air out."

"I'm not sure what's more disturbing, the thought of your dirty ass sitting right where my face is, or you watching the Kardashians."

Another long tug on his beer, followed by a rueful sigh. "That Kim has some ass. You know what I would do to that thing?"

"Can we not talk about you wanting to pound an ass while your baloney is staring me in the face, please."

"I'm beginning to think you like baloney…seeing as how you've turned down every honey pot that's come your way the last few days."

"You're a dick. You know that?"

"Yep," Nolan says proudly.

"Don't you have company to go entertain?"

"Left."

"Couldn't satisfy 'em?"

"Had to leave 'em able to walk." He chugs the rest of his morning beer—breakfast of champions. "They're bowlegged now, but they should be able to make it two blocks to catch the seven train."

"In your dreams."

"No, man, that's the thing…I'm *living* the dream. Unlike your sorry ass. If you weren't such a chick magnet, I wouldn't even hang out with you. Seriously. You're pathetic these days."

"Fuck off."

"Actually, this works out better for me. You're like one of those cute little dogs women love. You know, the kind a man would only be walking in the park with because he's pussy whipped. The chicks come over to pet it because it's so fucking ugly they think it's cute with that mop of stupid hair. But when they reach down, the little pebble-shitting canine bites her manicured hand." He grins and nods while he continues. "And I'm right there to console the pretty little lady."

"You're seriously disturbing."

"Wonder if Lucky likes puppies."

I bolt upright. "Screw you."

"Hit a nerve, did I?"

"Could you put some fucking clothes on!"

"Can you lighten up a little?"

"A woman I'm in love with got engaged. To someone else." I tear the blanket off and stand, rising to my full height so we're eye to eye. "I'm entitled to be an asshole for a couple of days."

Nolan flaunts a shit-eating grin. "At least you admit you love her now."

"A lot of good that will do me."

"We all told you the other day, we don't give a shit about opening for Easy Ryder. We get kicked off, something else will pop. Didn't like that fucker the first time I met him anyway."

"She's marrying the asshole."

"So you, what, give in?"

"What do you want me to do?"

"Quit being a damn pussy and fight for her."

I scowl at him, but he doesn't back down. "Try not to be drunk for our three o'clock tour-planning meeting at Pulse." I swing open his front door hard, letting it slam into the wall behind it, and don't bother to shut the thing behind me.

I glance down at the time on my watch as I push through the glass revolving door at Pulse Records. I'm ten minutes early, and since Nolan will likely not show until half past three, I probably have another forty minutes to wait before we start the meeting.

I told myself I wasn't going to look for her. In fact, the usual me would be late and I wouldn't have time to even consider stalking. Yet somehow I miraculously find myself heading down the hall to the studio I know she gives her lessons in.

Three days it's been since I last saw her.

If feels like a year.

The long hall is filled with mostly dark rooms. Until I get to the last one on the left. Bright light shines through the glass window. I'm not even sure if she's back from the west coast. Obviously, with me gone, there's no need for a coach any longer. Although maybe she decided to stay on the tour with *her fiancé*. The thought seriously causes a painful tightness in my throat.

Not wanting to be seen, I stand almost flat against the wall next to the door and lean my head forward just enough to peer in.

She's standing in front of a woman, motioning with her hands for the student to lift up at her chest, instructing her to sing through her diaphragm. Lucky's back is to me, but it doesn't matter, the tightness in my chest eases just from seeing her again. I may have been fighting the words that slipped out at Nolan's house today, but fuck if it isn't true. My body can't deny what it feels for her. It's been dead for three days and suddenly, just knowing she's on the other side of the door, it comes alive again.

But when I see her throw her head back and laugh, it feels like I got punched in the gut. She's at work—I know from experience that she enjoys teaching—yet for some reason, it's as though everything I thought we had must have been a lie. How can she be laughing when I've been walking around feeling like my dog died?

Of course, it's at this moment that my phone, which never rings, decides to go off. I narrow my eyes at Nolan's stupid grin flashing on the screen and swipe the call to decline. But the sound catches the attention of the student and teacher and I swiftly pull my head back against the wall. A minute later, light singing returns, so I chance one last glance and my eyes meet those of her student. Reluctantly, I head to my meeting before I get caught.

Upstairs, I'm surprised to find Nolan already in the lobby for our meeting. "It's only three." I stride past him and head to the reception desk. He follows me.

"I thought the meeting was at three?"

"It is. But I figured you wouldn't show for at least half an hour."

He grins. "Someone has to be the responsible party in this band."

I want to be pissed off, but I can't…he's just such a wiseass. With a chuckle, I say, "The last time we left any real responsibility to you, you ordered us ten thousand In Like *Finn* T-shirts."

He shrugs. "I don't see why you made a big deal out of that. You could have just changed your name to Finn."

"They were all ladies' size double XL."

"I like my ladies on the voluptuous side."

I snicker. "I give up. Let's go do this meeting, jackass." Arms hooked around my pal like we're back in elementary school, I follow the receptionist with the nice ass to the conference room, feeling like maybe, just maybe, things will turn out right in the end. The feeling is short-lived when we turn the corner and the glass fishbowl-like meeting room comes into my line of sight. A man I definitely was not expecting to see today is sitting at the table. Dylan damn Ryder. And he's smiling at me like a wolf about to pounce on a lame lamb.

chapter thirty-six

Lucky

"Thank you for helping out tonight." Avery lifts the security gate from the front of Lucky's and fiddles with the lock on the front door that has been sticking for more than ten years.

"Of course. It's not like I have a social life anyway."

"The way you look tonight, you *could* have a very busy social life. Maybe try smiling once or twice, so you don't look like you bite. You'll be all set." My best friend showed up at my apartment unannounced a few hours ago, declaring that if I wasn't going to *feel* good, she was going to at least make damn sure I *looked* good. So over a glass of wine, we raided my closet and I let her do my hair and makeup like we were back in high school. I wasn't into it at first—I actually did it to make her feel better. I've been so down, and she's been trying so hard, I wanted her to think she helped. But by the time we were done, she'd succeeded in not only making me look better, but actually feel a little better too.

Inside Lucky's we work like a well-oiled machine, restocking the bar, righting the upside-down chairs. When we're all set up, I sit on the other side of the bar while Avery counts out the register.

"I miss him like crazy," I sigh.

"I know." She pours me a glass of wine. "You need to talk to him."

"I don't want to ruin his career. Look at my mom and dad. He gave up everything to give me a life he thought was right for me. She walked away from us."

Avery pours herself a glass of wine and walks around the bar to sit next to me on a stool. "Your dad loved you more than anything on this earth. There was never a day he questioned if he made the wrong choice. Your mom made her choice, too. That's the thing...it was *their* choice to make and they both did what worked for them. You're not giving Flynn that chance."

"But what if he chooses me and stays for a year and then decides he made the wrong choice?"

"Like Iris did."

I nod.

"Is that what you're really afraid of? That he'll lose the tour and a year later he'll up and leave you for another one? That he'll break your heart?"

"I don't know."

"You didn't worry about the future with Dylan."

"I don't think I was ever really in love with Dylan."

She smiles. "It's about time you admitted it. I'm not sure what makes me happier, that you're in love or that you never loved Sleazy Ryder. But either way, you need to talk to Flynn. Otherwise *you'll* be the one wondering *what if* your whole life."

I raise my glass to her. "Thank you."

"For what?"

"For just being you."

"Remember that thought later," she mumbles cryptically and heads to the front door to officially open.

"What the heck does that mean?"

"Nothing," she throws back over her shoulder. But from her tone, I can tell that her fingers were crossed.

Before you're pregnant, you never notice all the strollers when you walk through the park. But then suddenly you see them all. It's not that they weren't there before, your brain just didn't point them out to you. Which is likely why it feels like every song is an anthem for love or breaking up tonight.

"If I hear one more song about losing the love of your life tonight, I may pull the plug," I yell over the bar while Avery makes my drink order. A blue-haired twenty-something is ruining Jewel's "You Were Meant for Me" on stage. But the lyrics taunt me.

Avery sings the chorus loudly (and completely off-key) in my face as she loads the drinks onto the table.

You were meant for me
And I was meant for you.

I stick up my middle finger and turn to deliver drink orders to table number eight.

It's almost midnight, the bar is near capacity, and I'm helping Avery behind the bar when a murmur comes over the crowd. A gaggle of women make a beeline for the door, a sure sign that a celebrity has just walked in. Even years after my father's death, it's not unusual for musicians to walk in and hang out. Lucky's truly has had some legendary musical guests stroll in unannounced.

"Who do you think it is?" I ask Avery as she looks toward the swarm of women blocking our view. It must be someone big; half the bar has taken notice.

"Ummm…" Avery bites her lip. "I might have stolen your phone earlier and invited…"

Suddenly, the figure the crowd has been hiding comes into view.

Dylan.

I turn to my best friend. "You invited Dylan?" I feel completely ambushed.

"No! I didn't invite him."

Dylan steps to the bar. Unsure of what to do, I remain frozen in place. We didn't exactly leave things on good terms. Unless calling me a whore and threatening to ruin my and Flynn's careers could possibly be considered a warm send-off in some strange universe.

"Can we talk?" Dylan asks with a weary expression.

I purse my lips together, but then nod. Avery grabs my arm, stopping me as I'm about to walk out from behind the bar.

"Lucky, you need to know something."

"What? You *did* invite him here?"

"No. But I invited Flynn to come tonight."

"You what?" My voice screeches.

"I might have told him you were miserable and said if he was miserable, too, you would be at Lucky's tonight."

After the initial shock of betrayal wears off, my stomach sinks at the realization that Flynn hasn't shown up tonight. Even though my mind is whirling, I know I need to process one thing at a time. While Flynn may not have shown up, Dylan *is* standing ten feet away. "I'm going to go out back where we can have privacy."

She nods.

Dylan's security clears the way to the back door and guards the exit as we slip into the alley.

"What are you doing here?"

He looks down at his feet. "I came to apologize."

When I say nothing in response, he lifts his eyes to mine. "For the things that I called you." He rubs the back of his neck. "Look, Lucky. I pushed you too fast. I get it now. But you hurt me. One minute I thought you said yes and the next you were taking it back."

"I didn't want to say no in the restaurant and embarrass you. I told you that."

"I know. I get that now. I can even appreciate it. But in the moment, I just wanted to hurt you back. So I said some pretty shitty things to get you back."

I nod. "Apology accepted. And I'm sorry, too."

He reaches out and takes my hand into his. "For what?"

"For the way things turned out. For everything." The guilt inside me escapes through tears.

Dylan takes it to mean I regret that things ended, rather than that I regret *the way* things ended. "Let's take a step back. I want to be with you, Lucky. I'll wait till you're ready."

He totally doesn't get that I'll never be ready to be with *him*. I've shown this man so much disrespect, it's time to be honest. "My feelings have changed, Dylan. I don't want to go back or forward. I'm sorry. I really am."

Rejection is definitely not something Dylan Ryder is used to. Shock registers on his face, then slowly morphs into something else. "It's because of *him,* isn't it? You really want to be with him?" He doesn't hide the utter hatred in his voice.

I nod. "But I haven't spoken to him since he left the tour. Please don't take it out on him and ruin his career because I fell in love."

"What?" he seethes.

"I'm sorry. It just happened."

"You're in love with that long-haired poser and you didn't *mean* for it to happen?"

I nod, and don't even attempt to try to tell him Flynn isn't a poser.

"So his dick just accidentally fell inside you?"

I have no idea if he knows for sure that we've been intimate, but he's lashing out and it doesn't matter at this point. I take it because I deserve it.

"I trusted you. I was going to make you my wife, for fuck's sake." His expression is filled with rage.

I'm relieved when he swings open the door and begins striding across the bar.

Until I see the man who's just walked in.

Flynn.

chapter thirty-seven

Flynn

After rereading her text for the hundredth time today, I walk into Lucky's with Nolan. She's miserable. I'm miserable. This is just fucking stupid. I know she loves her new job, but she's talented—any record label would be an idiot not to hire her. In fact, now that I'm in search of a new label for In Like Flynn, maybe we can set up a two-for-one deal.

My newfound fame delays my entry and I sign a dozen autographs as I try to make my way inside. Scanning the bar, my eyes find Lucky coming in from the back hallway. At first, I feel an overwhelming sense of relief just being in the same room as her. But then I squint and the sadness in her face comes into focus. It looks like she's been crying.

Brushing past the women swarming me, I'm focused on only one thing. Getting to Lucky and making her feel better.

Which is probably why I don't see the first punch coming.

chapter thirty-eight

Lucky

It all happens so quickly. One minute I'm walking back into the bar, Dylan a few angry steps ahead of me, then next I catch sight of a man I've been dying to see, yet suddenly dread being here. I watch the whole thing unravel, unable to stop it. My screams go unheard over the sound of the karaoke song blaring from the speakers.

Flynn registers me, but unfortunately doesn't see Dylan coming. The first punch lands square on his jaw, and I watch in horror as his head whips to the side from the force of the blow.

He staggers back, his hand going to his face, momentarily confused.

"You two fucking deserve each other. A whore who belongs on stage but doesn't have the balls, and a wannabe who has more balls than talent."

"Say what you want about me, motherfucker." Flynn's voice is eerily flat. "I probably deserved that first punch. But don't talk about Lucky that way."

Finally pushing past Dylan's hulking security, I scream again for them to stop, just as Flynn's fist connects with Dylan's nose and blood sprays everywhere.

The security team that was just standing there watching the chaos ensue finally jumps in when they see their guy get hit. Mayhem erupts and there's screaming and shouting, but the two men are at least separated.

"Get out!" I point in the direction of the door and scream at Dylan.

"No problem," he sneers, and wipes his nose with a towel one of his security got from somewhere. "Enjoy your fucking unemployed boyfriend, whore." He storms away, flanked by his guards.

Flynn's chest is heaving, but his eyes are glued to me. I don't know what to say or do. What other havoc could I bring down on this wonderful man? "I'm sorry," I whisper.

"Cell phones are snapping pictures a mile a minute and the cops are probably not far away." Flynn's friend Nolan tugs at his arm. "Let's get out of here."

"Wait," Avery shouts. I didn't even realize she was next to me. She tosses something to Nolan and he catches it. "Lucky's place. She'll meet him there in a half hour."

Flynn looks at me. He's hesitant to leave, so I give him a nod of assurance. "Go. I'll meet you there."

Only fifteen minutes later, the bar returns to normal, although there's still a buzz in the air and lots of whispering and staring at me. At least the cops didn't show up.

Avery hands me a shot of a gold-colored liquid. I don't bother to ask what it is. "This is for your nerves." She holds it up and tips her small glass in my direction. I return the sentiment. As soon as the burning in my throat calms, she takes the glass from my hands and looks me in the eyes, speaking with a stern tone. "Go home."

I pull her in for a hug, and afterward, she holds my shoulders, her voice apologetic. "I had no idea Dylan would show up."

"I know."

"Now go home and fix things with that mouthwatering man."

I smile and *finally* take my best friend's advice.

My hand shakes as I put the key into the lock of my apartment door. It's dark, and for a split second, I think he might not have showed. But then I hear his voice.

"So I take it you're not engaged anymore?"

I turn the living room light on and my heart leaps into my throat seeing him sitting on my couch. There's a bruise on his cheek and his jaw is already swollen. "Let me get you some ice."

Seeing as I don't find myself injured often, I don't have an ice pack. So I grab a bag of peas and sit next to Flynn on the couch, holding it to his face. He hisses at the contact. "Hurt?"

"I'll live. Nolan punches harder, and he loves me."

I smile. But when our eyes meet, I see his wariness. "I was never engaged."

His brows furrow. "I saw the pictures. Looked like a proposal and a celebration to me."

"It was. But it wasn't."

He waits for me to explain, rightfully confused.

"I was devastated that you were gone and told Dylan I was leaving. He asked me to have dinner with him to talk. So I did. I felt like I owed him that much. I was beyond shocked when he got down on one knee. I panicked. The entire restaurant was staring at us and he was waiting for an answer."

"So you said yes."

"No."

"Looked like it on the news."

"I actually just pulled him to standing and he hugged me. I never actually responded—but I didn't clarify I was declining either. At least until two hours later when we got somewhere more private."

"So you were really never engaged?" he asks again, like he can't believe it.

I shake my head.

"Why didn't you contact me?"

"Because Dylan told me he'd have you kicked off the tour. I didn't want to hurt your career."

"That was my decision to make."

I chortle. "You sound like Avery."

"Knew I liked that woman."

"And I guess you didn't contact me because you thought I was engaged."

He stares at me and shakes his head. "I wouldn't have let a ring stop me. Dylan told me he'd make sure you lost your job if I contacted you."

I nod. Guess we've both been manipulated.

Dylan's parting words finally register with me. I was so frazzled, I didn't stop to think what it meant when he said to "enjoy your unemployed boyfriend." "I'm sorry. I guess you lost the Easy Ryder tour?"

"Honestly, it's for the best. Even before we met, the guy had it in for me."

I take the frozen vegetables from his face and touch his cheek as I look deep into his beautiful blue eyes. "I'm so sorry. What a mess I've caused."

"I'm not sorry. I don't give a damn about the tour or the punch. All I care about is you." He brushes his knuckles along my cheek. The simple contact feels so good, I shut my eyes and breathe in a sigh of relief. If I were a cat, I'd purr. "Where does this leave us?" he asks.

My heart fills with hope. "Is there still an us? You left the bar with someone the other night. I thought maybe you'd moved on."

"Nothing happened with her." He weaves his fingers with mine and looks down. We're both quiet for a long moment. "How could anything happen with anyone else when I'm in love with you?"

My eyes jump to his. "You are?"

"I am."

Time stands still all around us. "I love you, too."

That slow, lazy, dimpled smile breaks through the last barrier of my heart. "You gave me my first screaming orgasm, I'm going to give you your last."

"Is that so?" I grin.

He stands and scoops me up off the couch. "We're never hiding again. And this time, there'll be no hand covering your mouth—I want to hear you moan my name while I lick every inch of you." He kicks open the door to my bedroom with his foot.

Setting me down on the center of the bed, he stares with a look that I can only describe as ardor. His voice is so soft, so heartfelt, so pure when he speaks again, I almost liquefy.

> *One step at a time, back behind the line*
> *We can't stop it, no, doesn't matter we try*
> *Walk to the blur, yes, you're gonna be mine*
> *Say we're still friends, we all know that's a lie*
> *You doubt it's true, but it's too late to turn*
> *The minute I touch you, our bodies align*
> *You're like fire, yet I run toward the burn*
> *We've crossed the line, now you're forever mine.*

"You finished the last verse."

He smiles. "Now do you believe me? There's no going back once you've crossed into the blur."

"I don't want to go back. I want to go forward."

"Me too, baby. Me too. But right now, I'm going to go up and down."

epilogue

Lucky

"I remember when my coffee used to be ready for me when I woke up," I tease as Flynn saunters into the galley area from the bedroom. He's shirtless, sweats hanging low on his waist. Seriously, the sight never gets old. Not for a minute.

He pours himself a steaming mug and refills mine before sliding in across from me. "What are you working on?"

I close the notebook I've been scribbling in all morning. "Nothing."

His eyebrows arch. "Nothing, huh? Then let me see."

"No."

He reaches and I swat his hand away.

"Why can't I see?"

"You'll see. Just not now."

He pouts.

"The pout isn't going to work either."

"No?"

"No."

He grins and leans forward, as if he's going to tell me a secret, then I feel his hand under the table slip inside the leg of my shorts. "How about this?" Truly, the man has magical fingers. And not just on the guitar and keyboard. His thumb presses into my clit and for a few seconds I succumb to my weakness—his touch. But then I realize his other hand is slowly slipping the notebook from my loosened grip.

"Not gonna work."

"Oh, it's gonna work. Give me a minute."

Dear lord, I'm in trouble when he pulls out the big guns—the cocky half grin and full dimples. His dexterous fingers dip below my panties and he runs two fingers up and down my center.

"Feels like it's already working."

I shake my head but don't try to push his stroking fingers away. When he lifts the fingers that he just coated with my moisture to his mouth and obscenely sucks them, I'm near opening the damn notebook and reading him what I was working on. Luckily, he's quickly forgotten the notebook, too.

"Spread your legs wider." He leans across the table so our mouths are lined up, but he doesn't kiss me.

Fortunately, I hesitate, because otherwise Nolan would have caught Flynn's fingers back inside of me. When will we learn to control ourselves?

"Mornin'," Nolan grunts.

"How many times do I have to tell you, put some fucking pants on before you come out here?"

He looks down, confused. "I do have pants on."

"No. That's underwear. And you're sporting morning wood."

Nolan scratches his head and looks down again. I turn my head, but only after getting an eyeful. "Oh. Sorry, man. I'm just grabbing some juice."

I take the opportunity to pack away my notebook and laptop, hoping out of sight is out of mind.

"We'll be there in about an hour," Flynn says. "Don't forget I'm crashing at your place tonight."

"Fine. But I'm not putting pants on in my place. You get to make the rules on the tour bus, I get to make 'em in Chez Nolan."

Flynn grumbles and Nolan goes back to his bunk. "You know this is ridiculous. Kicking me out of our place."

"It's tradition. The groom isn't supposed to see the bride before the wedding."

"Since when are we following tradition? I proposed in front of fifteen thousand people, and that little peanut growing in your belly isn't because you're a virgin."

I crinkle the napkin on the table and throw it at his nose. Flynn's not wrong. We haven't exactly taken the traditional route to get to where we are today. The day after the incident at Lucky's, our lives turned into a media circus. Pictures of the fight between Dylan and Flynn were sold to tabloids and our faces were flashing on TV for days. While it gave us an excuse to stay holed up in my apartment, I was nervous about what it might do to Flynn's long-term career. He, of course, was not. Unlike me, the man could seriously shrug off almost anything. He stayed true to his "everything happens for a reason" mantra and kept doing what he always did—writing songs, playing music and enjoying life day by day.

Not long after, the reason everything had happened came to light. Apparently, the old adage that there's no such thing as bad publicity is true. In Like Flynn's album sales doubled the week after the media frenzy, and within a month the band had its first *Billboard* Hot 100 top-ten hit. Things steamrolled from there. Instead of dumping In Like Flynn, Pulse Records asked the band to headline its own tour. It started out slow...twenty-two shows in smallish arenas...but with each city they visited, another two were added. By the time the band finished the last show yesterday, they'd played one hundred and eleven shows, and the last ninety were consecutive sell-outs.

Billboard just posted its predictions for the top-grossing tours of the year. In Like Flynn is slated to come in at number three—one rung above Easy Ryder. Speaking of which, four months after our split, Dylan Ryder wed a retired porn star—Jamie something—in a shotgun wedding. It wasn't confirmed how far along she was, but from the looks of her belly at the wedding, I'd guess she was already pregnant when we broke up. Everything happens for a reason.

Three months ago, Flynn proposed to me in front of a sold-out crowd in Miami. At the close of the show, I was standing stage-side when he told the audience that the American Airlines Arena was a very special place to him. His words were cryptic; he spoke of a fearless city and how the city had given him his first real kiss. Only I knew he was referring to me conquering my fear and walking on stage for the first time, and the first kiss we'd shared right in the very place he was standing. Then he treated the audience to an exclusive first—I hadn't even known he'd set the "Blur" lyrics we'd finished together to music. By the time he was done playing the song, I was an emotional mess. I was just so overwhelmed with love for the man and so joyful that I'd found him, I didn't realize what he was doing when he asked the audience for quiet and began speaking. I'm not sure who was more shocked when I ran onto the stage to accept his proposal...him or me. Who knew I was ready to make the final leap and walk on a stage in front of an arena full of people? Flynn, that's who.

I'm still not ready to sing on stage in front of a large audience. But I've made progress. Flynn and I even recorded a duet, which Pulse is producing and hopefully will be released in a few months. *Step ten, Dad. I'm almost there.* With Flynn beside me, I have no doubt step twelve is not too far away. Who knows, maybe I'll be standing next to Flynn when I finally stand on stage again.

Three weeks ago, I found out I was pregnant. It wasn't something either of us planned, but seeing how much Flynn adores his niece, I knew he wouldn't be upset. Turned out, he was the opposite of upset—completely over-the-moon ecstatic.

Neither of us wanted a big wedding, so we decided to do it as soon as the tour ended. That brings us to tomorrow.

"I don't remember you complaining when I told you last week. Avery is sleeping over."

"When did you tell me?"

"We were at the Emerson Hotel."

He leans back, sipping his coffee. "You had just flown in and we hadn't seen each other in two weeks."

"So?"

"Were you wearing black lace boy-short underwear, a T-shirt and no bra?"

"I don't know. Maybe?"

"I wasn't listening."

"What?" I'm thoroughly confused by this conversation.

"Your nipples were poking out through your shirt and I really love the black lace boy shorts."

"So?"

"I wasn't paying attention. I would have agreed to anything."

I chuckle. "I'll have to remember that for the next time we're arguing over something."

Taking my place at the back of the small aisle in the chapel, I pause for a moment. My dad should be giving me away today...walking me down the aisle. It's only about a thirty foot walk, but it seems I won't be making it alone anyway. I shouldn't be surprised when my barefoot husband-to-be walks to me and offers me his arm. Just like every day since the day we met, he's stood beside me. It's probably what made him the most irresistible to me. He doesn't want to carry me, he wants to walk side by side.

With Avery and Nolan as our witnesses, along with a small circle of close friends and family, including my Mom, we walk to the altar and stand in front of the minister, ready to become husband and wife. Beaming at us is the most adorable flower girl, in a tiny version of my dress.

We didn't discuss our wedding vows, so Flynn is surprised when I tell the minister I wrote my own. In sonnet form, I pour my heart out in fourteen lines of ten syllables. When I'm done, he wipes my tears and kisses me on the lips.

"Uncle Sinn." Laney tugs at her uncle's jacket and whispers loud enough so the rest of the room can hear her. "You're supposed to wait until he says you can kiss the bride."

Everyone chuckles, including the minister. But my soon-to-be husband leans forward with his usual cocky arrogance and reminds me, "Now that you're legally mine, I'll kiss the hell out of you in public, wherever and whenever I want."

Finally.

I found the man of my dreams. Only this time, he was real.

Dear Readers,

Thank you so much for all of your amazing support! Please sign up for my newsletter so that we can stay in touch, and receive this **FREE** short story!

Click here to sign up to receive Dry Spell FREE!
http://eepurl.com/bpzk-1
(You will only receive 4-5 emails per year and never be sold or spammed!)

acknowledgments

Thank you to all of the amazing bloggers that have dedicated your time to read my books and help share your experience with reviews. Without your voice, it would be difficult to find new readers.

A special note to some people I am incredibly thankful for—

To Penelope – Thank you for finding a productive use for our hours of chatting. How did I function before finding the other half of my brain?

To Julie – For being an opinionated New Yorker and always being honest—even when the truth sucks.

To Dallison – For reading my words, especially when the content isn't your favorite subject.

To Lisa – For organizing some amazing releases and telling it like it is.

To Sommer – for making this absolutely stunning cover!

To all my readers. Thank you for allowing me to tell you my stories. It is truly a gift and an honor to occupy your mind for a few hours. I love your emails and reviews, so please keep them coming!

Much love,

Vi

other books by vi

Throb
http://vikeeland.com/stand-alones.html

Worth the Fight
http://www.vikeeland.com/mma.html

Worth the Chance
http://www.vikeeland.com/mma.html

Worth Forgiving
http://www.vikeeland.com/mma.html

Belong to You
http://www.vikeeland.com/cole.html

Made for You
http://www.vikeeland.com/cole.html

Left Behind
http://www.amazon.com/Left-Behind-Vi-Keeland-ebook/dp/B000JM92LI

First Thing I See
http://www.vikeeland.com/ftis.html

connect
with vi

https://www.facebook.com/vi.keeland

http://on.fb.me/1uxLPTH

Twitter—@vikeeland

Instagram—@vi_keeland

http://www.vikeeland.com

CPSIA information can be obtained
at www.ICGtesting.com
Printed in the USA
BVHW081234120819
555664BV00024B/2373/P